I0743266

The Devil and the Dark:

Devil to Pay

Dead Reckoning

Enemy Colours

DEVIL TO PAY

R.M. OLSON

*To dad,
the only person I know who might love the age of sail more than I do.*

1

Silas

Silas tightened his grip on the small standard-issue knapsack he'd slung over his shoulder, glancing around one last time at the place that had been his home for the last two and a half years.

The tiny, cramped barracks room was hardly something to feel sentimental over. But it wasn't the room itself. It was what it represented: years of shipping before the mast before his superiors recommended him to the Naval Academy. Months of study to qualify for the entrance exams, and then two and a half years of classes here.

He'd have graduated in another six months, come out as a freshly minted officer, ready for his first command.

And instead …

He took a deep breath.

He'd never be coming back here. Hell, if they found out what he had in his knapsack, he'd be hanged for treason. He knew that perfectly well.

The thought sat sick in his stomach.

He'd thought this through a thousand times, sitting in class with a few hundred fellow officers-in-training, going over the location and name of every starship component in every naval-class ship, the history lectures, the strategy training. He'd gone through his options, over and over in his head, when he should have been focusing on his navigation homework or his lecture notes.

And in the end—this was the best chance he had.

He smiled bitterly as he turned away, letting his eyes brush over his neatly made cot, the small window that looked out over the academy courtyard, where dim lights from the lampposts glowed in the hazy fog of the night.

He'd spend his entire life believing that the Naval High Command was the closest thing in his world to God. That the Admiral could do no wrong. Even when he'd first found the information he was carrying in his knapsack, he'd thought perhaps it had been a misunderstanding. That getting it in front of the right people would change things.

And then he'd learned.

Thank God he hadn't done more than hint at rumours, rather than talk of irrefutable evidence, because had he done so, the lesson would no doubt have been permanent.

But then, he'd been raised to do his duty. He knew his life was a small price to pay for it. He just hadn't expected the ones claiming that price would be the people he'd spent his life serving.

He closed his eyes and took a long breath.

All that, he could worry about later. In the meantime, best to worry about getting out of here alive.

He stepped out into the silent hallway, closing the door carefully behind him.

For the briefest moment, he hesitated, glancing up and down the dorm corridor, his stomach tight. But no one was stirring. He'd timed this precisely—the cadets who were holed up studying for the upcoming exams would have already eaten and retired to their rooms—if not to sleep, at least to stare sightlessly at the dorm ceiling, equations and figures dancing in front of sleepless eyes. And the cadets who preferred to deal with the stress through other methods wouldn't be staggering back from the taverns for at least another couple of hours, if his experience held.

He straightened his shoulders resolutely and started forward at a brisk pace.

There was a heady excitement bubbling in his veins despite everything, a lightness to his steps. Maybe he was leaving this place, never to return. But by God, it felt good to be doing something finally, after weeks of thinking and planning.

His dorm was on the sixth floor. The lift wouldn't do—there were security cameras there that would make his flight all too easy to trace. But there was a maintenance stairway in the far back corner of the building that was almost never used. The security cameras there had malfunctioned a few months ago, and as far as he could tell, had never been replaced.

He'd gone in a few days ago and taped them as a precaution, so if someone came in to repair them in the intervening days, he'd see it.

He walked quickly, trying to keep his steps firm. If he was seen, he wanted to look like a man going about his business, not a thief slinking through the shadows.

And as to the fact that he was, actually, much closer to the latter than the former—well, that was something he could worry about once he was clear.

He'd almost made it down the hallway, his head dipped to avoid letting the cameras see his face, when the lift at the end of the hallway opened, and a familiar figure stumbled out.

Silas cursed under his breath.

"Silas!" The man slurred. He was noticeably unsteady on his feet as he stumbled down the hallway towards Silas. "What're you doing here, man? Shouldn't you have your nose in some book somewhere?" He hiccupped, and laughed.

Silas gritted his teeth. "Philip," he said in a low voice, trying to keep his tone civil. Any hint he was upset and Philip would be certain to remark upon it, loudly and at length.

"We were hoping you'd join us," the man continued, clapping a hand on Silas's shoulder.

Silas forced himself not to flinch away at the man's liquor-soaked breath. "Come now, shouldn't you be heading to bed?" he asked, removing the man's hand from his shoulder and trying very hard to keep the disgust from his tone. "You're on early morning duty, if I remember correctly."

Philip laughed loudly. He was in the same year in the academy as Silas, and Silas knew that the man had always been jealous of his entrance scores. He'd acted friendly, hung around Silas in classes, but never missed an opportunity to sink in a barbed comment, with a laugh as if he'd just been trying to be witty. "That's why 'm home early." He went to slap Silas on the shoulder again, but Silas caught his wrist.

"Well then, best get to bed. From the looks of you, you'll have a hangover tomorrow."

Philip gave an exaggerated grimace. "Where're you going at this hour?"

Silas sighed. "I'm going for a walk outside to clear my head, then back to my books. Nothing too exciting, I'm afraid."

Philip nodded, the motion almost enough to topple him over.

Silas turned him, none too gently, and pointed him towards his dorm room at the end of the hall. "Go on, we can talk tomorrow."

Philip muttered something in slurred protest, but Silas stepped briskly around him towards the stairways.

His heart was pounding. If he'd miscalculated, if more of the officer cadets were on their way home as well, there was no way he got out. And—he reached back to touch his knapsack, reassuring himself it was still there.

Someone would notice the documents were missing soon enough. The moment they did, there'd be a hue and cry about the entire Academy, and he knew damn well that he'd been incautious enough early on, asking the type of questions that shouldn't be asked, that he'd be high on the list of suspects.

He reached the stairwell and pulled the door open, just as the door to the lift opened again behind him.

He cursed and slipped inside the stairwell, peeking back through the window on the door.

Then he cursed again, louder.

It wasn't more drunken officer cadets. It was worse. The official Academy Guard. And Silas had a very good idea why they were there.

"Spread out," the commander barked. "It's somewhere close."

Dammit.

He swung the knapsack from his shoulders and hunted feverishly through it for the lockbox.

He'd checked for a tracer on it, found one and crushed it. That should have been enough.

But clearly, it hadn't been.

With fumbling fingers, he prised the case open.

No chip. The tracker must be set into the case itself.

He cursed again, and dumped the chips out into his hand, checking carefully that there wasn't another tracker hidden among them. Then he shoved them into his pocket and dropped the case on the floor.

They'd know he'd come this way, but there was no help for it now.

"Yes, Silas was here just now, my classmate. Went down the hall that way. He said he was on his way outside to clear his head, but he didn't take the lift …" Philip's helpful, drunken tones filtered through the closed door.

Silas jumped to his feet, yanked his knapsack closed, swung it back over his shoulder, and sprinted down the stairs, taking them two at a time.

He was down the first flight and swinging himself around the corner when the door above him was pulled open. "There he is!" someone shouted. Boots clattered down the stairs after him, and he could hear the commander shouting for her people to get downstairs to cut him off.

He swore through his teeth. The lift was too fast for him to be certain he'd beat it to the ground floor.

He yanked open the door leading to the fifth floor and pounded down the hallway. He had to get out of sight before they followed him out of the stairwell …

He reached the place where the hallway forked, and took a turn at random. There was a window at the end of the hallway, and he ran for it, pulling out his buck-knife as he ran. He came to a breathless halt when he reached it, glancing quickly over his shoulder.

They hadn't seen him yet, but he could hear footsteps and shouted orders behind him. He had a couple seconds at most.

He inserted the tip of his knife into the lock and twisted in a practiced motion. The lock popped free, and, holding his breath, he swung the window out.

It didn't squeak, thank God, and, before he could let himself think better of it, he swung his legs up onto the windowsill.

The building fell away below him, and he closed his eyes, bracing himself.

These windows didn't look out onto the grassy, well-maintained Academy courtyard. This side of the building looked out over the long, long drop off the edge of the Level, where the ground fell away under you and the swirling gases from the gaseous planet they lived on washed low and dangerous far below.

There were always a handful of students each year, around exam time, who used the windows on this side of the building to deal with their stress in a way that was much more permanent than either studying, or drinking, themselves into a coma.

Behind him, he could hear the door of the stairwell slam.

Out of time, then.

Holding his breath, he slipped down until he was grasping the edge of the windowsill with his fingertips, and carefully pushed the window shut. He wouldn't be able to relock it, if they checked. But considering the absolute stupidity of what he was doing right now, hopefully they'd check the easier options first.

And hopefully by the time they did check, he'd be either dead, or away. Although if he was being honest, he had a strong preference for the latter.

The outside wall of the barracks dorms was rough stone that, on this side of the building, had been eaten away over the years by the stray wisps of gas that would sometimes get swept up from the planet below, carving odd channels into the rock. Rumour said the ghosts of those who'd died from jumping lurked down there too, waiting to be swept up in an updraft. Silas could well believe it—the most common way to get into the Academy was to be recommended by your superior officer in the navy. Except for a handful whose family positions had got them a seat, most of the people here had traveled at faster-than-light speeds, and suffered the accompanying cellular damage that allowed them to turn ghost. And anyone willing to voluntarily face the depths of the gas planet was likely dealing with enough trauma that they'd turn the moment they died.

Silas shivered.

His ghost would be joining theirs in a few moments, if he wasn't careful.

Cautiously, he reached a hand out from the windowsill to a space between two of the stones, fitting his fingers inside and testing the handhold.

Not strong. But better than he might have hoped.

He tested a foothold, and cautiously shifted his weight.

A few more movements put him out of direct sight from the window, and he breathed a quick sigh of relief, despite the way his fingers cramped, grasping at the rock.

He glanced around quickly.

It was hard to find his bearings in the dark, with the moon half-hidden by clouds and the gas below shifting in odd, illogical patterns.

He tested another handhold, and shifted his weight again.

They'd be after him soon—it wouldn't take them too long to figure out what he'd done, and clinging to the side of the building like he was left him with no way to defend himself.

But he'd grown up clambering up ratlines on ships of the line, and he had a head for heights—you'd never survive in the navy otherwise.

He was climbing steadily, down and across.

Get around the corner of the building, where there would once more be blessedly solid ground underfoot, and get low enough that he could drop down to the courtyard without breaking every bone in his body. He could deal with the rest from there.

He let himself one cautious arms-length down, then another.

His hand slipped, and the jerk of his body pulled his foot loose as well.

He froze, hanging over the endless drop by one hand. His heart was pounding, his breath stopped in his throat.

His movements glacially slow, he lifted his hand and grabbed a rough outcropping in the wall, his palms slippery with sweat. He moved his foot back, feeling gently with the toe of his boot, testing the potential footholds carefully before trusting it with his weight.

His body slumped in relief when it held.

He glanced below him.

He'd made it probably two stories down, avoiding the windows. Once he got back to the courtyard, the drop would be survivable.

He gritted his teeth and edged farther along the building until at last, endless minutes later, his searching hand touched a sharp stone corner.

He let out his breath in relief, closing his eyes for just a moment.

He'd made it.

He worked his way carefully around the side of the building, then glanced down.

He'd managed to get a few metres lower, but that still left him at least two stories up.

The distance appeared much farther now that he was contemplating jumping.

He pulled in a quick breath.

No help for it. If he didn't get out in the next few minutes, he wasn't going to. And he'd already spent far too much time getting here.

He braced himself, adjusting his footholds for the best purchase. Then he shoved himself outward, tucking his body as he fell.

He landed hard, rolling over his shoulder, the breath knocked out of him at the impact of the fall. Then he scrambled to his feet and took off running.

The grass was damp under his boots, the cool wetness of it seeping through his clothing where he'd fallen. There was a stabbing pain in his right hip, from the fall, probably, but he didn't have time to worry about that right now. They'd spotted him—he could already hear the guards pouring out of the barracks after him.

He sprinted for the Academy gates. Not locked, thank God, but the usual guard was there, leaning casually against the wall.

Behind him, Silas could hear the clatter of the guards' boots on the cobblestone walkways.

The guard at the gate looked up at Silas's approach, then his face changed and he jerked upright.

"Shut the gates!" one of the guards behind Silas shouted. "Detain that man. That's an order!"

The guard at the gate raised his weapon. "Now listen here, boy, stop where you are. I don't want to—"

Silas slowed, and the man's hand on his stun-pistol relaxed a bit. "Good. Smart lad. Now—"

Silas drew back his fist and lunged forward, hitting the man in the jaw hard enough to send him staggering. Then he ducked past him, shaking feeling back into his hand, and took off down the narrow cobblestone streets that led to the ports.

He found he was grinning as he ran.

It had been too damn long since he'd done something like this.

Once he was out of the Academy and into the city proper, he

slowed a little, trying to catch his breath. His years of hanging around the ports as a child were paying off—there was no way they'd follow him through the maze of alleys and back streets that he knew as well as he knew his own home.

They'd guess where he was going soon enough, but with luck, by the time they did, he'd be long gone.

At last, he made out the port ahead of him through the night fog.

Even at this time of night it wasn't entirely deserted—ships that had come in from a long-haul voyage disembarking passengers and unloading cargo, the orange light of the streetlamps casting a shadowy glow over the place.

He avoided the more well-kept areas, where the wealthy ships would be docking, flooded with brilliant white light that was almost enough to approximate daylight, and slipped down towards the poorer section.

He glanced down at the note on his comm to check the directions, then, hoisting his knapsack higher on his shoulder, set off smartly across the narrow, cramped docks to the one he was looking for.

The ship was there still, its loading ramp down, the woman he'd negotiated passage with standing at the entrance, a suspicious scowl on her face.

Her hand went to her jacket pocket at the sight of him, and he slowed, raising his hands to show he was unarmed. "Just me," he whispered.

She narrowed her eyes, still not taking her hand off the pistol in her pocket. "You being followed?"

He hesitated. Still, better she knew the truth. He was paying her enough to account for the danger anyway. "Yes," he said. "I lost them in the streets, but they'll guess where I've come eventually."

She gave a short nod and jerked her chin to the ramp. "Get up, then. We're ready to head out, just waiting on you."

He nodded, and jogged past her up the ramp and through the hatch.

The inside of the ship was neither cleaner nor more glamorous than the outside—the wide belly of her crammed with cargo, strapped down in a haphazard fashion that, to his practiced eye, spoke of an intentional device to discourage inspectors from looking too closely.

Unless he missed his guess, this ship had more than its share of secret compartments.

Still, he wasn't here as a naval officer, he was here as a fugitive. And he wasn't going to complain about a captain smart enough to evade customs.

There were rickety stairways and ladders going up through the maze of ratlines, as well as a small lift for any of the crew who might not be able to take the stairs, and the typical ghost-locks, although on a ship this size it would hardly matter—one person turning ghost would take out the entire crew in a matter of minutes.

He shivered a little, and shook his head resolutely.

A dour-looking sailor looked up from his work, and beckoned Silas to a cramped set of stairs. Under it was a small trapdoor, and when Silas pulled it open, the cabin inside barely had space for a bed and a necessary.

"You'll stay there for the duration," said the captain, who'd come over to them. "I won't ask questions about who's after you or why, but I'm sure as hell not putting my crew at risk. It's a two-standard-day run. I'm guessing you don't have problems with faster than light, you being in the navy?"

He shook his head.

"Good. There's two days' worth of rations down there, along with a bed and a necessary. I'll tap on the door when you can come up, and you're paying before I let you off the ship."

He nodded.

She slammed the trapdoor behind him, leaving him in utter darkness.

He fumbled around on the wall until he found the light switch, and in its dim orange glow, he dropped down onto the bare, uncomfortable cot.

He closed his eyes for a moment as the ship shuddered under him, and sucked in a breath at the quick drop of his stomach as they lifted off.

He was free. He'd made it. And now …

He reached into his pockets, fingers brushing the small data chips that had come so close to costing him his life.

That had already cost him the life he'd planned out for himself.

Now he'd just have to hope like hell this had been worth it.

2

A sharp rap on the trapdoor above him jerked Silas out of a sound sleep.

He sat up, fumbling for his pistol. "Who is it?"

"It's the captain. We've docked."

He sucked in a quick breath of relief, sagging back against the wall. At last, he tapped the light and stood, scrubbing at his eyes. "I'll be up in a moment, just gathering my things."

"You have ten standard minutes," the woman said, voice brusque. "Not going to keep my ship here long enough for a tracker to pick it up."

"Understood," he called back.

He stretched, biting back a groan. He'd never been good at sitting still, much as he'd forced himself to in the Academy, and he'd thought the two-day trip would be a claustrophobic nightmare of waiting. Instead, he'd dropped into his bunk and slept through most of it—after the strain of the past few weeks, he hadn't realized how exhausted he was.

He didn't have much to gather, other than his knapsack. His clothes stank of sweat and grime, but he couldn't do anything about that, and in a port like this, with travellers coming in from long voyages, no one would expect better. On a wealthy ship you might be able to spare a recirc pump and reclaimed wastewater for washing. On a regular ship, that was an unimaginable luxury.

On a ship of the line, that luxury was reserved for the officers. Crew learned other methods to keep themselves fresh, none of which were either easy or reliable.

He sighed, and started up the ladder to the main deck of the ship.

The captain was waiting for him by the exit. He pulled up the credit chit on his comm to hover over his wrist and tapped it over to her. She glanced at it, then touched it against the comm on her own wrist, checking for authenticity. At last, grudgingly, she nodded. "Your credit's good, Level boy. Now go on, and good luck to you. Not staying in this place a moment longer than I have to."

"Thank you," he said, giving her a quick nod.

She nodded back, her expression losing none of its hostility, and he made his way down the ramp and onto the filthy streets of the dock.

The moment his feet touched ground the ramp behind him began to raise, and before he'd made it ten steps, it had slammed shut with a pneumatic hiss.

He glanced over his shoulder to see the ship lift off, hover a moment, and then make for the airlock exit.

He sighed to himself. His stomach was tight, his fists clenching unconsciously.

He'd just have to damn well hope this worked out the way he'd planned it.

He glanced around him quickly, taking in his surroundings for the first time.

Blackrock was … well, more or less what he would have expected of a pirate settlement.

The planet didn't have the atmosphere necessary to allow people up on the surface, so the settlement had been carved into natural caves in the semi-porous rock. Lamps were set at regular intervals into niches in the walls, guttering with the movement of the dank air through the caves, and here and there large fans, set into the ceiling, clanked and groaned, circulating the air to keep it from getting too stale. Dampness glistened on the walls and dripped from the ceiling, glittering in the flickering lamplight, and the moss and lichen and mildew tucked into the cracks in the wall told him the air here, at least, was clean enough to breathe.

He'd heard of the vats of algae they kept in the deeper caverns here to convert the oxygen—an intelligent fix for the problem on a planet without natural atmosphere and without the resources to terraform.

The port the captain had brought him to wasn't one of the larger ones—this was another of those small, badly kept ports where people who couldn't afford a proper berth ended up. But then, he wasn't here to be comfortable. He was here looking for one person in particular, and from everything he'd heard, this was the most likely place to find them.

He bit back the quick sting of guilt.

This wasn't something he was doing for himself. This was for the integrity of the navy, even if the Naval High Command didn't see it. And if it meant finding allies in Blackrock—well, there were those who'd done worse in pursuit of their duty.

The caves had been laid out in narrow, winding streets, houses and shops and whorehouses and taverns jumbled in a crowded mass around the port, where desperate sailors and pirates would be searching for something to distract them from the space-madness of being on a ship for too long—locked into a metal hull with only your crewmates for company, living with the chance that at any moment, any accident, a crewmate who you'd gambled or eaten with the day before might turn ghost and rip you to pieces with nowhere to go and no way to escape.

He shivered, pulling his jacket tighter around him in the cool of the deep caverns.

Even in the navy, they'd have a few cases of space-madness at the end of a long posting. And they had solid metal lock-doors to contain any potential ghosts, and at least a couple hundred people to share the endless hours with. He could hardly imagine it on a crewed pirate ship or poor merchant-class ship—seeing no one but the same seven or ten people for weeks or months on end.

He could hear, even from here, the noise drifting from the taverns at the end of the docks—raucous shouts, snatches of drunken song, the unmistakable sound of fists on flesh and the pained grunt of someone on the wrong side of the blows.

By the time he'd reached the crumbling raised walkways that led off the docks, he'd almost slipped twice in pools of something that stank badly enough that he had no wish to question their composition. His boots were thoroughly coated in slime, but—he shrugged wryly.

With the state of his clothes and hygiene at the moment, it would hardly make a difference.

He stepped onto the walkway, clutching his knapsack more tightly as the crowd of sailors and pirates, most of them at least half inebriated, jostled past him.

It was an odd, uncomfortable feeling, being here among people who'd likely slit his throat if they knew who and what he was. People who, under other circumstances, he'd be fighting on shipboard during a skirmish.

Ahead of him, at the end of the walkway, there was a tavern that looked like a place he might both be able to find information and avoid getting his throat slit. He put his head down grimly and began to shoulder his way through the crowd towards it.

He bumped into someone, hard enough to knock the wind from him, and looked up quickly, biting back a curse.

A woman who looked around his own age stood in front of him, swearing in language that would have caused a few blushes even in the Academy. She was tall, almost his height, and dressed in a rag-tag mish-mash of clothing that would have pegged her as a street-beggar back on the Level, but there was an impressive assortment of weapons tucked into holsters on her belt, and, if he was any judge, more distributed about her person. Her dark blond hair was pulled back into a ponytail, her eyes a startling blue, her naturally pale skin the blue-white pallor of someone with a fair complexion who spent all their time shipboard, where the closest thing you got to sunlight was the vitamin lamps you could sit under to keep from dying of vitamin D deficiency. She was pretty, her features fine and aristocratic, her face expressive.

And at the moment, the expression was decidedly irritated.

"Watch where you're going, sailor," she snapped.

He muttered an apology as she slipped past him, and went to hoist his knapsack higher onto his shoulders.

Then he cursed, and glanced back to see nothing but a cut strap.

He groaned to himself.

The woman had been a thief. He should have guessed. He scanned the crowd, but she'd already disappeared.

He patted his pockets frantically, weak with a sudden panic, but the information chips were still there. Thank God he'd kept the data chips in his pocket rather than his knapsack, at least.

But that had been far too close. Dammit, what the hell had he expected in a pirate settlement? Hell, in any port city. He was behaving like a damn landlubber.

He glanced around irresolutely, then slipped into a grimy side alley to take stock.

He double-checked his pockets, and breathed out a sigh of relief. She hadn't got any of the chips, which was by far the most important thing. But his knapsack had carried every possession he had to his name, although, granted, it wasn't much—his spare jacket and a change of clothing, his extra buck knife, the energy pistol he used ship-board, where a projectile would chance breaching the hull and killing everyone on board.

He still had his cutlass and his projectile pistol, which he'd shoved into the holster on his belt, as well as his sparker, which he always carried on his person. His regular buck knife was still in his pocket, and although he'd kept most of his extra credit chits in the knapsack, he still had the ones on his comm. Enough to keep him alive for a few weeks, at least, if not to buy him passage off this hell-hole.

And if he needed to do that, it would mean he'd failed. He'd gambled and lost, and he'd have no place to go back to, and he'd deserve whatever fate he'd damned himself to.

He forced his mind from dwelling on the thought. He still had the information chips, and God willing, that was enough. And if he saw that thief again, he'd show her the colour of his damn cutlass.

He turned, bracing himself to push back into the crush of the streets, when he heard a small, terrified gasp.

He spun.

At the end of the alley, an old man lay propped against the damp wall, eyes wide with terror. His long grey beard was unkempt, particles of food lodged in it, his clothing filthy and ragged, an open bottle tipped over beside him. Any other time, Silas would have dismissed him as a drunk sobering up after a bender.

But it wasn't the man that had grabbed his attention and held it.

It was the translucent shape that floated not a metre away from the old sailor.

Even from here, Silas could make out the ghost's features—an older woman, with kind lines on her translucent face that told him that in life, she'd been someone he'd have trusted on instinct.

It hardly mattered, though—when a person turned ghost, it left nothing of their personality, or thoughts, or instincts. A ghost was a reflection of past trauma, given form by the cellular degeneration caused by faster-than-light travel. And it wanted nothing more than to destroy anything it came across.

The man's face was bloodless with terror, and he whimpered as the ghost drifted closer.

Silas cursed under his breath. The man must be drunk—any sober and sane person knew better than to make a sound or move a muscle when there was a ghost nearby.

Even from where he stood, he could see the burning black pits that made up the thing's eyes, the mouth opening impossibly wide, gaping with sharp, translucent teeth that he knew damn well were enough to rip a person to shreds.

A ghost that was still forming was easy enough to dispatch with a sparker. But this one was fully formed, and deadly.

It was just an old man, a drunk in an alley. If this ghost missed him, he'd no doubt be killed by another next week.

But dammit, Silas had seen people killed by ghosts before. No one deserved that type of death.

He was running toward them before he could think better of it, yanking the sparker from his pocket and igniting the flickering blue tip as he ran.

He reached the man just as the ghost sprang. The man gave a long, quavering scream as ghostly fingers closed around his throat, and Silas jabbed the sparker into the thing, hunting for the spot where the spark of electricity would hit its core, dissolving it.

The ghost spun on him, letting go its grip on the man, and he jumped back.

His hands were damp with sweat, and he could feel the terror climbing up his spine.

He'd missed. It was difficult to kill a fully formed ghost with a sparker, even if you were experienced. Harder still when the thing was facing you, fear leaching off it like poisonous gas.

He shoved the sparker into the thing once more.

Nothing.

The ghost lunged, and he yanked his sparker free and shoved it forward one last time, desperately …

There was a soft, barely audible hiss, like a breath of air. For a moment, the ghost hung in front of him, a still-life painting of a nightmare, horrifying in its verisimilitude.

And then it dissolved, melting out and down from the flickering blue tip of his sparker into a mist that dissipated across the filthy alley floor.

Silas sagged back in relief. His hand holding the sparker was trembling so badly that the tip danced, making odd glowing-blue patterns in the darkness.

"Thank Our Lady." The old man's voice shook. "Thank Our Blessed Lady of the Ghosts, and thank you, lad. May Our Lady watch your path."

Silas replaced his sparker carefully in its holster with still-shaking hands. He was biting the inside of his cheek to hold back an almost hysterical laugh at the absurdity of it all—this man was a pirate, almost certainly. A drunk and a pirate. His commanding officers would have told him to shove a sword through the man's throat and save the ghost the trouble.

But there was something about the instant danger, the rush of adrenalin, that made him feel alive in a way he hadn't since he'd set foot in the Academy.

He drew in a steadying breath and looked up, holding out his hand to the man. "Come on, let's get you up. You have anywhere to go? Best not stay around here, I think."

"I agree with 'ee," the man croaked. He hesitated, then took Silas's outstretched hand, pulling himself heavily to his feet. Silas had to hold himself back from grimacing at the stench of the man as he leaned forward to slap Silas on the shoulder. "Thank'ee, lad. You saved my life there, you did."

"No more than what anyone would do," said Silas, trying to keep from wrinkling his nose. "Now go on, no point in giving the ghosts more targets."

"Ah, right enough." The man turned and made his unsteady way towards the alley entrance.

Silas hesitated a moment, then turned to follow.

Then he froze.

There was a figure in the alley entrance, watching him. And even in the uncertain light, he recognized her instantly—the thief from the streets.

She was backlit by the streetlights outside, but even in the dim artificial twilight he could see her eyebrows lift in amusement when she saw him looking.

He stepped forward, drawing his pistol. "I'd like my knapsack back," he said in a low voice. "Unless you'd like to become a ghost yourself."

Her mouth quirked in a mocking grin. "Fancy talk, Level boy."

He narrowed his eyes and stepped closer.

There was a pistol in her hand so quick that his eye could hardly track the movement. "Not so fast." She was still grinning. "Saw what happened back there. Why'd you save him?"

Silas shrugged. His shoulders were tight, and he wasn't sure if it was irritation at the pickpocket's brazen questioning, or at the fact that he couldn't have answered the question even if he'd wanted to. "You'd have left him to get eaten by a ghost, I guess?"

She shook her head, her expression going thoughtful. "Figure I wouldn't have. But more'n a few people around here might." She studied him a moment. "You're out of your depth here. I know a Level boy when I see one. What're you doing in a pirate harbour?"

"I hardly see that's your business," he said coldly.

She laughed. "Figure it might be, if you don't want someone to slit your throat in an alley."

"Someone like you?" he asked, voice still cold.

"Why're you here?"

He sighed. It wasn't as if he had any damn idea where to start looking. "I'm looking for Captain Mad Dog."

Her eyebrows raised higher. "You think Mad Dog'll talk to some Level boy?"

"I have information I think the captain would be interested in," he said through his teeth. "I came a long way to bring it. So yes, I would hope the captain would make time to see me."

She was watching him curiously now, her eyes scrutinizing the dirty clothes he wore. "Navy man, aren't you?" she asked at last.

He gave a humourless chuckle. "I was."

"Not anymore?"

He snorted. "You think I came out here on my leave? Spoke with my commanding officer and got permission?" He couldn't keep the bitterness from his tone.

She studied him a little longer. "Could be a spy. The navy's never been too particular about honour, least not when it comes to pirates." She shook her head with a little laugh. "Then again, if they were sending a spy, I'd expect something better than you."

He felt himself stiffen at the insult, and consciously forced his muscles to relax. No point being offended by a petty pickpocket. "Listen," he said, trying to make his voice remain reasonable. "If you know where I might find the Captain, I'd appreciate you showing me. If not—" He made as if to step past her, but she held up a hand.

"Easy there, Level boy." She paused, then shrugged, as if making up her mind. "Follow me. I can take you to someone who might be willing to introduce you to Mad Dog, if you get on her good side."

He hesitated.

His heart was pounding.

She shrugged again, still grinning. "Listen, the Captain's pretty well respected around here. By which I mean, people asking around after Mad Dog and Mad Dog doesn't want to see them are liable to end up dead. I can take you to see Gracie, and she'll make the call. That's the best offer you'll get."

He let out a short breath, shaking his head at himself.

If he had any sense, he'd stay away from this woman.

Then again, if he'd had any sense, he wouldn't be in this position to start with.

"Lead the way, then," he said.

She turned and plunged into the crowded streets, and he followed in her wake.

She led him down a veritable maze of side streets, until the bustling mass of humanity that marked the ports began to thin out. Soon they were weaving through only a handful of disreputable, suspicious-looking people, walking swiftly, hands on their weapons, wary gazes following their fellow travellers.

Silas put his hand on the butt of his own weapon, his heart beating more quickly.

At last the woman slipped through the door of an ancient tavern, the dark artificial wood of its exterior cracked and black with age, coated with mildew and rot. Even from the outside, Silas could tell it was the sort of place people went only if they were desperate.

And honestly—well, he couldn't argue he didn't fit that bill, at least right now.

He drew in a quick breath and followed her inside.

He looked around quickly as his eyes adjusted to the dimness.

The tavern wasn't crowded—a handful of weathered-looking sailors gambling on a cracked table in one corner, two or three others slumped over their drinks at the disreputable bar.

The woman he'd been following had made her way over to a small table in a darkened corner of the tavern. A figure sat there, slouched over a drink, and she beckoned him over.

Cautiously, he made his way across the tavern, his hand still resting on the butt of his pistol.

As he got closer, the figure raised her head, and he could make out her features for the first time.

Gracie was a little past middle aged, lean and weathered, dressed in the mismatched tunic and trousers that seemed to be the typical uniform in this place, and a long, oilskin coat that looked as weathered as she did. Her face was creased with the radiation-marks of someone who'd spent a lifetime among the stars, her skin the worn toughness of old leather, but her eyes were sharp and compelling. The tall glass in front of her was half empty, a dark amber liquid that looked much stronger than beer, but her hands seemed steady enough. She held the stump of a cigar between her fingers, and she lifted it to her lips as he approached, then turned her head to blow out the smoke. He found himself coughing at the acrid stench of it.

She studied him for a long moment, thoughtfully, then turned to the pickpocket. "What've you brought me, Ari?" Her voice was a low rasp that wasn't unpleasant, and her tone was mild, but Silas tightened his hand on the pistol in his belt.

"Level boy I found wandering around the port," said Ari, grinning. "Said he was looking for Mad Dog. Thought I'd bring him here, let you decide if you'd introduce him to the captain."

"Ah." Gracie raised her eyebrows and turned back to study Silas again.

"Picked his pocket earlier, wanted to see what he was doing here." Ari pulled his knapsack from the small duffel she carried, and he opened his mouth in outrage as she emptied it on the table in front of the woman, then forced it closed again.

He knew well enough that his outrage would have no effect whatsoever on the thief.

Gracie must have noticed, because he saw a touch of amusement in her expression as she glanced over the items. "A naval man," she said at last, leaning back in her seat. "The Admiral send him, you think?"

Ari shook her head. "Don't think so. Admitted he used to be navy, and he hasn't got a story nearly good enough for a spy." She paused. "Saw him save Old Man Evans from a ghost back in an alley by the port. Only reason I stopped long enough to talk to him. Thought you might want to hear what he had to say for himself."

Gracie turned to study him again, a sharp interest in her eyes that almost made him want to squirm.

He crushed the impulse ruthlessly, and forced his face into an impassive expression. Her mouth twitched in amusement, and she gestured to a rickety seat. "We don't stand on ceremony here, lad. Sit."

Stiffly, he did as he was told.

She took another long pull on her cigar, watching him with interest as the silence stretched.

He gritted his teeth and returned her look with an impassive gaze. He wasn't about to be bated into some trap by the woman who, he was increasingly beginning to suspect, was Ari's employer.

At last she nodded, blowing out a long stream of smoke. "So, boy. You're looking for Mad Dog."

He nodded. His teeth were still clenched.

Even if this woman was a thief, it was possible she knew the pirate captain.

"I see. And you just turned up here, hoping you'd stumble across the captain. Mostly spends time on the *Sweet Jenny*, Mad Dog does."

He nodded. "I know. The *Sweet Jenny* was spotted by a ship of the line three weeks ago in the Wolf sector, and then again a week and a half ago in the Haley sector. With travel time, she'd have been out of port for at least two months. Made sense that she'd dock here for a bit to resupply."

Gracie raised her eyebrows. "Not a bad guess. The *Sweet Jenny* docked here two days back."

He gave a short nod. His breath was still coming too quickly. "I imagine Captain Mad Dog won't stay in port long. So." He leaned forward. "Will you introduce me?"

Again, Gracie raised her eyebrows. "Why would I do that? Mad Dog isn't someone I'd want to cross, if I had the choosing of it. Even if I did introduce you—a naval man studying to be an officer, from the looks of you—what makes you think Mad Dog'll see you, rather than just order your throat cut?"

"Because I have information," he said through his teeth. "I risked my damn life to get it, too. And I think Mad Dog might find it interesting enough that I won't lose my head for it."

Gracie tipped back her drink, draining it in a long swallow, then set the empty glass back on the table with a click, leaning forward. "What sort of information might that be? It'd need to be good enough for me to be able to spark the captain's interest."

He gritted his teeth again. "I have information on what happened back on the Level, twenty-five years ago during the court trials. I know what really caused the Starfire naval disaster."

Gracie watched him a moment longer.

The tavern keeper had come over as well, a wide-necked bottle in her hand. Gracie smiled up at her, holding out her empty glass, and the woman filled it, then turned to Ari, handing her a bottle of what looked like cheap beer.

She turned to Silas. "And what will the fine young man have?" Her voice had a tinge of mocking to it. "A beer like our Miss Ari?"

"He's my guest, Abigail. And he's looking to talk with Mad Dog." Gracie's voice was mild. She glanced at Silas, a quirk of amusement at the corner of her lips. "Give the boy what I'm having. Don't water it down. We'll see how much of a sailor he is."

The tavern keeper smiled slyly, pulling out another glass. "Right you are," she said, placing it on the table in front of Silas. She filled it expertly from the same bottle she'd used to fill Gracie's glass, then turned to leave.

Ari uncapped the beer bottle on the edge of the table and brought it to her lips.

Gracie watched her for a moment, then turned back to Silas. "You're right," she said at last. "Mad Dog might be interested in hearing that, if it's what you say it is." She turned back to Ari. "Make sure the boy gets a meal in him, he looks like he's had nothing but ship's rations for too long. Then bring him by." She picked up her drink and raised it in a salute to Silas. "I'll get you an audience with the captain, lad. And then you'd best hope what you have is enough to hold Mad Dog's attention."

She tipped back the rest of her liquor, placed the glass down on the table, and pushed back her chair.

Silas's heart was pounding.

He had no idea if she could do what she said, or if she was simply stringing him along to rob him blind and cut his throat. But this close to his goal, he knew damn well he wasn't going to let common sense stop him.

Ari put down the bottle of beer and grinned, watching Gracie go. "Well, you heard her. Let's get you fed. Abigail don't always do meals, but she's a good cook, and she'll do it if Gracie asks her."

He frowned, picking up his drink as Ari beckoned the tavern keeper over.

"Well?" Ari asked, turning back to him. "You going to drink it, or you going to let it go to waste?"

He put the glass to his lips carefully.

Ari snorted. "Cautious one, aren't you?"

He glared at her and tipped it back.

Then he put it down again, coughing. "What the hell was that?" he managed, when he could speak.

Ari and the tavern keeper were clearly trying to hold back their amusement.

"It tastes like syrup!"

"Just cold black tea, with about half a kilo of sugar stirred in." The tavern keeper chuckled. "Likes her tea sweet, does Mad Dog."

Silas turned to stare at her. "What?"

The tavern keeper gestured out the door where Gracie had disappeared, still grinning. "Mad Dog Gracie Madox. The one you were talking to."

Silas stared for a moment.

Then he spun on Ari. "What the hell?"

She laughed, holding up her hands. "You wanted to see Mad Dog. I got you a meeting with Mad Dog."

He glared at her, his heart still pounding far too quickly.

She grinned. "Go on, finish your tea and Abigail'll bring you something to eat. We don't want to keep the captain waiting now, do we?"

3

Gracie

Gracie looked up at a tap on the door, pulling her attention from the holomaps hovering over the battered table in the small room above the tavern that was unofficially reserved for her.

"Come in," she called, glancing over her shoulder.

"It's me, Captain. 'M bringing Silas. The Level boy."

She smiled to herself. Ari's Stacks accent always grew thicker when she was trying to put one over on an unsuspecting target.

"Bring him in," she said, pushing her chair back from the table.

A moment later, Ari stepped into the room, the young man from the Naval Academy close on her heels.

He looked furious.

She bit back a smile and gestured at a small stool. "Take a seat."

To his credit, he hesitated the barest moment, then did as she asked.

Despite the anger steaming off him, the boy knew how to rein himself in and listen to orders.

That was promising, at least.

"Captain," he said, irony dripping off his tone. "I'm flattered you agreed to meet with me."

She finally allowed the smile to reach her lips. "The pleasure's mine."

She let the silence hang for a few moments while she studied him.

She'd never been afraid of silence. Most people were, and she'd found the most effective way to get people to talk was to simply sit them down across from you and say nothing. It didn't take most people long to start babbling out whatever came into their heads to avoid the awkwardness, and often enough it was something they wouldn't have said if they'd been thinking it through.

The boy didn't, though, just met her eyes, a stubborn irritation glowing in his expression.

Her smile broadened, just a little.

"Well, Silas," she said at last, stretching the kink from her back. She'd been pouring over the charts for long enough that her muscles were beginning to protest. "You've come quite a ways to talk to me, from the sounds of it. So tell me." She leaned forward, resting her forearms on her knees. "What is it you've come all this way to say?"

He watched her, head cocked to one side, eyes narrowed. "I'd heard rumours that Captain Mad Dog was the most well-known pirate in Blackrock," he said at last. He gestured around him. "From what I've been told, the navy, all the way up to Admiral Judith Usher herself, has been personally hunting Mad Dog for years, to no avail. Ships that come after the *Sweet Jenny* have a habit of turning up on the radar as ghost ships, or disappearing completely." He shook his head. "Excuse my incredulity, but this hardly seems like the lodgings of a pirate captain with that sort of reputation."

She watched him a moment.

"Fair enough," she said at last. "I would have thought that after we met in the tavern, you'd have realized that things aren't always what they seem at first glance. But—" She shrugged. "If you'd like proof, this should be proof enough, I think." She pulled back the sleeve of her shirt, exposing the symbol burned into her skin.

The mass of scar tissue was in the shape of the mark attached only to those who ended up in prison on the highest government charges of treason. The symbol that meant "traitor." If you weren't found guilty after your trial, it was removed. But if you escaped, crossed the prison barriers while it was still attached to your skin—it burned itself into your flesh, a permanent marking you could never get rid of.

The burns were a faded white by now, the scars of them old enough that she would hardly have noticed them if she hadn't thought about it. The pain of the damaged nerves still woke her at night sometimes from a sound sleep, itching and aching under her skin, even after so many years. But even that had become habit enough that she'd just turn over and fall back asleep, rather than lie awake dreaming of revenge.

Silas's eyes had gone wide, his face growing a shade paler.

She pulled her sleeve back down, covering the old scar. "So," she said pleasantly. "If we've proved my identity to your satisfaction, I'd like to hear why I shouldn't slit your throat and get Ari here to drag you back into an alley for the ghosts to feed on."

Silas had brought himself back under control impressively quickly. His face was still a little pale, but he nodded. "Understood," he said. "I'm sorry for questioning you."

She smiled a little. "I admit, I'd have been disappointed if you hadn't."

He sat up, leaning forward so his posture matched hers, a restless energy humming through the lines of his body. "I'm not going to beat around the bush," he said. "I know the real story of what happened back in the court trials twenty-five years ago, with the Starfire naval disaster. I know why you turned pirate."

She raised her eyebrows, watching him. "You do, do you?" she asked at last. "Enlighten me, please."

He reached for his pocket.

Her pistol was in her hand before his hand touched the fabric of his trousers, and behind him, Ari's pistol was cocked at his head.

He froze.

"Good," said Gracie, keeping her voice mild. "Now. Put your hands back where we all can see them."

She didn't think the Admiral would have sent someone as stupid as this boy after her, but she couldn't afford not to take precautions. She knew perfectly well what a prize she'd be for anyone willing to risk it.

Slowly, hands spread wide to show they were empty, Silas held his arms out in front of him. "I'm not reaching for a weapon, I promise," he said, keeping his voice low. "I have some information chips I thought would interest you. I was going to pull them out of my pocket."

Gracie considered him for a moment, then nodded at Ari.

"Get up," Ari snapped, shoving the pistol into his back. He cast her an irritated glance, but got to his feet, still holding his hands out in front of him.

"Which pocket?" Gracie asked.

He made a curt gesture with his chin.

"Don't mind me," said Ari, holding the pistol with one hand and reaching into his pocket with the other.

Silas kept his eyes on Gracie, gaze steady, eyes narrowed, and she found she was smiling a little despite herself.

Fool this boy may be, but she found herself liking him.

"These them?" Ari asked a moment later, pulling out a handful of chips.

He nodded. "Be careful with those. I risked hanging for treason to bring them here." His tone was short, and she couldn't in honesty blame him.

"I apologize for the inconvenience," she said, gesturing him back to his chair. "What's in these documents that's important enough to risk hanging for?"

He leaned forward again, his expression going from sullen to intense in a moment. "Those are the records of the trial. The ones that weren't made public." His voice was low, but she could hear the vehemence in it. "It was the biggest naval disaster in the last century, but the trial was behind closed doors, and the only records ever released to the public were heavily redacted. We got the official story, nothing more. But these?" He gestured to the chips in Ari's hand. "These tell a bit of a different story from what we've all been told." He glanced up at her again, catching her eye. "Captain. Those chips contain proof—irrefutable proof—that your parents were set up. They weren't the ones who were responsible for that disaster, or the thousands who died from it. They were executed as part of a coverup, and everyone involved in the trial knew it."

He stood and ran his hand through his hair, a second away, she assumed wryly, from starting to pace.

"And you. You were in the Academy, weren't you? Your records were erased, but I found enough of a track to know you were there. They took you out, tried you for treason. And Admiral Usher—I'd always wondered why she hated you so much. She was one of the ones who testified against you, wasn't she? You escaped, and I can't blame you for what you did after that. But it was all a setup, from the top down. You were innocent, and so were your parents. And the people who were responsible—the people whose damned negligence caused the whole thing—are still sitting in their Admiralty seats."

Gracie sighed, watching the young man.

She could feel a hint of the old anger flaring up again, the fire she'd so carefully banked. The sick fury at the Admiral—not an admiral then, and she hadn't been a pirate, just two women studying in the Academy and dreaming of a career in the Navy—that had become a cold hate burning under her skin, a fire she'd thought, once, would consume her.

But it was old. The pain was old, and the anger was old, and the desperate hurt of it was old, old, old.

"And?" she asked at last, when he didn't continue.

He glanced down at her, a hint of confusion on his face. "Didn't you hear me? I said, I have proof!" He gestured at the chips in Ari's hand. "If you're nearly as powerful and dangerous as they say you are, why not take this? Take it back, shove it in the faces of the people in power, release it to the public. You could take them down with this. You're a pirate, but surely once there's incontrovertible proof of what drove you to it, to save your own life, you'll get a pardon. And you can take them down, all of them. Every last one of the people who killed your parents, ruined your life. And if they don't want to do that, there'll be people who'll fight alongside you, I swear it. There are people out there, like me, who believe the Level navy should be what it damn well promises it is."

She almost smiled at that. Instead, she shook her head. "And then?" she asked.

He stared at her. "You could get your revenge. You could clear your name, make them pay for what they did to you!"

She watched him for a long time, tipping her head to one side.

He believed it. He truly believed, in his young, idealistic way, that you could turn back the clock, heal wounds that had long since scarred over.

Had she ever been that young? She must have been, once. Once upon a time, she must have been just as stupid and idealistic as this boy in front of her.

At last, she shook her head. "I'm sorry, lad."

He frowned, brows furrowing. "What?"

She pushed back her chair and rose. "I'm sorry." She gestured around her. "I've got everything I need right here. I have a good crew, a berth to call home, a ship. I'm well respected, and nothing happens around this port without my say-so. Why would I give that up for revenge?"

He was still staring at her, his face a mix of blank astonishment and anger and bewilderment.

She gave him a humourless smile. "You say I could get my revenge, take your documents and burn across the Level like vengeance sent by Our Lady of the Ghosts. Perhaps I could. And supposing I was very lucky, and I did that without being killed myself, I took down Admiral Usher and everyone in the Naval High Command who was complicit in the Starfire disaster—maybe with half of the people who'd followed me still alive afterwards—supposing I did that. What happens next? No matter what your documents say or don't say, they wouldn't give me back a career in the navy. And I couldn't rightly go back to piracy after that either, could I? I'd be a curiosity at best, you a pariah, because if you've turned on the navy once, you'll do it again, and they know it. You think the rot in the navy is just one or two up at the top? You think the rest of them would cheer you on for rooting it out? If you think that, lad, you don't know them like I do. No, I'm too old to dream of that sort of revenge."

She glanced at his face and sighed, pulling her chair around and straddling it. "Tell me, lad—why does this mean so much to you? You're right, I was in the Naval Academy once. I know damn well what you risked to come here. So why? A pirate hardly merits this kind of attention, I think."

He was still glaring at her. "Doesn't matter, does it?" he said stiffly. "You've already said you're not interested. Is anything I say going to change your mind?"

She shook her head. "It won't. But indulge an old pirate, won't you?"

He glared a moment longer, then at last, reluctantly, he sat back down. "My parents," he said at last, his voice low. "They were killed in the disaster. Both of them. I was too young to know anything about it. I was raised by my aunt and uncle. But my parents died in that incident." She could hear the hardness in his tone, and she recognized it well enough. "Those same people who set up your parents to die for treason so the important people involved wouldn't have to face the consequences of their own negligence killed mine as well. And they got away with it. They killed thousands of good sailors, and there's no one in the Academy who'll risk their necks to bring out the truth. No one but me."

She raised her eyebrows. "Why come to me, then? Why not bring this to the reporters? Spread it out on the airwaves?"

He snorted. "You think I'd have lived long enough to do that? I barely escaped with my life as it was. I was raised to know my duty, to my parents' memories and to the navy. I've spent every moment I could shipboard since I was twelve years old trying to live up to it. But I can't do that if the navy's rotting from the inside. I'd happily die for it if I thought my death would make a difference, but it won't, not alone. You were my best chance. With Captain Mad Dog backing this, people would have listened. But—” He gave a sardonic shrug. “I should have known the great captain would be too comfortable to listen to anything I had to say.”

She was still watching him. “So what now?”

He gave another one-shouldered shrug. “Hardly matters, does it? I’ve already given up everything. I go back, they’ll find some excuse to jail me, or have me executed for treason.”

“You’re going back, then?”

He snorted again. “What else is there for me? Turn pirate, like you?” He shoved back his chair and stood. “I gambled, and I lost. I’m man enough to accept that.” He shot her a humourless smile. “Best of luck to you, Captain.”

She waited until he was almost at the door before she held up a hand. “Wait, lad.”

He stopped, but didn’t turn.

“I have a proposition for you.” Her voice was mild, but she could see him tense at it.

She might be misjudging him. But she didn’t think she was.

“What sort of proposition?” he asked at last, still without turning.

She sighed and stood. “Been looking for a sailor to crew with me. Lost someone in a skirmish back in the Helix sector a couple months back, and I’ve been flying short-handed. We may not see eye to eye, you and me, but you’re a brave lad, and a resourceful one. Don’t know more’n a handful when I was in the Academy could have done what you’ve done—steal classified documents, escape the guards, make it here. Add to that, Ari says she saw you step in to kill a ghost to save a man you didn’t know. I could use a man like you on my ship.”

For a few moments, he stood where he was.

When he did turn, at last, there was a weariness under the stubborn expression on his face. "I have no intention of turning pirate."

She shrugged. "Well then, how about this—I'm flying a job. I'm short-handed, and you have no way off this rock. I accept that that's partly on my account. So you come on this one job. Maybe in the meantime you convince me you're right, and I should come back and take my revenge on the Admiral and the Level. Or maybe I convince you that piracy isn't as terrible as you've been led to believe. And if neither of those things happen—" She shrugged again. "I drop you on a resource planet somewhere where you can find a ship back to the Level. Maybe you sign on with a merchant crew, know a handful of those who'll see your credentials and not ask questions. Always looking for a sailor who's trained to fight, they are, and you'd be back in the sky, at least."

He closed his eyes. There was a weary slump to his shoulders that almost made her feel sorry for him.

But then, he'd made his choice. No one had forced him into it, and that meant he was better off than at least three quarters of the people on this dripping rock.

He straightened, meeting her eye. His jaw was clenched tight, and she could still see the anger burning in his expression. "Captain. Believe me—I risked hanging to bring you these documents. I'm not afraid of facing consequences. Don't think you can threaten me into signing on with a pirate crew." He paused a moment. "But I'll sail with you, on one condition. You don't want to help me bring to justice the people who murdered my parents and hanged yours. Very well. But if I sail with you on this one job, help you take whatever prize you're after—then you'll swear to at least look at the documents I brought, and hear me out."

She considered him for a long moment.

He'd been willing to risk hanging to bring her the documents, true enough, but then, she'd found most people's bravery evaporated somewhat when they were face to face with the immediate prospect of death. Not many would have had the gall to try to strike a bargain with Captain Mad Dog. Then again, Ari had said she'd seen him save a drunken sailor from a ghost. It took nerve enough to do that.

She wasn't interested in his idea of revenge, no. And she wasn't young enough and a fool enough to think the navy had something in it worth saving. But no harm in hearing him out. He'd be trying to convince her, she knew that well enough, but a few weeks on a pirate ship and he might be open to being convinced himself.

And there was just a chance she could use what was on those documents. As much as she knew the old wounds reading them would cut open, perhaps there was something there she could use.

At last, she nodded. "Very well, lad. You have yourself a bargain. We take the prize, I'll agree to review your documents and sit down and listen to your plan."

He stared at her, as if he hadn't been expecting the answer. She cracked a smile. "Go on, Ari'll be waiting for you outside the door. Tell her you're coming along, and I asked her to get you kitted out. We're leaving tonight."

"Tonight?" He frowned.

She raised one shoulder in a shrug. "Bit of an urgent job. Usually we take more time planet-side. Ari'll give you everything you need to know. You'll get the standard crew contract—you're the newest crew member, so you get a one-twentieth share, plus whatever bounty you earn during the trip. You can ask Ari for the record. I believe in being transparent with the earnings."

He gave a terse nod, and stepped out the door.

Gracie watched him go.

When he was gone, she sighed and pulled her chair around, turning back to the charts.

He'd be a decent crew, she'd seen enough of him to guess that, and there was something behind his burning intensity, naive as it was, that intrigued her.

But it wasn't that that'd made her offer.

She recognized his type. He was officer material, that boy. And losing someone like him would be a blow to the navy. To the Admiral, God damn her eyes. She'd hear the reports, sooner or later, hear that he'd left, and he'd signed on to Mad Dog's crew.

Silas wouldn't be the first officer-material Gracie had turned, and he wouldn't be the last, but every blow to the Admiral was one Gracie was happy to strike.

The lad was only half-right. She hadn't been interested in his kind of revenge, the kind that would risk everything she'd spent the last twenty-five-odd years building up from nothing, and would gain her at best a pale shadow of what she was owed.

But she'd never forgive them.

Her name was already a curse in the Admiralty. And she intended to ensure they never stopped fearing what she'd do next.

4

Silas

Gracie had been right—Ari was waiting outside the door. From the slight trace of guilt in her expression, she'd been listening in.

He hardly cared.

"Captain says you're to kit me out," he said through his teeth.

Ari raised her eyebrows at him. "She signed you on as crew?"

He gave a terse nod, and Ari grinned. "Look at you. Less than a day on Blackrock, and you're already turning pirate."

He turned to her. "I'm not turning pirate." He was still speaking through his teeth, enunciating his words so they'd be impossible to misunderstand. "I'm going along on one job with you. That's it. And I'm doing it because your captain made a bargain with me."

The shock of Gracie's refusal was still jangling through his muscles, turning gradually from despair to anger.

But under the anger—there was a bright thrill of excitement.

He shoved it down ruthlessly.

He'd been in the Academy two and a half years. And every damn day of those two and a half years he'd swallowed down the desperate, aching need to be out in deep space again, where he could finally breathe, feel a ship's deck under his feet and ratlines under his hands. Because what he was doing in the Academy—preparing himself to be a commissioned officer, to serve the navy the way his parents had—was worth the sacrifice.

That was all this was, too—a sacrifice he was making in pursuit of his duty. Nothing more than that. And he could ignore the sharp, clean joy that came at the prospect of finally damn well doing something—of action, of testing himself against the elements instead of against the bland exams set by the teachers, of no longer having to measure every word and thought, or force his muscles still and bite his tongue until it bled because that was what was expected of an Academy student.

Ari was watching him, eyebrows still raised. At last, though, she shrugged and jerked her head towards the rickety stairs. "Well, if you're coming with, we'd best get you dealt with. Going to have to sign onto the crew for the voyage, and from the look of your knapsack, you didn't bring much kit with you." She grinned. "And what you did bring, you lost about ten steps off the ship."

He glared at her, and she snickered. "Hey. If it hadn't been me, it would have been someone else."

He frowned. There was something under her accent, that blend of the Stacks and resource-planet tones he'd come to expect from pirates. Something much more cultured. He'd heard traces of it once or twice as she spoke before, but now that he was listening for it, it was unmistakable.

"Come on, told you we haven't got much time," she said, starting down the stairs.

He followed, his boots clattering loudly on the creaking steps.

The noisiness of it was probably intentional—difficult to sneak up stairs like these, and from what he'd seen of Gracie, she wasn't one to leave things to chance.

He could still feel the hot, unreasoning anger burning under his forced calm.

Damn her.

He'd heard stories of Mad Dog. They'd all heard stories of Mad Dog, how when the *Sweet Jenny* sent out her ID mark, ships in the navy would turn and run. The captain was a legend.

And he'd believe them. He'd eaten up the tales like a child eating sweetmeats, and he'd gambled his entire life on their veracity.

And then he'd come here to find … what? A coward? Maybe. He still wasn't sure. He'd been expecting a larger-than-life hero, and he'd found a middle-aged woman with crows-feet around her eyes, who smoked the foulest cigars he'd ever smelled and drank sweet tea instead of hard liquor.

And then, like the idiot he was, he'd signed on to her crew. Even if it was just for this one job.

He cursed himself under his breath.

But better this than the alternative. Better this than accepting that he'd failed, accepting the corruption in the navy as something inevitable and unchangeable.

He'd go with Mad Dog on this one job, and he'd do everything in his power to make sure they succeeded. She'd promised to hear him out then, and he'd figure out a way to convince her. And then he'd damn well fix what had been broken twenty-five years ago, in the organization he'd given his entire life to.

He wasn't sure how he could do otherwise, and still face himself in the mirror.

He reached the ground floor of the tavern where Ari waited impatiently, the tavern-keeper beside her. "Go on," Ari said, gesturing at the woman. "Give her your sizes. Abigail is the one who keeps us all kitted out, she knows where to find things at a decent price. And no one dares cheat her, because they know Mad Dog deals with her, and Mad Dog isn't one to let something like that slide."

He gave the woman his size for boots and trousers and shirt in terse tones, but she looked more amused than offended at his temper.

"I'll put word out to my people and have the lad's kit back within a couple hours," she said to Ari, as if he wasn't standing in front of her. "None of the sizes are that uncommon, so we should be able to make do."

"Good enough," said Ari. "We're shipping out at eight bells, though. If your people are late, the captain'll have your ears for making her crew watch the boy wandering around deck naked."

Abigail laughed, and Silas shot Ari a dirty look.

She grinned innocently back at him, and gestured him to a table. "Sit. Abigail'll get you kitted out well enough to satisfy the captain, and meantime, I'll get you signed on to the crew."

She rummaged in her duffle and pulled out a small box Silas recognized instantly as a copy of the ship's manifest. She tapped it, and a note sprang up, hovering over it.

She waved it across to him, and he glanced it over quickly, stomach tight.

Standard crew duties, compensation set out as Gracie had told him. It wasn't an unfair bargain, truth be told. He'd sailed in the navy long enough to know that that size of share was unthinkably generous in naval terms, if somewhat more standard among pirates.

Still, in the navy you drew regular pay, and the chances of getting shot out of the sky or torn to pieces by the ghost of one of your former crewmates was much less pronounced.

"Good?" she asked, when he looked up.

He nodded. "Fair enough."

It hardly mattered, really.

Ari pulled up a blank note and set it hovering over the box. "This'll upload to the ships databank," she said. "You can go ahead and speak into it. Repeat the words after me."

He nodded again.

His heart was pounding in his chest, and he wasn't sure whether it was because of Mad Dog's refusal, or because of what he was about to do.

But he'd already given up everything for this. He'd already given up his future, his eventual officer's posting, his life in the navy.

"I … go ahead and say your full name," Ari began.

"I, Silas Hunt," he repeated.

"Do hereby sign on with the crew of the *Sweet Jenny* for the duration of the voyage, leaving from Blackrock and returning to Blackrock."

He repeated the words.

"I do hereby swear my loyalty to the *Sweet Jenny* and to her captain, to follow any duly given orders, and to otherwise provide my services as set out in the crew manifest."

Again, he repeated the words.

"I agree that should I forfeit my responsibilities, save for good cause as set out in the crew manifest, I shall forfeit my life or my freedom, judgement to be carried out by the captain."

Again, he repeated the words, ignoring the cold in his chest.

He'd said similar words a thousand times, each time he joined on the crew of another naval vessel. But on each of those vessels, as brutal as the captains may have been, he knew that they'd have to ultimately report back to their superior officers and justify their actions. A captain was the law and the god of their own ship, he knew that well enough, and there was no recourse when you were trapped onboard, light-years away from any other human. But there was always the chance that the ship's records would be pulled, the tamper-proof ship's black-box examined, and he'd seen captains censured when their discipline was too harsh even for the standards of the navy.

Here, though, the saying was entirely true. Captain Mad Dog was the law and the god of the *Sweet Jenny*, and from what he'd seen, there was no one and nothing to rein her in but her own sense of fair play.

"Good," said Ari, tapping the box. The note with the transcript of his words disappeared, and a button flashed on one corner.

Ari rummaged in her pocket and handed him a pin. "Prick your thumb and give us a print, and then you're signed on."

He nodded silently.

He could wrestle with the decision all he wanted. But in truth, he'd made his decision the moment he'd decided to steal the documents. All of that had led here, whether he'd known it or not.

He could feel the sick irrevocability of it sitting in the pit of his stomach.

He pricked his thumb and squeezed it until he had a small, scarlet bead of blood. Then he pressed down carefully on the screen.

A small light on the box flashed, and then his thumbprint disappeared, downloaded onto the system along with his DNA mark.

Ari wiped the place clean carefully with the corner of her shabby shirt, then looked over at him, still grinning. "There. Everything fixed and official. Let's take you to meet the crew."

He grabbed her arm as she went to drop the box back into her duffel. "I'm crew now. First, I want to know about this job."

Ari hesitated a moment. At last she shook her head. "Captain'll explain the job when she's good and ready. In the meantime, you and I do what we're told."

He studied her face a moment. His most recent experiences with Gracie hadn't exactly made him trust that either she or Ari wasn't trying to pull something on him. But the look on Ari's face was as close to sincere as he'd ever seen it.

"I'm not lying to you, Level boy," she said. "Captain has a reputation. You know that well enough, or you wouldn't have come out here looking for her. And she does things her own way, and if you want to damn well stay on her crew and stay alive, you shut your mouth and follow orders."

At last, he nodded.

He'd just signed away his life and his freedom, at least until the voyage was done. It had been on a pirate vessel, yes, but he knew well enough that the pirate ships and the merchant ships had an uneasy one-way truce in the matter of crew—no merchant that valued its cargo would knowingly sign someone who was sworn to a pirate crew until they were released. It wouldn't keep them safe, perhaps, but it would at least ensure that they weren't the most tempting target available.

The navy had no such scruples, but then, the navy was probably currently calculating how high to hang him if he ever showed his face at the Academy again.

He had to bite back the sharp sting of regret.

It didn't matter.

He knew what he knew. And he could never have done what everyone else who knew did—keep his head down, let the past stay in the past. Not try to damn well fix it. He'd never have been able to do that. He'd have spoken up, shouted loudly enough that they couldn't ignore him anymore. And then the tattoo burned onto Gracie's arm would have been implanted in his own, and he'd have gone down in the books as either a traitor, or yet another sailor with strong potential who'd succumbed to space-madness and started spouting nonsense that would get people killed.

Either way, he'd be put down like a stray dog.

"Come on," said Ari, zipping her duffle and pushing herself to her feet. "Crew'll see your pledge upload and be wondering what's happening."

He took a deep breath and nodded. "I'll follow you."

It took all his concentration to stay with Ari as she ducked through the backstreets down to the port. She made no effort whatsoever to make it easy for him to keep up.

"This is the *Sweet Jenny's* private dock," she said at last, as they stepped out of the narrow warren of dim streets, packed with bodies and lit with flickering orange lantern light, and back onto the docks.

The docks here weren't like the ones on the Level, hanging out over the swirling gas of the gas planet, creating the illusion that they hung over nothingness—that once you crossed the oxygen barriers, you could step off the docks and into the very space the ships would be taking you to.

These docks were as cramped as the rest of the filthy pirate city, carved out of the rock and dripping with the ever-present moisture, the ancient airlock doors above them the only things that differentiated them from the rest of the caverns.

The dock that held the *Sweet Jenny* was no different, at first glance, from any other dock along the row. But when he looked closer, he could see the heavy airlock doors set into the ceiling of the small cavern were big enough to admit one ship only.

He'd only spent a few hours in the pirate settlement, but it was enough to tell how valuable a private airlock entrance like this would be.

The Sweet Jenny herself was a sleek craft, her sides bearing the burnished score-marks of FTL travel, her shape unmistakable from Silas's years of sailing for the navy—the ship every young recruit was told stories of, in whispers, by the older petty officers.

He almost laughed. What his old crewmates would say if they saw him now …

Ari shot him a smug grin, then stepped out onto the dock. "Hey," she called through her comm. "Open the damn doors, got our brand new cabin-boy with me."

He turned to glare at her, and she smirked as the ramp lowered.

She led him through the hatch into the main deck of the *Sweet Jenny*, and he glanced around him, impressed despite himself. The ship was small, but every part of her was designed for maximum efficiency—from the walkway that formed the main deck, jutting out over the cargo belly of the ship, to the narrow catwalks and ratlines that connected each layer of the ship to the next, to the small, lock-tight doors on the captain's and crew's quarters and the med bay, useful in case someone turned ghost.

"So this is Silas Hunt."

The clear contempt in the words made him look up. A small cluster of people stood on one end of the main deck. Every one of them was watching him, hostility clear in their gazes.

The woman who'd spoken had cold green eyes, a weathered face, and dark hair cropped short. She was wiry, and short enough that if she was standing next to him, the top of her head wouldn't reach his chin, but she was glaring at him, eyes narrowed and arms crossed on her chest. "Level boy, are you? Served in the navy, sounds of it." She turned and spat on the deck, her face broadcasting pure disdain.

Ari was still grinning. "Silas, this is Vee. Vee, Silas." She turned to him. "Vee's our cook and our medic. You don't want to get on her bad side, all I'm saying."

Silas glanced at the woman.

He was clearly already pretty damn far on her bad side.

"This is our first mate, Toothpick."

Silas looked over in surprise at the man's Stacks name.

He should have been expecting it. People who turned pirate didn't often do it because the life they were leaving was comfortable, and he knew damn well that most of the people here were from resource planets or the Stacks—the ghost-haunted repurposed mining platforms that lay below the Level, home to those who had neither the money nor the family nor the political pull to get out. The navy had always used sailors from the Stacks—easy enough to find, as they mostly didn't have a better option—but they seldom made a higher rank than ordinary sailor. He was accustomed to people who were from the Stacks doing their best to hide where they were from.

Neither Ari nor Toothpick seemed to have any concern about broadcasting Toothpick's origins.

He was a tall man, lean, with dark skin and greying hair, and piercing eyes that seemed to cut right through Silas. He nodded, but didn't speak, and Ari gestured to the woman beside him, seated in a hover-chair. "That's Freddie, our mechanic."

Freddie looked a little younger than Gracie, but not by much. She was a wide woman, with light brown skin and straight black hair pulled back into a ponytail. Her legs were thin from disuse, but her upper body was powerful, the muscles in her arms and shoulders clearly defined. She had a broad face and a pleasant grin, and there was a restless energy about her that he could all but feel.

"And then we have Jumper over there, and Temple beside him.

Jumper's weapons, Temple's our pilot and works our tech."

A small man with olive skin and grey hair, who looked to be in his sixties, nodded at Silas when Ari said the name Temple. Beside him stood a young man who looked a couple years younger than Silas. He had pale skin, wide eyes, and a face that was probably normally friendly, but was currently drawn into a scowl. He gave Silas a small nod, then looked quickly away.

"Jumper don't talk. Mostly uses signs, so you'd best learn 'em," said Ari casually. "Might be young, but he's the best damn weapons tech around, and you miss what he's trying to tell you, you're liable to get yourself killed." She grinned. "By me, if not by the enemy. I'm second mate, me, and I'm over the crew. And that's all of us."

She turned back to the others. "Sil here signed on for the one voyage only. He's getting a bunk and a locker, same as the rest of us, and Captain'll be pissed if she finds you killed him on accident."

Silas bit back a retort.

He could say he'd been shipping out in deep space since he was twelve years old, and he knew damn well how to handle himself. But he doubted that would impress the people standing in front of him. Honestly, he had no real desire to do so. These were his unwilling shipmates for one voyage. He'd treat them with civility, and he'd expect the same in return, but there was no call to try to make friends.

"Come, I'll show you your bunk," said Ari, gesturing. She jumped up on the railing overlooking the cargo hold, grabbed a ratline, and slid down a level to the crew quarters. "Ladder's over on the side, Level boy," she called back over her shoulder.

He found, suddenly, that he was grinning.

He vaulted the rail, catching the ratline, and slid down to join her, landing neatly on the narrow walkway beside her without so much as a stagger.

Yes, he was on a pirate ship. But after two and a half damn years in the Academy, he hadn't realized how much he'd missed being ship-side, down to his bones.

"Crew bunks together," Ari said, tapping a lock on one of the doors. "Captain don't want to take risks with ghosts, so the door locks. Never get the whole crew at a time in the bunks, so it means some of us would live through it even if we didn't finish the ghost off, and the med bay locks down right quick too."

He glanced at her curiously as he tossed his jacket across the hammock she pointed out to him. "You're from the Level."

She flushed, and looked away.

"You are, aren't you? I can hear your accent."

She was scowling, and in other circumstances, he might have been willing not to press her. But after the day he'd had, he wasn't feeling particularly charitable, at least not when it came to Ari's feelings.

At last, she turned back to him. She was still scowling, but she gave him a short nod. "Grew up on the Level, yeah."

He raised an eyebrow. "Family?"

Again, she hesitated.

He gave a wry snort. "Not like I'm going to be able to take back news of you. I show up back at the Academy, I'll deserve everything I get."

She sighed. "Yeah." For a moment she was silent. "My last name was Davenport."

He frowned, then his eyebrows shot up.

The Davenport family was one of the most prominent families on the Level, and for a moment, his brain tried to superimpose Ari, ragged and piratical and grinning, across the pictures of the Davenports on the pages of the society papers, and failed utterly.

She was staring at the floor, her jaw clenched, and for a moment, he almost felt guilty for bringing it up.

But she'd stolen his knapsack, and played him for a fool. She hardly had grounds to complain.

"Well," he said at last, with a weak attempt to lighten the mood. "Could be worse. You could have been in Victoria and Robert Davenport's family."

She looked away, her expression pained.

He stared. "Wait. You are?"

He pictured the photographs he'd seen in the papers—Victoria, with her long blond hair and fine features, Robert's glare into the camera. And between them, their son—a slender, pale, miserable-looking young man.

"I thought they only had the one son. I heard he died in an accident when he was a teenager."

Ari finally met his eyes, her smile small and bitter. "They only ever had a daughter. They just weren't willing to accept that. My parents don't do well with things not turning out the way they expect."

Silas frowned, studying her.

Now that he was looking, he could see the resemblance between her and the photograph—the same fine features, high cheekbones, startlingly blue eyes. But there was nothing of the misery that had bled across the youth's expression in the photograph. This woman was confident to the point of cocky, her mouth always on the point of twitching up into an irreverent grin or turning down into a challenging scowl.

"Ran away as soon as I could figure out a way, shipped off-planet. Found my way here, and Gracie signed me on to her crew. Got me what I needed to transition." She shrugged. "Not uncommon around here. Not in the Stacks, either, from what I hear, or on the resource planets. Just the high-class bastards on the Level who think nothing should ever change as have a problem."

He huffed out a small, bitter laugh. "You're right about the Level High Society being afraid of anything that challenges their preconceptions," he muttered, half under his breath. He looked up and caught her eye. "I'm sorry they didn't listen to you."

She studied him for a moment, expression challenging. Then at last her face relaxed into a grin. "Better this way anyways. Can you imagine me trying to flounce around to all the events and make pretty small talk with Levellers?"

He snorted again, louder. She laughed, head tipped back, posture relaxed, and he was struck once again by how pretty she was.

He shook his head at himself. That was the last thing he needed to be thinking about right now.

After he'd stowed his few belongings, she took him on a short tour of the ship, pointing out the weapons and the tech he'd be expected to learn.

There was nothing here different enough from what he'd shipped with before to be unfamiliar, thankfully, but he paid close attention anyway. He knew from experience how easily the slightest miscommunication or fumble in a battle could get people killed.

He'd barely made it back to the deck when a sharp clang rang through the ship.

He glanced up, startled, to see Gracie standing on the main deck, her hands clasped behind her back.

The rest of the crew clearly understood the signal, because a few moments later they'd assembled on the main deck. Gracie caught his eye, and he could see a trace of amusement on her face, but he looked away resolutely, jaw clenched.

"Toothpick," she said, turning to the tall man. "Are we ready to ship out?"

The man nodded. "Aye, Captain. Ship's in good order, supplies laid in." He jerked his head at Silas dismissively. "Ari took the lad around, showed him the ship."

Gracie nodded. "Good." She paused a moment. "I've told none of you yet where we're going. There's a reason for that—if word had got out, even a whisper, we'd be fighting our way through other pirate ships to get to it. No call to be shooting our own when we could be shooting the navy." She gave a small smile. "Any rate, there's a reason for the secrecy, and a reason for the hurry, and the next time we dock, you'll all get your full shore leave."

Her smile widened, and for the first time Silas could see the danger behind Gracie's mild expression. "There's a ship bringing in a load of weapons for the military, the *Agate*. Seems their FTL drive has broken down. They're drifting out too near a black hole for comfort, and their captain was frightened and called in. We're going to go pick up those weapons, fit out the *Sweet Jenny* with what we can, and sell the rest—they'll bring a pretty profit, and these are the best weapons money can buy. Maybe make the navy think twice about coming after a ship that's carrying weapons like that."

Silas could feel his muscles tightening as she spoke, his fingernails digging into his palms.

Naval weapons, in the hands of pirates. He knew damn well what that meant, and how many good sailors would die for it.

He'd known, when he'd agreed to sign on to Mad Dog's crew, that whatever she had in mind, it wouldn't be something the navy would approve of. He'd taken the chance of signing on, knowing she could be meaning to take a merchant ship and kill everyone on board, or go up against a naval ship he'd shipped on in the past. He'd given up his right to protest the moment he agreed to her terms. It was the only option he'd seen open, and he'd known exactly what he was doing when he signed the crew manifest.

But he couldn't sit idly by while the people who'd been responsible for the disaster that killed his parents, who'd knowingly sent out the ships with untested FTL drives, never suffered a moment of consequences for it. While the official naval reports laid the blame on innocent people accused of treason. He couldn't do that.

He had a duty, dammit. That, at least, had been pounded into him deep enough he wasn't likely to forget it.

Gracie glanced around at her crew. Her expression was still mild, but her eyes were sharp. Her gaze didn't rest on him for any longer than it did on the rest of her crew, but he saw the evaluation in her eyes.

He met her gaze defiantly, and again, he saw that hint of humour in her face.

"One other thing you should know," she said at last. "The ship's put out a distress call. It's almost certain the navy will be sending a ship out after it to tow it back to the Level. These weapons will be as important to them as they are to us. We'll have to watch our backs, and there's a good chance we don't end this without some sort of fight."

And there it was.

The chance he'd be fighting against a ship he'd served on, fighting against sailors he knew and had grown up with.

There was always going to be that chance.

And he'd agreed, knowing that. He'd agreed anyways.

He couldn't very well have done otherwise.

"I've passed the last known coordinates of the ship through to the main controls," said Gracie. "Temple, set us a course. The rest of you, prepare to cast off."

The crew turned away to their assigned duties.

"You. Sil. Check the ratlines, make sure they're secure," Ari called over her shoulder.

"Aye," said Silas. Despite his years of training, he found he had to work to keep his tone respectful. She'd assigned him the most menial task on the ship, usually given to the youngest of the new recruits. "Right away."

He turned off to his duties, jaw still clenched tight, as under him, the *Sweet Jenny* purred to life.

5

Hollis

Hollis closed her eyes for just a moment as the piped military tune drifted out of the wide-open hatch ahead of her.

She checked her posture, checked the way she was standing—legs apart, hands behind her back. Her shiny black boots, brand new for the occasion, rubbed against her calves.

She'd get a blister there, if she wasn't careful.

Her coat hung the way it should—it ought to, she'd been up far too late the previous night starching and ironing it. The other new captains she'd studied with had turned theirs over to the launderers. That wasn't an option for her. She'd gone without her noon meal for over a year simply to afford the gold-lacquered buttons on the coat. She could have foregone the buttons, left them regulation blue, but she knew well enough that wherever she went, there would be whispers already—the captain candidate from the Stacks.

She'd be damned if she gave them anything more to gossip about. "Captain?"

The voice came at her elbow, and she opened her eyes with a

start, cursing internally.

The person standing next to her was taller than she was, but not by much. They weren't broad-shouldered, either, but their wiry frame looked anything but delicate. They had dark, curly hair pulled back neatly into a regulation ponytail, light brown skin, a smooth face, either regulation clean-shaven or naturally beardless, she couldn't immediately tell, with pleasant, even, androgynous features, a light voice, and an outfit starched stiffly enough that it would probably stand up on its own.

"Yes?" she said, her voice coming out short with nerves.

She cursed again, quietly. She couldn't afford nerves. She couldn't afford to let anyone on this ship guess that she wasn't completely confident.

"I'm Foster Price. Your first mate."

She nodded brusquely, turning to face forward again.

She recognized the name, although she hadn't met its owner before now.

Foster Price. Non-binary, late twenties, born on a resource planet, worked their way up through the ranks without the benefit of the Academy. First mate was as high a position as they'd merit without Academy training, but it was a good deal more than most sailors achieved. That spoke to either talent, or important friends. And since they hadn't been recommended to the Academy, Hollis was willing to assume it was sheer talent. That, or luck.

"They're ready for you, I believe, Captain." Foster's voice was mild, with enough of the required formality to avoid disrespect, but not enough to be stiff.

They'd have needed a veritable expertise in bootlicking, if they'd gotten to the position of first mate without Academy training. She could hear it in their voice—patently inoffensive in every way.

Hollis nodded again, forced her clenched fists loose, and strode forward, her boots ringing off the hard surface of the ship's loading ramp.

Her ship. Her first command.

Pray to Our Lady that it wouldn't be her last.

The piping increased in volume as she stepped through the hatch and onto the ship's main deck, a loud, shrieking cacophony she'd heard often enough when the captain appeared on deck.

It was different when she was the captain.

The former feelings—awe, resentment, envy, longing—had all been subsumed into one massive wave of nerves.

She paused at the head of the deck, head high, hands clasped behind her back, boots regulation distance apart, and waited. Foster paused beside her, standing deferentially half a step back.

When the last of the shill notes died away, she looked out over the assembled crew.

For a moment, her mind went a static white-blank.

There were so *many* of them. Rows on rows on rows of bodies, standing in neat lines, dressed in assembly-neat uniforms, faces turned up towards her. She couldn't focus on the faces, just a blur of skin-tones and hair-colours, featureless blobs sitting atop sailor's uniforms.

She was responsible for every one of these sailors. If one of them didn't make it home, turned ghost, killed their crewmates, it would be on her. Every life, every death would be her responsibility.

At her elbow, Foster cleared their throat softly.

She drew in a breath—she couldn't help herself this time—and stepped forward.

The sound of her boots on the deck was impossibly loud in the silence.

"Crew of the *Verity*. I am your captain, Hollis Ives."

The sailors below her were looking up at her, watching her steadily. The only sounds were the shuffle of feet, the brush of fabric, the soft in-and-out of hundreds of breaths.

Three hundred and fifty, to be exact. Three hundred and fifty-three, including herself and her two mates. A full complement for a ship of the line.

She cleared her throat. "Sailors. You have each signed onto this ship with your mark. You have pledged your loyalty to the navy. And I will expect each one of you to live up to the pledge you've made. There will be no slacking, there will be no disorderly behaviour, there will be no drunkenness. This is a fighting ship, and we will be in fighting form at all times."

She'd practiced this speech over and over again in front of the small, uneven mirror hung above the washbasin in her Academy dorm.

They would already be underestimating her, before she set foot on the ship. She was well aware of it. She needed to ensure they understood she would brook no insubordination.

"Our duty, sailors, is to keep our system secure. We are the vital lifelines. We protect the merchant ships from pirates, we regulate trade, we allow the lifeblood of the system to flow. It is the honour and the duty of each of us to do so, and to do so in a manner befitting the weight of our responsibility." She paused, letting her words sink in. "And I will expect no less from each of you," she finished at last. "There will be no leniency for those who do not comport themselves as befits sailors sworn into service."

Her voice didn't shake.

There was a long moment of silence, as she looked at her crew and they looked at her.

She could see the resentment on their faces, the mistrust, barely masked.

She hadn't expected any less. She was from the Stacks, and every sailor here knew it.

Her hands tried to clench into fists behind her back, but she refused to let them.

She wasn't afraid of a fight. She'd never been afraid of a fight—if she had been, there was no way the Admiral would have plucked her from the nameless ranks of sailors with an Academy recommendation.

There was no way she would have survived the Academy itself.

It was an open secret she'd left another officer candidate on the point of death, after a dead-of-night duel. They couldn't prove her guilt, and the other candidate, to his credit, had refused to rat her out. The Admiral had told her, sternly, that should there be another incident, she'd be unceremoniously removed from her position.

She hadn't done it because she'd enjoyed the fight. She'd done it because she hadn't had a choice. Because if she hadn't all but killed him, someone would have killed her.

She was from the Stacks. And she knew exactly what it took to survive.

When she judged the silence had lasted long enough, she strode down the ramp to walk between the ranks of sailors, Foster at her elbow.

They turned to watch her as she passed, and she could feel the weight of the eyes on her back.

She was the law and the god of her own ship, and out in the far, far reaches of space, the fringes of the known universe where pirates or ghosts or simple space-madness could wipe out an entire crew without word of their death reaching the Level for weeks or months after—there was very little a captain could do that would merit censure from the powers that be in the navy.

But law and god of her ship she may be, there was always the threat of mutiny—of a crew who didn't trust their captain, or whose hatred and fear overwhelmed their fear of punishment when they returned. And if there were a mutiny on this ship, she wasn't sure who she could trust.

No. She knew damn well she wouldn't be able to trust anyone.

But she couldn't punish the sailors for resentful glances, much as they made the back of her neck prickle with the inherent, unspoken threat.

She could have gone around the captain's walk to get to her cabin, but she intended the crew to know that she was not a captain who was afraid of the lower decks. She'd been a sailor herself before the Academy, and she hadn't forgotten her way around the ratlines, if necessary.

She was almost at the end of the endless row of sailors standing at attention when she caught the voice from behind her, in a whisper clearly meant to be overheard. "You can smell the Stacks on her, can't you?"

She spun abruptly, and Foster stepped back smartly, just in time to avoid the ceremonial sword at her hip striking them.

"Who said that?" she demanded, her voice harsh and sharp in the sudden silence.

No one spoke.

Hollis narrowed her eyes. Her heart was beating loudly enough that she wondered if the sailors around her could hear it.

"Who said that?" she asked again. Her tone was quiet, and deadly calm.

The sailors shifted uneasily, but again, no one spoke.

"Very well," she said. Her voice cut through the quiet like a blade. "If you will not tell me who spoke, I will ensure that every member of this crew suffers the punishment."

There was a small scuffle to one side or her, and she refrained herself, with an effort, from glancing reflexively over, refrained herself from putting a hand on the comforting grip of her pistol.

She would not show fear. She would not allow this crew to believe she was afraid of them.

"It was me, Captain. Sorry, Captain. It was only a joke, Captain."

She turned.

A young man stood before her, eyes downcast, but there was the hint of a smirk under his solemn expression, a hint of mockery under his respectful tone. A petty officer, clearly someone from the Level. Probably with an important family.

She let the silence hang for much longer than was comfortable, until the young man was shifting uneasily under her gaze. The rest of the crew was silent, watching the tableau play out.

"It was a joke, was it?" she asked at last, her tone cool.

"Yes, Captain. Just a joke, is all." There was still that smug mockery under his tone.

She looked him up and down again, deliberately, letting her gaze sweep over him as if she were inspecting livestock.

"What's your name, sailor?" she asked.

"Midship officer Blakely, Captain."

"Very good, Officer Blakely." She injected a knife-edge of disdain into her voice. "You're on watch-and-watch-again for the next week. In that time, you're on inspection duty on the outer hull."

The man's head jerked up, his face gone suddenly pale. "Captain, it was just a bit of a joke. I'm sorry—"

"You will obey orders, sailor, or by God I'll have you flogged." She bit off the words.

Around her, the crew murmured in quiet protest.

She could well have sentenced him to death. Depending on the course they set, it was easily possible that a sailor on double-watch on inspection duty on the outer hull would be weary enough that they wouldn't notice the alarm for an approaching meteoroid or bit of debris in time to get themself out of the way. There was a reason the outer hull inspection duty was split so that no sailor had to take it more than once in a fortnight, and even so, it was the watch with the highest number of casualties.

And if he did die, when she returned, she'd face his family.

That didn't matter, not right now.

She turned slowly, examining the crew. Her hand itched for the grip of her pistol or the hilt of her cutlass.

They quieted under her glare.

Her heart was pounding so quickly that she could hear it in her ears, feel it in her fingertips.

"Is there anyone else who'd like to say something? Anyone who disagrees with the punishment?" she asked into the quiet.

No one spoke.

"Very good." She turned to Foster. "Mate Price, please see to it that this sailor's punishment is carried out."

"Aye, Captain," Foster murmured.

She couldn't tell from their voice whether they approved or disapproved of her actions.

In the end, though, it hardly mattered.

She was from the Stacks. She'd have to fight for every scrap of respect, and she couldn't afford to let her crew think, for one moment, that she was weak.

She let her gaze sweep over the crew one last time. Then she turned and started down the row of sailors once more, the only sound her boots clicking against the metal of the deck.

From the corner of her eye, she saw Foster's hand relax from where it had been resting on the grip of their pistol.

An eternity later, she reached the end of the line of sailors. She turned up the short ramp to the captain's quarters, tapping the control as she approached. The doors slid back silently, and she stepped through, Foster ducking in after her.

She strode over to the large table in the centre of the conference room and sank down into the large, comfortable captain's chair. "Mate Price. The Captain's Log and the Seal, if you please?" she said, holding out a hand imperiously.

"Of course, Captain." Foster stepped up beside her, handing her the ceremonial seal, coded to her fingerprint, and the thin rectangular case that was the Captain's Log.

The moment she inserted the seal into the log, she'd have access to her mission instructions.

The moment she inserted the seal into the log, she'd trigger the ship's black box to begin recording—a failsafe should the unthinkable happen, and the ship not return—the ship's hatch would seal, and the three hundred and fifty-three souls on board would be committed to the depths of space.

Foster stood respectfully back, but she could feel their eyes on her.

Her hands were trembling as she pulled the cap off the seal and inserted it into the slot in the captain's log, but she was able to get it in on one try.

She could feel the faint hiss of the ship under her as the command whispered through the ship's control systems—the ramp pulling up, the hatch preparing to seal shut.

A holograph sheet appeared, hovering over the log, and she

scanned through it quickly.

Then she scanned through it again, more slowly, forcing herself to read each word.

A ship bringing in naval weapons, the *Agate*, stranded in the Adrian Sector. Too near a black hole for comfort. They were to reach it and retrieve the ship, if possible, the cargo and crew if not.

That was enough of a challenge for a first-time captain, certainly. More than she'd feared, or hoped, lying awake at night on her thin mattress in the Academy dorms.

But that wasn't all of it.

Underneath the official notice, there was a scrawl of handwriting that she recognized, from her time serving under the woman.

"We have intelligence that a pirate channel may have picked up the distress broadcast," the Admiral had written. "This will not be a simple retrieval mission. Be prepared for a skirmish. Best of luck, Ives."

Hollis closed her eyes for a moment, breathing in through her nose.

She'd been in enough pirate skirmishes, in her time as a sailor—bloody, nasty things, and you never came back with as many crew as you went out with.

This wasn't a simple first mission at all, then. That far out in empty space, with no help and no backup should things go badly, this had the potential to be a death-trap.

But then, she'd never asked for a simple first mission. She couldn't afford to. She was from the Stacks, and she couldn't afford even a moment of weakness, or the wolves from the Level, the ones who already believed she should never have been given a captain's post, let alone one on a three-hundred-and-fifty-crewed ship of the line, would devour her whole.

She opened her eyes and looked over at Foster, keeping her expression bland, despite the way her heart was racing. "Mate Price. Please send the coordinates to the bridge and instruct them to chart a course." She split off the piece of the note that held the shipping coordinates to the last known location of the *Agate* with two fingers and sent it to hover over Foster's wrist comm. "Instruct Second Mate Greene to ensure the ship is in fighting order, and to oversee daily drills. There is a chance we'll be meeting with pirates, and I'd like the crew prepared. I will join you on the bridge shortly."

"Yes, Captain," said Foster, ducking their head respectfully.

They turned and stepped out of the grand conference room, and the door slid shut behind them.

When they were gone, Hollis allowed herself, finally, to slump in her seat. Her hands were shaking so badly that she had to clasp the legs of her trousers to steady them.

She closed her eyes and tipped her head back against the fine back of the chair, swallowing down the taste of sick in her throat.

This was her ship. She was its law and its god while the voyage lasted. This was the position she'd been dreaming of for as long as she could remember, the position she'd fought and bled for, from the time she was a child in the Stacks, fighting to survive the ghosts, from the time she was a skinny fourteen-year-old and had stowed away on a merchant ship, from the time she was sixteen and had managed to sign onto a naval ship, through sheer stubborn determination. From the time the Admiral had recommended her to the Academy, an impossible, absurd stroke of luck that had left her feeling giddy and weightless and disoriented. The position no one in the Academy, except perhaps the Admiral herself, had believed a woman from the Stacks could or should achieve.

And she'd had no idea, on a three-hundred-and-fifty crewed ship of the line, how utterly, entirely alone that position would leave her.

6

Silas

Silas had shipped before the mast since he was twelve years old. He knew, logically, that a pirate ship would be different from a ship of the line, but it wasn't until the organized chaos of liftoff that he realized exactly how different.

He was used to manning his post, running up the ratlines to the various levers and mechanisms that needed to be held down or checked or adjusted. He was used to a ship of the line, and a crew of hundreds.

Here, it was the eight of them.

Once he'd finished checking the ratlines, Ari had asked him, tersely, if he understood pressure charts. When he'd nodded, she pulled him down below the ladder to the lower deck and shoved him into the tiny, claustrophobic pressure room. "I'll notice if the pressure is off, and I'll send Freddie down with a knife to slit your throat and get you the hell out of the way," she'd snapped before striding off.

He took a deep breath and studied the gages. He didn't know the

Sweet Jenny, but the setup was easy enough to figure out if you were used to faster-than-light ships.

Above him, he heard Ari's clear voice shouting out orders, the noise of footsteps and the crew hauling themselves up and down the ratlines, the hiss and groan of the ship as it lifted off its dock, and above them, the heavy, ringing *clang* of the first airlock doors slamming open.

He checked the pressure and adjusted the levers as they swung wildly, the ship's engine running higher. There was the delicate sensation of the ship lifting into the airlock proper, the *bang* of the airlock door slamming shut behind them.

A pause.

He glanced over at the pressure chart one more time to check his calculations, wiping the trickling sweat off his forehead on the back of his sleeve—the pressure rooms were always the hottest part of the ship. Under him, he could hear the low growl of the ship's engines preparing for liftoff.

He adjusted his hands on the levers, eyes glued to the pressure gages.

It was a thankless, mundane task, keeping the pressure—probably the reason Ari had given it to him—but it meant the difference between a smooth liftoff and a jerky, half-cocked disaster. Bad enough pressure stabilization could even lead to a crash, although Ari'd catch something like that long before he had time to get them in too much trouble, even if he were inclined to do so.

"All hands, ready for liftoff," Ari called, her voice drifting down from overhead.

"Aye," he shouted back over the line, joining the chorus of "Aye"s from various parts of the ship.

"Strap in!"

He reached back, pulling out the harness straps—properly stored, he noted in the back of his mind, and if not new, at least well-maintained.

"Toothpick. Crew's ready for the countdown," Ari sang out.

"Ten. Nine. Eight." Toothpick's voice, quiet and steady, floated through the ship's amp system.

Silas checked the gages, readjusting one to sit just a hair lower.

"Seven. Six. Five. Four."

He moved his hands back to the levers, fingers hovering over the one he knew he'd have to hit first.

"Three. Two. One. Going up."

The ship shuddered and lurched beneath him, throwing Silas back against the straps. He grabbed for the pressure levers, fingers flickering over them as the acceleration shoved him back and down, the harness straps cutting into his shoulder.

On a ship of the line, the acceleration was less noticeable, more ponderous, measured out across a ship that was twenty times the size of this one, and the docks on the Level were built in such a way that there was very little atmospheric pressure to contend with once a ship had sealed its hull.

Here, they'd have to gain the speed to get through the atmosphere, thin as it may be, and contend with the gravitational pull of the small moon, enhanced with an art-grav core.

The ship trembled, as if trying to shake itself to pieces, and he grabbed for another of the pressure gages, feathering it higher.

Then the shaking stilled, the noise of the ship's engines cut suddenly, and there was a brief weightless moment before the ship's artificial gravity switched on.

Silas sighed in relief and sagged back against the harness straps.

Then he straightened, checking the gages. All running well, and all at the correct pressure.

He let out a quick breath, and smiled ruefully at himself.

He felt like a ship's boy on his first voyage.

He checked them one more time, then unstrapped his harness, stowing it neatly back against the wall. Then he stepped out of the small room and onto the main deck.

The rest of the crew had already unstrapped and were going about their duties quickly and efficiently, and for a moment he stood where he was, feeling slightly lost.

He'd been used to knowing exactly where he was supposed to be and what he was supposed to be doing, every moment of the day or night since he was twelve years old and had first shipped off with the navy, the tight, claustrophobic structure of it as galling as it was familiar.

The loose informality of the pirate ship left him feeling oddly disoriented, the freedom of it itching under his skin, like an animal he'd been keeping caged for as long as he could remember stretching and lashing its tail.

"You. Level boy. Ari said you're working under me for as long as I need you."

He glanced up to see that Freddie had maneuvered her hover-seat over to him. "Got new ships parts in, they need labeling and stowing. And then I've got plenty of joint seams for you to grease and gear-hoods for you to clean. Weren't on shore long enough to get everything done."

"Aye," he said, nodding his head. He managed to keep both the word and the gesture respectful, despite his rapidly rising irritation.

He'd been sailing since he was twelve. He'd spent the past two and a half years studying everything he'd need to know to run a ship of the line, and he'd likely have been granted one of the coveted captain's posts when he graduated the Academy—he'd already been hearing rumours.

And they were treating him like a cabin boy.

Well, so be it. He certainly wasn't going to give them the satisfaction of seeing his annoyance.

Freddie snorted. "Don't stand much on ceremony around here, lad. Come on, let's get you working, see if you're any good."

He followed her as she maneuvered her chair expertly through the ratlines, using them to lower herself between decks at a speed and with a skill that took Silas some effort to keep up.

At last they reached the bottom deck, where a large storage compartment sat, boxes stowed haphazardly on every surface.

"Know your way around ship's parts, boy?" she asked.

He nodded again.

"Good. Check the shelves to see how I've got them organized, and get them stowed properly." She shot him a sharp glance. "I've seen people turn down the room grav to stow boxes, make it easier on themselves. And then the grav comes back up, or we get up close to a star or a black hole, and suddenly the parts are all over the floor and pieces are broken. This ain't a military ship, we don't got extras. Need every last thing on board here, much as your life's worth if we lose one. Understand, boy?"

"Understood."

She was still watching him, and he took the opportunity to study her back.

Her broad face had creases on it that spoke of a smile being more at home there than her current scowl, and she had bright eyes, and a repressed energy that reminded him of some of his wilder crewmates when he was a young man shipping before the mast.

"What you staring at, boy? Get to work," she snapped, but now that he was listening for it, he could hear the hint of humour under her tone.

"Aye," he said, nodding again respectfully, and turned away.

Behind him, he could hear her snort again, half under her breath. "Lad's navy through and through. Told you, we don't stand on ceremony here. Once you're done, call in through my wrist comm, I'll get you polishing."

She turned and maneuvered her chair expertly out through the opening, and he sighed, glancing around at the boxes.

It was going to be a long damn day.

It was. His back and arms were aching by the time he finished the boxes, and then Freddie had him greasing and polishing the seams along the bottom hull. "Get you outside the ship, check 'em and clean 'em on the outside soon as we get to a jump-pause," Freddie commented. She herself was half-way inside one of the thruster motors, working on something he couldn't see, her hover-chair tipped up sideways and hovering gently just over the deck, and her voice floated out to him slightly garbled through the purr of the running engines.

By the time dog-watch was called he had to blink against the brightness when he stepped out on the deck again, his hands and forearms stiff from squeezing the grease-gun and his shirt damp with sweat from the heat of the lower decks.

"Sil and Jumper on dog-watch," said Ari, glancing over them. Her gaze on him was appraising, but he was too tired to try to parse the meaning behind it.

Jumper nodded, glancing over at Silas nervously, then away. He signed something, and Silas closed his eyes in frustration.

Of course. Jumper didn't talk. And Silas didn't know the signs, and he wasn't likely to without some help, and no one on this ship seemed inclined to help him.

The rest of the crew left for supper, and as Temple slipped past him, the man took him gently by the arm. "A word, lad?"

Silas turned, frowning. "Yes?"

Temple tipped his head in Jumper's direction. "Lad wasn't treated well growing up. He's a bit nervous of new folk, but he's the best weapons tech you'll find." The man's voice was mild.

Silas nodded, still frowning.

"He don't like loud noises, and he don't like being shouted at, and he don't like being touched if he don't ask for it. But thing is, Gracie signed him on because he was damn good at what he does. She don't take kindly to people mistreating her crew. And nor do I. You upset the lad, and I'll slit your throat myself, I will." His tone was still the same calm as before, but there was a hint of steel under it that told Silas he wasn't posturing.

When Silas glanced down, the man opened his hand long enough to show a gleaming shiv.

Silas fought back the impulse to reach for his own weapon. That wouldn't make the situation any better.

"Understood," he said flatly.

Temple smiled, that same mild expression he usually wore, and patted Silas's shoulder. "Good lad, good lad. Just thought I'd warn you. Explain how things work around here."

Silas nodded again, shortly. His teeth were clenched, hands in fists at his sides, but he forced them to relax as Temple moved away.

When he glanced up, Ari was watching, her eyebrows raised a little. She caught him looking and gave him a cheeky grin, then slid down the ratlines to the crew deck.

Silas sighed and turned back to Jumper, who was avoiding his gaze.

As far as he could remember, Jumper could hear, he just didn't talk. And he'd caught the way the rest of the crew signed while they spoke, but until he knew his way around whatever signs Jumper used, that wouldn't help him much.

"Jumper, I'm Silas," he said. Jumper wasn't looking at him, but he could see by the slight tensing of the boy's shoulders that he'd heard. "Temple told me you don't like loud noises or shouting, and you don't like being touched without permission. I don't intend to do any of those things. I just want to get through the watch without any of us getting into trouble. Got it?"

Jumper gave a quick nod, still not looking at him, and signed something that Silas had no idea how to interpret.

He paused a moment, trying to figure out how to ask.

At last, Jumper did look up at him, a trace of annoyance in his face. He jerked his thumb in an exaggerated gesture to the starboard deck, then pointed at himself and jerked his thumb to the port deck.

Silas nodded, his face clearing. "I'm on starboard, you're port. Understood."

Jumper began to sign something else, then cut himself off, the gesture clearly frustrated. He took a deep breath, then glanced at Silas. He pointed at Silas's chest, then shrugged, tipping his head from side to side as if asking a question.

Silas frowned. "Do ... do I know what to do?" he hazarded at last.

Jumper nodded impatiently.

"I believe so," Silas said.

Jumper waited.

Silas sighed. "I'll be watching the screens for any sign of a meteoroid collision or a pressure drop. I'll be checking the pressure gage readout and the starboard engine readout to make sure all's well. I'll be looking at the mechanical readout, and checking for any hull damage from space debris."

Jumper nodded and turned away quickly.

Silas sighed and turned to his duties.

The dog-watch was the shortest watch, and he'd only just got the hang of the various readouts and sensors by the time Vee came to relieve him. She scowled when she saw him and didn't bother to speak, just gestured him down to the crew deck with a jerk of her thumb.

Silas and Jumper ate their cold supper in silence—some sort of reconstituted stew he didn't recognize, but tasty enough, and a hell of a lot better than he'd expected ship-board—and then turned into the crew's bunk.

The rest of the crew were there, minus Vee and Temple, who were on watch, and Gracie, who had her own cabin.

"You're over there," said Ari, glancing up at him as he walked in and tipping her chin towards his hammock in the corner. "You'll want to strap in before you sleep—we're going to make an FTL jump in a couple hours."

She turned back to the game of dice, and he stepped over to the hammock. There was a locker in the floor underneath, and when he lifted it, his kit had already been stowed neatly.

He sighed and sat down on the swaying hammock, closing his eyes and letting the weariness of the day wash over him.

Behind him, he could hear the soft clink of dice, the quiet laughter of the rest of the pirate crew. There was a sharp alcohol smell to the air that told him grog rations had been passed out.

He hadn't been given any, and he was confident he should have been. But it hardly seemed worth complaining over.

He'd been the new man on a ship before. You picked your battles, and you fought them hard enough that no one would come after you again. But this battle wasn't one that was worth fighting, at least not yet.

A soft, haunting note made him open his eyes.

Jumper had pulled out a small flute, and was playing a tune Silas recognized.

He smiled despite himself, humming the tune under his breath.

"You know how to play?"

He looked up, startled, to see that Ari had crossed over to him. She was holding out a battered mouth organ.

He stared at her, and she offered it again. "I said, you know how to play?"

He glanced down at the instrument. It was old and worn, and he hadn't played since he'd joined the Academy, but …

"I do." He took it and polished it on his trouser leg, and she gestured him over with a jerk of her head.

"Come on, then, been a long day. We could use a song or two."

He followed her over to where the rest of the crew was gathered around the dice. Jumper glanced up at him, and nodded towards the mouth organ.

"Play me a few notes, I'll come in," he said, and Jumper picked up his flute again, tapping his hand against his thigh to set the rhythm.

This time, it was a song Silas was less familiar with, but the tune was simple enough, and he picked it up quickly. By the time it ended, he and Jumper were playing in harmony, and he'd even added a couple embellishments of his own to the tune.

Jumper glanced over at him with a quick smile as the tune came to an end, and tapped his hand on his thigh again, setting another rhythm.

They played for a while longer. Silas closed his eyes and let himself get lost in the rhythm of the music, his body relaxing for the first time since he'd left his dorm room back in the Academy days previous.

When at last Jumper put up his flute, Silas handed the mouth organ reluctantly back to Ari.

"You're not too bad on this," she said grudgingly. "Surprised you don't have one of your own."

He smiled a little. "I used to. Not much use for one in the Academy, and when I left, I only took what I'd need to stay alive. No point in carrying extra weight when you're running for your life."

Freddie looked up, then gestured at Toothpick with a jerk of her head. "Move aside, make room for the lad. Lad who can play the mouth organ can probably play dice, I'd wager."

He raised his eyebrows as the others moved aside to let him and Jumper in, and sat down beside them.

Ari handed him the dice. "We're playing hazard," she said. "You know the rules, I guess?"

He grinned. "Lost everything but my socks in a game of hazard when I first shipped onto a crew. I learned the rules after that."

Toothpick glanced up, the ghost of a smile on his face—the first time Silas had seen him smile. "Let's see if you learned anything useful, then," he said.

They played a few rounds, but Silas was fighting a losing battle against weariness. "Sailors," he said at last, standing and brushing off his trousers. "I'm for my hammock." He paused. "Thank you."

Freddie looked up. Her gaze was piercing, but not hostile. "Had my doubts about you—don't get on with Level folk much myself, but you didn't do a bad job today."

He nodded, and hesitated a moment. "Temple's a Level name, no?"

Freddie smiled, showing her teeth. "Temple's from the Level, yeah. Signed on to a merchant crew, he did, shipped with them for a while. And then one day they got into a skirmish, a couple of his crewmates were killed. He saved the ship, saved the lives of the captain and most of the crew, but got a nice injury to show for it, and watched his crewmates die in front of him. So when they got back, they gave him the legal fee and sacked him." She shrugged, still grinning. "You're from the Level, boy. You think he could find another place to work after he'd been a sailor, traveled faster than light, seen some trauma? Temple hates the Level as much as any of us."

Silas stared at her. And then he nodded slowly.

It made sense. On a naval ship, you had sailors who'd traveled faster than light and who'd seen enough trauma to make turning ghost inevitable. But the ships were sectioned off, ten or twenty to a sealed compartment, so if someone died and turned, the worst case was you lost a few dozen. On a merchant ship, they'd never spend that money and weight if they didn't have to. If you were a civilian sailor who saw trauma—well, you were unemployable after that. It might be different for him, someone trained on a weapon, whose usefulness might outweigh his liability. But for a regular merchant sailor? No one would risk you, and most of the time you ended up in the Stacks.

There were enough ghosts in the Stacks already that one more would hardly matter.

It made a sick sort of sense. Accidents happened in space, people died. And one of the crew turning ghost could easily kill off the entire ship. It happened often enough, even on ships with their crew trained in weapons and who knew how to use a sparker, that the salvagers were always busy clearing out and bringing in ghost ships.

But it was a hard way to repay a man who'd saved his captain and crew.

"I guess I can hardly blame him," he said at last.

Freddie just nodded, still watching him, and at last he turned away.

He dropped onto his hammock, weary enough that he barely had the energy to pull off his boots before he fell back onto the rough surface. The soft swaying of the hammock at the vibrations of the engines was a familiar, comfortable feeling. He closed his eyes, listening to the sounds of the ship around him, and he realized, suddenly, how much he'd missed this.

He'd been recommended to the Academy, which was a high honour in itself—although not, perhaps, completely unexpected, considering his family. And he'd gone willingly, as excited as any young sailor at the prospect of one day captaining a ship of the line.

But that had meant two and a half years shore-bound. Two and a half years of his muscles aching to move, of keeping a desperate, iron-tight grip on every thought and word, of forcing himself into the patterns and life of a student. Two and a half years he'd had to become accustomed to sleeping on a cot that sat firmly on the ground, instead of a swaying hammock, to silence after lights-out instead of the familiar, comforting hum of ship's machinery.

And until now, he'd had no idea exactly how much he'd missed this, through every atom of his body.

Around him, he could hear the rest of the crew standing and stretching, putting away the dice and getting ready for bed.

Temple was from the Level, he knew that, and so was Ari. Freddie and Vee would be from resource planets most likely, judging from their names, and Jumper and Toothpick were Stacks names if he'd ever heard them.

He frowned a little, picturing the rapid flicking of Jumper's fingers as he signed.

If he was from the Stacks, his signs were probably at least some variation on the standard Stacks sign language.

He groaned and rolled over, pulling up a note over his wrist com. He scrawled in a quick request, and a moment later his comm pulled up a diagram of some of the more common Stacks signs.

He looked them over, shading the soft glow from his comm as best he could to avoid keeping his shipmates up—although from the sound of it, they'd been asleep by the time they'd hit their hammocks.

On four-hour watches, he'd get used to falling asleep instantly soon enough, he knew that from long experience. But for now, despite his weariness, his body was accustomed to the regular sleep-and-wake cycle that they used shore-ward.

He sighed.

On a ship like this, the chance for uninterrupted time would be scant, and Ari was right—if he couldn't understand Jumper, that could mean the difference between life and death if they were in a bad situation.

He squeezed his eyes shut to try to blink the sleep from them, and settled down to pour over the long list of diagrams.

When he was woken for watch in the middle of the night, he felt as if he hadn't slept at all. He rubbed the sand from his eyes, yawning, and staggered to his feet, shoving his boots on more by feel than anything else as he stumbled out of the crew decks and groped his way up the ratlines to the main deck. By the time he finished his watch, it was breakfast, and he slid down the ratlines to the mess hall. Vee was handing out bowls of something steaming, and he took one and crossed over to a corner to sit. He passed Jumper as he went, and tried out a smile. "'Morning," he said, signing clumsily with the hand that wasn't holding his bowl of food.

Jumper raised his eyebrows and signed something rapid that Silas couldn't quite make out.

"Sorry," he said, signing as he spoke. "Still learning."

Jumper paused. Then he signed again, a little slower this time, the motions exaggerated. Silas frowned in concentration, mouthing the signs he knew. "… *morning. Anything happen … watch?*"

"Nothing happened, just routine. The central starboard pressure sensor went wild about midnight. I managed to get it back under control, but we may have to send someone out to check this morning. But nothing too worrying," he said, signing along to his words as best he could.

Jumper nodded, turning away, but Silas caught the hint of a smile on the boy's face that hadn't been there before.

He dropped onto the deck, pulling the small mess utensil out of his pocket and flipping out the spoon.

The food was bland, but still better than what he'd usually get for breakfast on a naval ship, and he ate quickly, the hot of it burning his mouth.

"You're with Temple today, got some repairs he wants done," Freddie called over to him from the corner where she was seated, her bowl balanced in her lap. He nodded. His body ached from the previous day's labour, and he could feel the weariness from lack of sleep seeping through his muscles.

Today was going to be another long day.

But perhaps—just perhaps—he'd survive this after all.

7

On the fifth day out of Blackrock, Silas woke to the blaring of alarms. He rolled out of his hammock, cursing. Around him his shipmates were doing the same. He stubbed his toe pulling on his boots, and swore softly, limping as he followed Jumper out onto the main deck.

"Navy scouting ship to port," Ari snapped over the comm line as they assembled on the main deck. "Jumper, get on the guns, take Vee with you, Gracie says light guns only. I'll be up soon as I get everyone ordered. Sil, you're with Freddie in the engine room, Toothpick, you're with me. Temple, you're in the cockpit with the captain."

The crew separated to their duties with military rapidity, and Silas found himself the last one on the ratlines as he followed Freddie down.

His heart was pounding faster than usual.

He was shipping on a pirate crew. It was inevitable, probably, that they'd have a brush with the navy.

It was in pursuit of something worthwhile, it was his duty, he'd thought this through a million times.

But it was easier to be certain when it was a hypothetical situation.

"They'll be firing to hit the FTL drive, 'less I miss my guess," said Freddie. She was already bent over the engine controls. "I want you on the sensors. They get close, you pull all the power so's we don't start a chain reaction."

He nodded, turning to the sensors Freddie had indicated.

Through the ship's comm, he heard Ari's count, then her call of, "All guns, fire!"

The ship lurched and shuddered as the weapons discharged, and Silas grabbed for the wall to keep from being thrown backward.

Freddie turned, thrusting a harness at him. "Strap in, lad, you'll be no use to anyone if you split your head open on the floor."

He grabbed the harness and struggled into it, keeping his attention fixed on the sensors.

He should have thought of it himself, honestly, but he was used to a ship of the line, large enough that even a broadside wouldn't shake her like this.

"Incoming," Ari snapped, and then the ship jolted again. He managed to clip the harness to the wall before the rocking sent him stumbling, and he jerked the straps tight.

The sensors had gone wild, but they steadied as he watched. "Close, but no direct hits," he called over his shoulder. Freddie gave a quick, preoccupied nod, and he turned back to his task.

"Fire on my count," Ari called over the comm, and Silas braced himself. Another broadside from the *Sweet Jenny*, and moments later, another shout of, "Incoming!"

One of the port engine sensors spun wildly, and he grabbed for the control, yanking it all the way down.

"Temple, swing us around to fire on their port side." Gracie's voice through the comm was as mild as ever. "Ari, we're looking to disable, not kill."

Silas raised his eyebrows, a small, rueful smile on his face.

The rumours had completely misrepresented the pirate captain, apparently.

And despite the fact that it was unquestionably a good thing, considering they were currently firing on a fifty-crewed naval scouting ship, he couldn't help a small, sharp pang of something like disappointment.

"Freddie, when they come around for another salvo, I want you and Sil to take the FTL offline the moment there's a shot close enough to make it believable. Take the nearest running engine offline as well."

"Aye, Captain," Ari called, and Freddie echoed her.

Silas shot her a questioning glance, and she shrugged. "Captain does as she pleases, and we follow orders, lad. Can't be that different from the navy, now, can it?"

He blew out a breath and turned back to his work.

Through the comm, he could hear Ari calling orders, felt the ship shudder as the weapons deployed, and then felt the jolt of a direct hit.

"Now!" Freddie snapped, and Silas glanced at the sensors and pulled the rear starboard engine offline as Freddie powered down the FTL.

"Done, Captain," Freddie called up through the comm.

"Very good." Gracie's voice was still mild. "You and Sil get up to the cockpit, please. Ari, Toothpick, you too."

"Aye, Captain," Freddie called back, and jerked her head at Silas. "Go on, you heard the captain."

Silas unclipped his harness and stowed it quickly, then followed Freddie up the ratlines and onto the main deck.

By the time they reached the cockpit, Ari and Toothpick were already there. Ari gestured him to silence as he stepped through the door, and he realized Gracie was bent over the ship's comm.

"This is the *Intercept,* paging the *Sweet Jenny.*" The naval captain's voice through the comm was sharp and arrogant. "Your FTL is down, and you've lost your rear starboard running engine. I demand that you turn yourselves in. I repeat, stand down and turn yourselves in."

Silas glanced at Ari, frowning, but she just gestured him to silence again.

"As you say," said Gracie, her voice unusually grim. "We've lost our FTL and our rear starboard running engine. But we haven't lost our guns. That was a warning volley. I'll tell my gunner to disable you if you come at us again."

"And then what, Captain Mad Dog? You're far enough out that without your FTL, you'll never make it back to civilization." He paused. "A pirate like you deserves to be shot down just like the mad dog you're named for. But if you stand down, I'll offer you a negotiated surrender, just like I'd offer any other ship. That's the best you'll get from me."

The silence in the cockpit stretched.

At last, Gracie bent over the ship's comm again. "Very well. A negotiated surrender. We'll be waiting for you at the airlock." She sounded wearier than he'd ever heard her.

The comm clicked off, and Gracie turned to the crew gathered in the cockpit. "Ari, Temple, you know what to do," she said. "The rest of you, with me. They'll expect my crew with me when I offer my surrender."

Silas frowned at Freddie as they followed Gracie out of the cockpit and down to the airlock. "What's she playing at?" he whispered.

Freddie raised her eyebrows at him. "Captain don't much like navy scout ships to think they can get away with harassing pirates, is all. Figure she's planning to give them a bit of a lesson."

Silas thought back to his first day on Blackrock, and gave another small, wry smile.

They reached the airlock, and waited as the skiff took off from the scout ship. At last, the captain's voice came through the ship's comm. "Paging the *Sweet Jenny*. Request you open the airlock."

"Go ahead," said Gracie quietly, nodding at Freddie.

A moment later, the outer airlock door hissed open. There was the rough metal-on-metal sound of a ship locking on to an airlock, and then the harsh sucking sound as the airlock sealed around the skiff.

Gracie nodded to Freddie again. The inner airlock door hissed open, and Silas could see the naval captain, flanked by his first mate and a dozen heavily armed sailors.

"Captain," said Gracie, stepping forward as the man approached. Ari and Toothpick stepped up beside her.

"I'm here to accept your surrender," the man said brusquely. "You'll be brought back to the Level and taken to a fair trial before you're hanged, which is more than what you've done for far too many a good naval sailor."

Gracie nodded, and reached down to unstrap her cutlass. "Won't apologize for what I've done to survive, Captain," she said. "But ..." She glanced up, and when she did, Silas noticed that Temple had moved inconspicuously around so he was standing behind the shoulder of the first mate.

Gracie nodded, a quick dip of her head.

Temple yanked out his short steel shiv and plunged it into the throat of the first mate.

The man gave a gurgling scream and dropped to his knees, blood spurting between his fingers as he clutched at the wound, and Ari stepped forward, bringing her cutlass down in a short, sharp blow that sliced through the chest and stomach of the sailor on the other side of the captain. There was a hiss as the airlock doors slammed shut, and Silas realized, suddenly, that when Gracie had stepped forward to meet the captain, she'd timed it so most of the sailors would be still behind the inner airlock door.

The captain started to turn, a shout of alarm half-formed in his throat.

Gracie pulled out her pistol and shot him through the head.

"Cycle out the oxygen in the airlock, Freddie," she snapped, turning, as Toothpick dispatched the last of the sailors who'd made it past the airlock.

There was a familiar sucking sound, and a shrill, terrified sob, choking and horrified, from inside the airlock, the sound of someone banging on the inner airlock doors.

Silas stood where he was, feet glued to the deck in shock, staring at the bloody bodies on the ground.

The blue plasma of a forming ghost gathered over one of the bodies, but Toothpick stepped forward and dispatched it quickly with his sparker before it had time to form.

The pounding on the airlock door had grown more feeble, and at last it petered out altogether.

Silas felt sick to his stomach.

"Jumper, heavy weapons, please. Take the ship down. I want no survivors." Gracie's tone was cool and dispassionate.

The *Sweet Jenny* staggered, a series of quick jolts as the heavy weapons fired. Ari had pulled up a screen over her comm and was studying it. "He's taken it down, Captain," she said at last. "Nothing left but space dust."

"Good," said Gracie. "Freddie, unhook the skiff from the airlock, please. Don't close the airlock door until you're sure there's no bodies or ghosts left inside."

Freddie nodded.

Through the plex viewport in the inner airlock door, Silas could see the skiff detach, see the bodies sucked out into the blackness after their ship.

"Poor devils," muttered Temple. "It's a mercy they're unconscious." He reached down and pricked the pad of his thumb on the tip of his blade, smearing the blood along the crude drawing of Our Lady of the Ghosts carved into the side of the *Sweet Jenny*'s airlock. "Our Lady take them safe, and their ghosts not come back."

Ari came to find Silas a few hours later, while he was scrubbing blood from the floor outside the airlock. He'd given the bodies their last rites and sent them out the airlock after their companions, and now he was finishing with the decks.

She watched him for a while. He ignored her, focused on his task.

He still felt faintly sick to his stomach, a shakiness through his muscles that reminded him of the first skirmish he'd ever been in, as a boy in the navy.

He wasn't a boy any longer, and he'd seen more deaths than he wanted to count. But for some reason, he could still hear the pounding on the airlock door, growing fainter and fainter, hear the cool dispassion in Gracie's voice as she told Jumper she wanted no survivors.

Fifty naval sailors and their captain, all dead.

"Never killed a pirate on your naval ships, Level boy?" Ari asked at last.

He closed his eyes and sucked in a quick breath. "Yes," he said shortly. "I've killed more than one, in a fair fight."

She gave a small laugh. "You said you weren't a naval man anymore. Still talk like one, though."

He straightened, glaring at her. "Gracie's a pirate. I understand that. That doesn't mean I have to like her luring a captain onboard the *Sweet Jenny* with the promise of a surrender, and then shooting him in the head."

Ari grinned. "You think she should have told him first? Or you think she should have taken the *Sweet Jenny* against them nose to nose, got her shot to hell before we took down the ship? Honour's a cold comfort when you're floating in space with your line cut."

He shook his head sharply. "I'm sorry if wanting a fair fight bothers you."

She watched him for a while, leaned up against the wall, and finally, he turned back to his task. The blood had soaked into the tracks of the airlock doors, and it took some scrubbing to get it out.

"You know why the ship is called the *Sweet Jenny*?"

He looked up again, startled. Ari was still watching him.

"Should I?" he asked.

She gave a one-shouldered shrug. "Captain don't talk about it much. Don't know why you would." She paused. "Guess you know already that the captain was a naval woman once, in the Academy and everything. And guess you know about what happened next, on account of that's why you came out here in the first place. But back in the Academy, captain had a lover. And when Gracie was arrested for treason, on the Admiral's testimony, she lost her position at the Academy. She was stripped of her rank, and she watched her parents hang. She lost everything. But the only thing she can't forgive is losing Jenny." She shook her head and slid down the wall to sit cross-legged on the floor. "Captain don't drink much anymore, but she did a bit when I first signed on with her. No more'n any other sailor, but more'n she does now. And from the time I met Gracie, there was only one time when I was afraid of her. It was when she'd been drinking, and I asked her about Jenny, asked if she'd left during the trials." She gave a soft, humourless laugh.

"Thought maybe she'd pull out her pistol and shoot me through the head, just like she did that captain. 'I've lived through a hell of a lot in my life, Ari, and I'll live through more, but I swear on my blood I'll kill the person who says a word against my Jenny,' she said. Only time I ever saw her really angry. Don't know what happened to Jenny during the trials, and I know better'n to ask. But whatever it was, it damn near broke Gracie. And I think if she kills the Admiral one day, that'll be why." She shook her head. "You know what she lost, Sil. You know what the Admiral and the Level took from her. You think that was fair?"

Silas sighed, swallowing down a thick mix of guilt—guilt at killing naval sailors, guilt at serving in the navy that had done what he knew it had done. "That captain wasn't part of it."

Ari shrugged. "Maybe not. But Captain ain't going to play by rules Levellers only abide by when it suits them. Level don't fight fair, Sil. Maybe you did. Know you well enough by now that I figure I can say I believe you on that point. But Gracie ain't fighting the captains that come out after her. She's fighting the damn Level, and she plays by her own damn rules. And I'm not one to blame her for it." She paused a moment. "Anyway, came to tell you that Freddie wants you down in the engine room when you're done here, got some repairs she wants to take care of before our next jump."

"Yeah," said Silas shortly.

The sickness hadn't left the pit of his stomach, and he wasn't sure it would anytime soon.

Ari's words made too much sense.

He couldn't blame Gracie. That was the whole reason he'd come out to Blackrock in the first place, and he'd told her, to her face, that he couldn't blame her for what she'd done to survive.

But it was one thing to hear about it in stories. It was another to look into the face of a naval captain as he watched his first mate die, the second before he himself was shot through the head in a mission he'd been promised would be peaceful.

And it was another thing still to realize that he, himself, was as complicit in the man's death as any pirate on this ship.

He gritted his teeth and turned back to his work.

He'd signed onto Gracie's crew for a good cause—a cause that was important enough he'd been willing to give up his whole damn life for it. It was the right thing to do, it was only right that the people who'd killed his parents and so many other sailors be brought to justice.

But what had happened here sure as hell hadn't been justice.

He damn well needed to keep his mind on why he was doing this, or he'd lose his own damn soul.

8

Gracie

"Captain."

Gracie looked up, and beckoned Toothpick to enter.

He came in, dropping into the chair next to her.

The screens in front of her showed charts of the space they'd be passing through, highlighting the path Temple had calculated for them. She pulled them forward over the desk, expanding them so Toothpick could see them.

He looked over at her, a questioning expression on his face. "I heard the broadcast we intercepted overnight," he said at last.

She nodded, keeping her face expressionless.

She'd heard it as well, the moment it came in. She always slept lightly when they were on a mission—it was the only thing that had kept her alive as long as she'd lived.

"And?" she said, her expression mild.

He smiled at her wryly. "Captain. I've shipped with you long enough."

She smiled back, then sighed and gestured at the maps. "They've already sent out a naval ship. They acted faster than I'd hoped, but it wasn't unexpected."

Toothpick frowned at the charts. "They'll be taking the straightest shot," he said, tracing his finger along the marked shipping route. "I'm guessing they won't bother with the shared lanes, just use the naval shipping course. Which means they won't have to pause to re-calibrate, like we will."

"Yes," she said absently, attention fixed on the charts. "Their ship won't be as quick as ours, but they have less to lose." She glanced over at him, her face grave. "Don't want to get into a fight with a three-hundred-and-fifty-crewed ship of the line if I can avoid it. And we can't afford for the navy to have proof it was pirates as took the weapons."

He nodded again. "I heard." His voice was as grave as hers. "They're taking this seriously."

She gave a soft huff of laughter. "Did you see the cargo manifest? Of course they are. This ship is carrying enough firepower to wipe out Blackrock completely."

He raised his eyebrows at her. "You think that's what they intended to do with it?"

She studied him a moment, then gave a wry shrug. "I don't think so. It's possible, but the Admiral knows that if she takes out Blackrock, she won't stop piracy. We'll just spread out, be harder to track down. Right now, they know where to find us. If Blackrock is gone, she has no idea what will happen next. And you've seen what's happening in the navy right now. They're preparing for war, or I'll eat my hat."

"You think so?"

She shook her head. "Go over their broadcasts for the past few months. It's more than obvious. That boy who signed on with us would have made captain in six months, or I miss my guess. And they'd have needed him, badly."

Toothpick nodded again, turning back to the chart. "So they'll be moving as fast as possible, and if they sent someone out that quickly, they probably know their broadcast was intercepted." He frowned at the chart again. "Don't see how we get there before they do, though. Unless …"

She smiled just a little, running her finger along a line on the chart.

He looked up at her. "You'd take us that close to a star? We'd have to pause and recalibrate right in front of it. Our ship won't be able to hold against the heat for long."

"It won't need to. We'll stop, recalibrate, perform any necessary repairs, and move on. It shouldn't take more than about two standard hours, and our hull will hold up for at least three." She glanced over at him. "It's a risk, I know. But I'll be damned before I let the Admiral have those weapons." Her voice came out hard and flat. She knew Toothpick had heard the tone in it by the way his posture straightened.

He'd been shipping with her for almost two decades. Longer, even, then Ari. He knew when to push, and when to leave well enough alone.

"It's not revenge I'm after," she said, softening her tone a little. "We need those weapons. We need the payout it'll buy us, after the damage we took in the skirmish that killed Bray." She leaned forward a little, meeting Toothpick's eyes. "And I'm not damn well letting the Admiral use those weapons to kill us. Because you know as well as I do that's exactly what she'll do. If there's a war coming, first thing she'll want to do is clear out the skies, give herself a little breathing space and put her new captains through some training.

She won't take out Blackrock, I think, but the skies'll be swarming with naval ships, all kitted out with shiny new tech. And I'll be damned if I'll let her have this. I'll be damned if I let her go after us without the teeth to bite back."

Her tone was still mild, but Toothpick knew her well enough. He nodded. "Right you are, Captain. I'll go tell Temple to set us a course. You're right, if we make our stops short enough, we should still get there before the naval ship can. If the *Agate* has lost its FTL drive, it'll likely have lost most of its long-range weapons with it, and we're well-equipped. We should be able to take the cargo and get out before the naval ship arrives."

She gave him a brief smile. "They're too close to a black hole for the captain's comfort, so I hear. We'll nudge her in that direction before we leave. If she's close enough that the naval ship won't risk going in after her, they'll have no proof what happened or who did it. Admiral can make all the fuss she wants, but no one in government will agree to send out ships to fight and die against pirates if she doesn't have the evidence to make her case."

Toothpick nodded again, pushing back his chair. "Aye, Captain." He paused a moment, then turned to her with one of his rare smiles. This time, though, it was shot with steel. "And Captain? Even if this was just to spite the Admiral—I think I can speak for the crew when I say, you'd hear no complaints from us."

She nodded, returning his smile, and he turned and left the cabin, ducking under the door before sliding it shut.

Gracie sighed and turned back to the charts.

There was a tight knot in the pit of her stomach.

They'd be cutting it close. Toothpick was right to bring up his concerns. But she'd been right as well—they had no other option than to get there before the naval ship. And if she was any judge, what was on that ship was enough new weapons tech that she'd be dooming more than one pirate ship if it came through. Possibly her own.

It was each captain for themself on Blackrock, and well they knew it. But she didn't have the reputation she did only because of her crew, or her past victories. Everyone on Blackrock knew that she'd do her damndest to keep the Admiral off their track. They knew that she'd never hesitate to strike a blow against the navy, and that she'd do it in a way that would keep the Admiral from retaliating. That was what had given her her reputation among the pirates.

Maybe they didn't all know her history with Admiral Usher. But they'd guessed well enough the cold hate behind it.

She sighed and leaned back in her seat, closing her eyes wearily.

Now that there was a war in the offing, the naval ships were coming out with increasing frequency. And from her own self-interested perspective, the fewer pirate crews captured and killed, the more the navy had to spread out its operations, and the easier it was to take an unguarded merchant ship.

But it wasn't just that.

She opened her eyes, smiling wryly.

Maybe that boy, Silas, had the right of it after all. A clean, simple revenge. Something easy and neat, that would tie everything up in a tidy bow—the heroes and the villains.

She was no hero, though, and she had no desire to be. And revenge and hate were a much, much messier business than Silas would ever understand. You couldn't afford to focus on revenge if you wanted to stay alive.

But God's eyes, she sometimes wished you could.

9

Hollis

"Mate Greene. Please ask the sailors to run the drill again, but this time in a manner that a damn pirate ship wouldn't have time to come in under our guns and board us while our crew prepared to fire, please."

"Aye, Captain." Emmett's tone was respectful enough, but she could hear the note of resentment under it. He turned back to the crew. "You heard the captain. Run the drill again, quick-time."

Hollis stood on the captain's deck, her hands clasped behind her back, and watched the crew run a weapon's drill once more—the fifth time they'd gone through it today.

They weren't bad. But not bad wasn't enough, not with the near certainty of a pirate skirmish in their future.

And, truth be told, she had no guarantee her sailors would follow her orders if things went poorly.

Best to have them trained to the point that the reactions were all but automatic.

She watched her second mate as he called out orders to the crew.

He was a tall man, older than she by a good decade, with pale skin and pale hair and a face lined from years of the radiation exposure inherent to life in the navy. She'd looked up his service record—he'd been given second mate's position out of the Academy. It wasn't an insult—there weren't nearly as many captain's posts as there were Academy graduates, and a second mate's position on a three-hundred-and-fifty crewed ship of the line was generally considered a respectable post.

But Emmett was serving under a captain from the Stacks, and a first mate who'd never studied at the Academy. Hollis couldn't blame him for his simmering resentment.

But nor could she trust him.

The crew finished the drill, and stood at attention.

"Better," said Hollis, looking over them. "Again."

She could hear the quiet muttering as they turned back to their tasks under Emmett's barked commands, but after the last few days, at least, the crew knew better than to audibly complain about their captain's orders.

Hollis could feel the tension riding between her shoulder blades, and she consciously tried to relax.

It was no use. She'd known it wouldn't be. She wasn't sure, honestly, if she'd slept more than a few hours in a stretch since the *Verity* had left port.

She sighed, pushing back her weariness. "Run the drill twice more, please, Mate Greene," she said. "I'll expect it perfect tomorrow."

"Aye, Captain," he said, and turned back to his work.

Hollis turned and strode off the captain's deck and back down the corridors to her cabin. The sailors moved smartly out of her way as she passed, but even after almost a week on shipboard, she could feel a prickling between her shoulderblades when she stepped past them.

She doubted anyone on her crew would risk trying to kill her, not now, at least. Not while things were running relatively smoothly. But she still wore a long scar on her back from her previous life in the navy, when a fellow petty officer, drunk and resentful, had tried to knife her in her sleep.

She'd learned, since then, to sleep lightly, and with a shiv clutched in her hand.

It wasn't until she reached the empty conference room and dropped into her chair in front of the massive table that she finally let herself relax. She closed her eyes and tipped back her head, letting her weary brain go blank for a few blessed moments before she forced it back to the task at hand.

Captaining a ship of the line was, when you came down to it, an almost monotonous regularity, at least while they were simply keeping course and there were no skirmishes in the immediate offing. And the *Verity* was big enough and well enough armed that no pirate ship would see her as easy pickings. They'd only get into a pirate skirmish if Hollis led them into one on purpose.

Which, it appeared, was exactly what the Admiral had tasked her to do.

No, it wasn't captaining that was keeping her awake at nights. But then, she'd never been worried about her ability to run a ship, or even about a pirate skirmish.

She'd been worried about surviving her own damn crew, should they decide they didn't trust her.

She groaned softly and pushed herself upright, pulling the charts in front of her once more. She'd been looking at them long enough that they were all but burned on the back of her eyelids in the few hours of sleep she'd managed to snatch between watches, but she still had work to do on them.

"Captain. I have the reports you asked for."

She looked up, blinking. Foster stood respectfully at the door.

She sighed, and pushed aside her charts. "Come in, Mate Price."

She still had no idea how to read Foster. Her first mate had never been less than respectful, but there was something appraising in the way they watched Hollis, and it set Hollis's teeth on edge.

Foster stepped forward and placed a narrow rod on the table, and when Hollis tapped it, a cluster of reports sprang up over it.

She glanced through them quickly.

Nothing too alarming, at least.

"Midship Officer Blakely has completed his watch-and-watch-again that you assigned to him, Captain," they said when she glanced back up at them. "With your permission, I'll set him on regular rotation again."

Hollis had to pause a moment to recall what the hell Foster was talking about. Then she had to bite off a quick sigh of relief. There had been so much to do that she hadn't had time to think of him since.

He was still alive, thank God. One less thing to worry about when she brought the ship back into port.

"I take it he survived being put on outer hull inspection duty, then," she said tartly. "Yes, you may put him back on regular rotation. But ask Greene to keep an eye on him, please. I imagine he's not happy with his punishment. I don't want him spreading insubordination."

Foster frowned, just the slightest crease between their eyebrows. "Aye, Captain, I'll do that." They paused. "I … don't think it will be as necessary as you think, though. The lad wasn't happy, but he lived through it, and I think he thinks the more of you because of it."

Hollis turned to stare at her first mate.

Foster was watching her, that trace of appraisal in their expression. "He knows what he did merited punishment," they said. "He didn't think you'd dare give it to him. And once you did—" They shrugged.

Hollis was still staring.

For the first time, she saw the hint of a smile on Foster's face. "Captain. If I may. The crew doesn't hate you as much as you seem to think they do. You've not been unfair, and if you've been pushing them hard, it's not so much as they can't understand why." They paused a moment. "There are some of us, Captain, that are on your side, if you'll believe it. The Admiral herself assigned you this ship, and all of us know it. And she's not one to miscalculate."

Hollis was still staring at her first mate, trying to make the words they'd said compute.

Trying to decide if she could believe anything they said, and whether they deserved gratitude or censure for saying it.

"If there's nothing else you need from me, Captain, I'll go down and talk to Greene about getting Blakely reassigned." They dipped their head respectfully, and stepped out of the room, leaving Hollis still staring after them.

10

Judith

"Admiral."

Admiral of the Fleet Judith Usher looked up from the interlacing stacks of holonotes hovering over her desk. She had to push them to one side to see the man who stood there, his eyes respectfully downcast.

"Come in," she said, closing down the handful of war briefings she'd been studying.

They weren't common knowledge, not yet, and she had no intention that rumours should start to spread before she'd had time to craft a suitable response.

Rumours were already spreading, she knew that well enough— whispers between captains, whispers throughout the crews of the ships of the line, whispers among the merchant sailors. Whispers in the halls of government, where she'd have to present her report presently. And it wasn't just rumours of a resource war with the Rosette System—already there were those speaking out stridently against any possibilities of conflict, and against anyone who brought up the contents of the briefings. There was a threat, it was undeniable, but until she had a firm response crafted, she'd prefer not to get into those weeds.

Vice-Admiral Edwin Wright stepped inside, saluting smartly. She returned the gesture, and nodded at him to take a seat.

He dropped into the proffered chair with a sigh of weariness that made her glance at him more closely.

His hair, already going to grey, was touched with a frosting of white at the temples, and the deep lines and radiation-spots in his face, the ones that marked those of the naval corps who'd seen years of service over the ones who'd worked their way up through a desk job, were more pronounced than usual.

She had the same marks, the same lines in her face in skin worn prematurely from years of space radiation from traveling on faster-than-light ships.

Surely, though, even with the exhaustion of the last few weeks and months, she didn't look as weary as he did. Did she?

"Admiral Usher. I … apologize for stopping by without an appointment." His tone was weary as well. "I didn't wish to alarm you, and honestly, the news I'm bringing is probably something that only you will be in position to appreciate the significance of."

She sighed and pushed the notes hovering over her desk farther to one side, giving her an unobstructed view of his face. "Edwin. I appreciate your concern, but I am a busy woman. If you have something to say to me, say it."

He paused a moment before he continued, and it was that more than anything that told her exactly what his news concerned.

"There was a young man, an officer candidate. I'm certain you'll have heard of it—a few days back, he stole some classified documents and ran."

She frowned. "I had heard of that. The documents weren't anything too sensitive, I hope?"

Edwin shrugged. "I don't think he has any current classified information, if that's what you're asking. Older records, although I haven't verified yet exactly what they contained. Be that as it may, though, we've recently been able to track where he's gone. The last word we've heard of him, he was heading for Blackrock."

Judith closed her eyes for a moment. "Let me guess—he was captain material."

"One of our brightest. His instructors were planning to recommend him for a three-hundred-and-fifty-crewed ship."

Judith slammed her palm down on the desk. "We can't afford to lose officer candidates, not with war as close as it is! You know that as well as I do. What the hell were his instructors thinking? Do they not monitor the officer candidates these days?" She blew out a short, frustrated breath. "When I was in the Academy, we couldn't sneeze without the instructors questioning us on our health the next day. And this boy somehow found classified documents, stole them, and ran off without anyone noticing."

This had Mad Dog's fingerprints all over it. Judith suspected, sometimes, that the damned woman kept herself as up-to-date on Level politics as Judith did, watching for an advantage. Between the pirate's strategy of sabotage on one side, and the politics of the upcoming war on the other, and the unrest in the Stacks added to that, she was fighting battles on multiple fronts.

She couldn't damn well afford this, not right now.

Edwin gave her a humourless smile. "That's the trouble with people intelligent enough to make good officer candidates. They're harder to control than the loyal, stupid ones."

Judith nodded. Her jaw was clenched hard enough that it ached, and she relaxed her muscles consciously.

The same traits that would have made the boy an exceptional officer—independent thought, intelligence, the ability to think for himself rather than simply trust the accepted wisdom—were the traits that would have made him unpredictable, and a tempting target for Mad Dog.

But she had to outfit more additional ships off the line than she really wanted to think about, and she needed officers who would be talented and skilled enough to adapt quickly to changing circumstances when war inevitably broke out. The older captains who'd spent their careers fighting skirmishes with pirates were useful enough for what they were good at, but she had her doubts that all of them would be able to switch their mindset quickly enough to be ready for a war.

"So," she said at last. "We've lost another promising captain candidate. That's unfortunate news, yes, but I hardly see that it warrants a personal visit in the middle of the afternoon."

He shook his head. "That's not all, I'm afraid." He leaned forward a little. "You remember Captain Hollis Ives?"

Judith nodded, frowning. She'd personally recommended the woman to the Academy. And her instincts had been proven right. Ives was from the Stacks and hadn't started in the navy until she was sixteen, a good four years later than most of her peers. But she was whip-smart, and canny as hell, and exactly the type of officer material Judith had been looking for.

"You assigned her to pick up the weapons ship that was stranded in the Adrian Sector, didn't you?"

Judith nodded again, slowly. "She needed a solid first command. There are likely to be pirates after it, we got word the transmission had been intercepted. She should be capable enough to handle a skirmish, and it'll give her some legitimacy in the eyes of her crew."

"We got word of the identity of the pirate ship that went after the *Agate*," he said, his voice grim. "It was the *Sweet Jenny*."

Judith stared at him for a moment as her mind processed his words. Then she swore violently. "You're certain?"

He nodded. "Unfortunately. My sources were very confident in their information." He shook his head. "Admiral. You need to call Ives back."

Judith hesitated a moment, her chest thick with dread. "I can't," she said at last, her tone brooking no argument. "We need those weapons. I won't pull her out."

Edwin frowned. "You'd send an untested captain against Mad Dog? She won't stand a chance. You told me you needed good captains. How can you afford to sacrifice one like this?"

Judith drew in a breath. "Mad Dog is only one woman. She may be dangerous, but she'll be going up against a ship of the line, with three hundred and fifty crew. I trust that Captain Ives can handle herself. Had I not, I would never have recommended her for her own command. Besides, even Mad Dog will be well aware that if we have proof that pirates took the weapons ship, that will give us the impetus we need to redouble our efforts against Blackrock. She won't risk a pitched battle."

"Admiral." Edwin's voice was heavy with concern. "This is Mad Dog you're talking about. Pull Ives, send in a seasoned captain. That's our only chance to avoid another ship lost, captain and crew."

"No." Judith let her voice go fully flat. "I will not be pulling Captain Ives. She has her orders, it's up to her to complete them in a satisfactory manner."

Edwin studied her for a few moments. At last he sighed and stood. "As you say, Admiral," he said, turning away.

She waited until he'd gone, and the door closed behind him.

Then she slumped in her seat, swearing quietly.

Her shoulders were so tight that she could feel the strain up her neck, merging into the beginnings of a headache at the base of her skull.

She couldn't even warn the *Verity*. The only warning that would reach a ship of the line after its first FTL jump would have to go through the emergency channels, broadcast on every open comm line.

She trusted Ives. She didn't trust that the crew of the *Verity* wouldn't mutiny if they knew what they'd be facing, especially with an untried captain, and one from the Stacks to boot.

And if she pulled Hollis, she'd lose a captain just as readily as if Mad Dog shot her down. She'd save a ship of the line, yes, but she'd lose the weapons, and she'd lose a captain. The moment she sent out the command, she'd be broadcasting to all and sundry that she didn't trust the woman. That would be enough to hamstring any new captain, let alone the first commissioned captain from the Stacks.

She cursed again, viciously.

If she let Hollis go on, there was still a chance the woman would pull through—rescue the *Agate* and get back. And to be perfectly honest, she needed a captain more than she needed three hundred and fifty sailors. Sailors were easy enough to come by—anyone who'd sailed on a merchant ship was spoiled for any other career, and desperate bodies were plentiful in the Stacks, where every day was a chance of getting torn to pieces by a vicious ghost. She didn't like it, she was well aware of the unfairness of it, but it was currently her saving grace—they always had as many sailors as they needed to fill their allotments.

But captains—good captains—were few and far between. And she couldn't afford to lose Hollis.

She closed her eyes for a moment, rolling her head from side to side to try to loosen the tension in her neck.

She could picture Gracie's face, her small, mocking smile.

Mad Dog Gracie Madox, who'd killed more good sailors and captains, downed more ships than Judith could recall without looking.

The woman was a legend in the navy, her name spoken in a whisper and with a glance over your shoulder. If the crew of the *Verity* had any idea who they were going up against, they'd mutiny.

If Hollis had any idea what she was going up against …

Judith shook her head and opened her eyes, turning back to her documents.

She'd simply have to hope the woman was as scrappy as she'd seemed, back when she crewed under Judith. And she'd have to hope whatever the hell a Stacks captain prayed to was listening. Because her decision not to pull Hollis might well be sending the entire ship to its death.

But she wouldn't unmake it. She couldn't.

11

Silas

Silas cursed as he struggled into the bulky suit, clamping the breathing tube between his teeth. The slim, fitted suits they used for skirmishes, the ones most sailors took to wearing under their uniforms when fighting was imminent, were enough to protect you from the pressure and temperature changes inherent in a battle in a ship's airlock. But for a repair job on the outer hull, he'd need a bulkier suit, where the level of protection made up for the loss of maneuverability.

"We're stopped for exactly one hour." Freddie's voice filtered in through the soft protective hood he was wearing.

He clipped the suit shut and bent to grab the helmet from the ground at his feet.

"That means you'll need to be fast. It'll be hot as the devil's asshole out there, so you won't want to stay any one place too long, or your boots'll start melting."

He nodded tersely, fitting the helmet on carefully and feeling around for the neck clasps.

"It's the devil's seam we need taken care of." She handed him the torch, and he fastened it carefully to his utility belt as she lifted the tank up behind him, clipping it on to his shoulder harness. "You've worked on the devil's seam before?"

He nodded again.

He'd done repairs on the devil's seam more times than he could count as a young man in the navy. It was hard, brutal, dangerous work, and he'd managed to mostly avoid it as he'd moved up in the ranks.

Now, on the *Sweet Jenny*, he was back where he'd started.

The difference was, of course, that in the navy they didn't do repairs on the devil's seam unless they were in a quiet place in space, and the radars showed no approaching space debris. And in addition, they never sent out a crew of less than three, two to keep watch while one worked.

Here, he had an hour to repair the seam, and they were close enough to a star that even from inside the ship he could feel the heat of it, making him sweat under his heavy suit even inside the airlock. Freddie would be keeping watch from inside the ship, but they had neither the crew nor the time to send someone out to watch with him.

"You alright, Level boy?" she asked. Through the earpiece in his suit, he couldn't tell whether she meant the question to be sarcastic or sincere.

It hardly mattered. The job had to be done, and he wasn't about to give them cause to think a naval sailor any less competent than a pirate.

He gave her a thumbs up, and she nodded, pushing her chair forward to the airlock controls. "You'll be able to call in through the suit, but I'll be keeping an eye on you from here. Got my own things to fix on the inside, but there's an alarm that'll sound if you're in trouble or if there's trouble coming up. And if you see something, hit the panic button on your suit, and it'll send an alarm back so we can pull you in. Got it?"

He nodded again.

"Good. On my count, I'll hit the airlock. You'll want to be in and out as quick as you can." She paused. "Three. Two. One. Inside airlock opening."

The doors slid apart, and he stepped inside the small, pressurized area.

He readied his anchor line, preparing to wrap and fasten it to the external setting. On the newer ships of the line there were automated anchor lines. They made it harder to miss your knots and accidentally send yourself out into space with no way to get back. But they were less maneuverable. With the hand-tied anchors, it was easy enough to pull yourself in, switch your anchor line, and move out again in a different direction. It made a difference on a fighting ship, and he'd been in enough skirmishes to value the adaptability. Besides, if he was going to trust his life to an anchor line, he'd just as soon do it to one he'd tied himself.

He tapped his helmet, activating the comm line. "Ready to tie in."

"External airlock opening, on my count."

He moved over to the exit door, taking a firm grip on the handholds.

"Three. Two. One. Outer airlock door opening."

There was the hiss of machinery, and the doors slid open.

There was a sharp sucking sensation from inside the airlock as the pressure stabilized, and then he maneuvered his way carefully out through the airlock doors and onto the outside surface of the ship, keeping a tight grip on the handholds.

The heat from outside hit the moment he was through the doors, and he could feel the coolers on his suit kick in. The airlock he'd exited was facing the star, and already the heat was making the surface of the ship hot enough that his boots felt tacky against the surface.

He secured his anchor line quickly, wrapping it three times around the hook and tying it in, then tapped his helmet. "Anchor secured."

"Outer airlock door closing on my count. Three. Two. One. Outer airlock door closing."

Behind him, the doors slid silently shut.

He glanced around, taking his bearings. He'd need to work quickly, but he couldn't afford to make a mistake. Freddie was monitoring, but she had work of her own to get through in the hour break they had while Temple charted their new course.

Carefully, using the anchor rope to brace himself, he adjusted the mags on his boots until they gave him solid contact with the hull without impeding his movement. He tugged on the anchor line one last time out of habit, testing the knot, but he'd been tying anchor knots since he was twelve years old.

He stepped forward, working his way towards the devil's seam.

The long seam that traversed the length of the hull was heavily reinforced, but the strain of faster-than-light travel put impossible amounts of pressure on it. There had been some recent merchant ship designs that had managed to eliminate the seam, but none of them had proved overly practical—without the give of the seam, you sacrificed maneuverability and speed, and in the worst case, risked tearing the ship apart in an FTL jump. On the naval ships, the hull itself was reinforced to the point that they could manage several consecutive jumps without checking the seam, but they also had the luxury of set jump courses that were kept free of debris. Smaller ships, like the *Sweet Jenny*, were simply unable to build up that level of reinforcement, and they traveled courses that made collisions with space-junk much more likely.

It took him a few endless minutes to get to the end of the hull. Still, he'd been a sailor for long enough to know how important it was to start at the tip of the seam, because a missed centimetre could be the difference between a ship that could hold up to a FTL jump, and a ship that would split down the middle like a ripe fruit.

"I'm at the end of the seam," he said over the comm, pulling up the vid broadcast on his wrist. If Freddie wanted to watch, she'd be able to see his progress as he went, and the vid would be uploaded to the ship's record if anyone needed to check his work later.

He unclipped the wand from his belt and cued up the roll of reinforcement patches, and began the slow, painstaking work.

By the time he'd been out twenty minutes, sweat was already dripping down his back, gathering between his shoulder blades, trickling down his hairline and into his eyes. The temp control in his suit hummed diligently, but it wasn't enough against heat like this. He blinked back the sweat, the salt stinging his eyes.

It was … odd, really, to be outside on a ship so close to a star. The brilliance was like daytime back in the Level, but a hundred times brighter, a sharp contrast to the black of space around him. Like he'd imagined some of the resource planets, the warmer ones where food production was more important than mined minerals or trapped gasses. The other children he'd grown up with had always talked about how exciting it would be to live on a resource planet.

But Silas's mind had been wholly occupied with sailing, on a ship of the line out into the far reaches of the known universe. Out to the edges of space, where no one knew exactly what you'd find, what dangers or beauties drifted endlessly out beyond human imaginings.

He shook his head and turned his attention back to his work.

He was more than halfway done.

He glanced at his timepiece, and gritted his teeth.

More than halfway done, but more than half the time gone as well. One hour, they'd told him, and he was forty minutes in.

He stood, stretching the cramp from his back, and fed another roll of reinforcement patch into the wand. He glanced over his shoulder as he worked, squinting even under the protection of the sun-shielded helmet.

He'd made it farther than he'd thought, now that he was looking. Maybe he had a chance to finish this off before the hour was up after all.

He turned back to his work.

Behind him, there was a flash of … something, and the brilliant light that he'd been squinting against brightened momentarily. He squeezed his eyes closed, and the heat and the exhaustion and strain had slowed his thoughts enough that his brain hardly registered the danger until Freddie's voice shouted through his earpiece, "Solar flare! Get back inside, now!"

He sat stupidly for a moment. And then his brain kicked into gear, panic flooding through him.

"How long until impact?" he snapped through his com.

"You have four minutes, forty-three seconds."

He glanced over to the airlock door, and then shook his head, cursing.

There was no way he'd reach it in four and a half minutes, not like this. And if he didn't—he'd seen pictures of sailors who'd been caught outside in solar flares. Peeling skin, vomiting, seizures. Death, if they were too close, and their suits lacked sufficient protection.

He closed his eyes for a moment, trying to slow his racing heart.

He'd never make it back walking. He could try to make the other side of the ship, that might shelter him enough to keep him from the worst of the radiation poisoning, but it wasn't a given. He might still die, and if he went that way, he'd give up his chance of making it inside.

Four minutes and ten seconds.

He gritted his teeth, leaned down, and dialled the mag clamps on his boots down to zero. He took a sturdy grip on the anchor line, pulling in a quick breath.

In naval training, that was the first thing they taught you—never turn your mag clamps off, not in a fight, not ever. Because the moment your only link with the ship was your anchor line was the moment you were vulnerable to anything—flying debris, a kink in the line, worn equipment, a single stroke from an enemy's rapier or heat-knife.

The moment you were trusting your life to only your anchor line, you put yourself in the hands of chance.

He looked ahead to the airlock door, calculating his trajectory. Then, carefully, he pulled the anchor rope taut and pushed himself off the side of the ship and towards the airlock door.

The moment his feet left the surface of the ship, he grabbed for the line and began hauling himself in, hand over hand.

Four minutes left until the solar flare hit.

He reached the place halfway up the hull where he'd tied in to re-secure his line and grabbed for the tie-in, jerking the knot free with one hand. Then he pushed off again, making for the entrance.

"Standing by at the airlock. Call in when you're here. I won't be able to hold it open long." Freddie's voice through his earpiece was calm, but he could hear the fear under it.

He closed his eyes, swearing under his breath.

She was risking enough as it was, to even consider opening the airlock door this close to a solar flare.

He pulled himself forward again. Almost there, he'd be there in less than a minute …

And then the line went oddly soft in his hands.

He stared at it for a moment, horror welling in his stomach, then followed the line with his eyes to where it was tied down on the anchor loop outside of the airlock.

Then he saw it—a tiny sliver of metal protruding from the smooth edge of the anchor loop, likely the result of a glancing collision with a bit of space debris.

He'd normally have checked the loop before he tied on. But he'd been in a hurry, and he'd been short on time, and he hadn't.

And now, it had rubbed the anchor cord almost through.

In regular circumstances, that would have been frightening, but manageable—with his mag boots on the deck, he could bring himself in slowly, not put any additional strain on the line.

But now—he'd been pulling himself in on the line, every jerk of his arms sliding it across the rough surface. And the sliver had cut through two of the three loops of the knot.

He glanced behind him.

The wave of the solar flare was visible now, an odd ripple in space, glowing with radiation energy. In a moment, the outer edges of it would hit him.

The outer edges weren't enough to kill him. But when the full force of it hit, even if he'd have survived the radiation sickness, the energy of it would be enough to push him free of the ship, and easily enough to cut through the remnant of his worn anchor line.

He could reactivate the mags on his boots, there was always the chance he could work himself close enough to the ship to clamp on.

But if he did that, there was no way he'd make the airlock in time, and the wave of the solar flare would probably be enough to shove his boot clamps loose, even if he dialled them all the way up.

He closed his eyes for a moment, tapping his helmet. "Freddie," he said quietly. "Stand down. My anchor line's compromised. I'm not going to make the airlock."

There was a moment's silence on the other side of the line.

He couldn't help glancing over his shoulder again.

The flare was less than a minute away. Already, he could feel himself being pushed gently out and away from the ship.

He drew in a long breath.

This wasn't how he'd thought he'd die. But then, everyone who signed onto an FTL ship knew that death would come for them sooner or later—in a skirmish with pirates, killed by the ghost of a bunkmate, radiation sickness, having your anchor cord cut—there were a million ways to die in space. He'd been careless, and he knew damn well he deserved what came next.

"Lad! Can you hear me?"

The voice was crisp and sharp, and he looked up quickly.

The airlock was open, and a figure was pulling their way out, hand over hand. He didn't recognize who it was from the bulky suit, but the voice through his earpiece was unmistakable.

"Captain?" he said blankly.

"I'll catch your line." Her voice was calm and businesslike. "I've told Freddie to close the airlock before the flare hits, so be quick, or you'll trap us both out here." There wasn't even a hint of fear in her voice, at least none that he could make out.

Even from here, he could see she wasn't strapped in. She wouldn't have the time to strap in, nor the time to untie. They had perhaps thirty seconds.

She held the edge of the anchor loop with one hand, and with the other, she grabbed the frayed end of his line, wrapping it around her glove. "Pull yourself in, lad, quick-time."

His brain finally registered what she was doing. Frantically, he grabbed at the rope, yanking himself towards her as fast as his arms could pull him.

The strain must be intense—she was holding him anchored with nothing but her own grip, and already the solar winds were trying to tear both of them away from the ship.

And then he was there. He clasped her wrist in one hand, and with the other, cut loose the end of the line.

"Good lad," she said. She dragged them both inside the airlock just as the doors slammed shut, plunging them into darkness.

For a moment he simply lay there, panting, as the airlock chamber re-pressurized and the gravity field established itself. Gracie was breathing hard as well, he could hear her panting through the open channel in his suit comm.

At last she unclipped her helmet, shaking back her hair, and looked over at him. "You alright, lad?"

He took a deep breath to steady himself and unclipped his own helmet. His hands were shaking. "I'm alright, Captain," he said, glancing up at her. "I … Thank you." His voice choked a little over the words.

Her eyes held that same sharp perceptiveness he'd noticed when he first met her in the tavern in Blackrock. "You signed onto my crew, Sil. I don't leave my crew to die, not if I can help it." She turned away, unstrapping her suit. "Best we get inside. The hull is rad-shielded, but we'll be better off inside the second airlock. I don't want a bout of radiation sickness if I can avoid it, and I don't want you vomiting your insides out when I need you on watch."

"Aye, Captain," he murmured, but he found himself staring after her, something tight and uncomfortable twisting in his stomach.

She should have left him to die. If this had been a navy ship, he'd have been left to die rather than endanger the ship or one of the crew. He'd been careless, and he'd have deserved it.

But she hadn't. She'd risked her life to save him.

He'd watched her shoot a naval captain in the head in cold blood, with no sign of remorse. And then she'd saved his life, when he knew damn well he didn't deserve it.

At last, he shook himself out of his revery and got to his feet.

Gracie was speaking into her comm, and a moment later, the inner airlock door slid. Freddie waited at the entrance, her face a little paler than usual, Ari at her shoulder. There was no hiding the relief on either of their faces when Gracie stepped through. "Captain," Freddie said, her voice catching a little. "Glad to see you in one piece."

Gracie smiled wryly. "Glad to be in one piece."

Silas stepped out of the airlock door after her, and to his shock, Freddie looked almost as relieved to see him as she had to see the captain. "You too, Sil," she said. "Glad Captain pulled you in."

"As am I," he murmured.

He still wasn't sure why she'd done it.

Ari was watching him, a calculating expression on her face. "Thought she'd leave you out there, didn't you, Level boy?" she whispered as he passed.

She must have seen in his face she'd guessed right, because she smirked. "Captain don't do that. There's a reason every damn one of us here'd die for her, for all that we're not your Level navy sailors. She don't leave her crew to die."

"She killed fifty naval sailors in cold blood," he whispered back.

Ari raised her eyebrows. "Weren't her crew, though, was it?"

Silas scowled at her. The shakiness of the moment before had turned to an odd anger. "They didn't deserve to die. I did."

Ari grinned. "You did, did you? For following orders to get out there and patch the seam, that's why?"

"I was stupid," he hissed. "It was my own damn fault."

"Maybe. But I figure ain't a one of us here who haven't made a mistake before." She sighed. "We take care of our own, Sil. I lived on the Level, remember? I know what it's like. You don't like the Captain's morals, maybe, but hell, least she's not one to see her crew in trouble and cut their line." She turned away. "Anyway, best get going. Figure Captain's not going to be happy when Freddie gets done talking to her."

A few minutes later, they'd gathered in the engine room, where Freddie had pulled up the diagnostics. "Solar flare came before we had time to put up shielding after the jump," she said.

"What's the damage?" Gracie's voice was measured.

Freddie flipped through the glowing holographic pages in front of them. "There's a lot, but most of it I can fix—swap out a few electrical components, and we should still be able to fly her. But it fried the circuits on the long-range guns. Those, I won't be able to fix without a dry-dock. We can still fly, but we're not going to win if we get in a spitting match with the Navy."

Gracie nodded, her face grim. At last, though, she turned to Toothpick. "We're not losing this cargo. We'll go on, and we'll just have to be sure we make it before the naval ship does."

"Aye, Captain," said Toothpick. "I'll get Temple to calculate our next jump." But Silas could see the worry on the man's face as he turned away.

12

Hollis

Foster was waiting for her as Hollis pulled herself up the ratlines and onto the bridge deck. She could have gone around, but the tone in her first mate's voice had told her this was urgent.

"Mate Price," she said, straightening and shrugging into the jacket she'd flung over her shoulder. "What is the emergency, please?"

Foster had already started down the corridors towards the bridge at a brisk pace, and Hollis fell into step behind them. "A solar flare, Captain," Foster said as they walked. "We'll pass right through the middle of it on our planned jump."

Hollis nodded, and then they were at the bridge. She stepped inside, and the organized chaos quieted at her arrival.

The silence was expectant, less respectful than wary.

Fair enough. As long as there was silence, she'd not question its origin at the moment.

"What do we have?" she asked as she reached the control deck. Emmett turned at her approach.

He hadn't tried to challenge her authority, and his looks of resentment had diminished over the last couple days, and for that she was grateful. But he still seemed to be under the impression that his experience was worth more than her own, and while he never outright questioned her judgement, he'd come close enough to it on more than one occasion.

"Here, Captain," he said, tapping a point on the glowing screen. "There was a solar flare in the Helix sector, which normally is too far to affect us. But if we take the planned route," he traced the jump corridor with his finger as he spoke, "we'll go through the centre of the burst. I suggest we lock down and wait it out, come out of FTL until the screens show clear again, and then move on. Alternately, we could take this route." He traced his finger along a circuitous route through three more jump channels. "If we do that, we should avoid the worst of it."

She frowned at the screen, calculating. "Wilkes. How long is the fallout from the flare expected to last?" she asked briskly, turning to the navigator.

The woman frowned. "We can't tell exactly, but it was a large one. To be safe, we'd want to lock down for at least twenty-four hours."

Hollis turned back to the screen in front of her.

She hadn't done the calculations on the alternate route Emmett had pointed out, but from the looks of it, it would add at least that, if not more.

Twenty-four hours.

It was standard procedure, drilled into all the officer candidates in the Academy.

But she knew damn well what a twenty-four-hour delay would mean.

They'd gotten word that there had been a pirate ship that had set out from Blackrock shortly after the broadcast was intercepted.

Pirates couldn't travel as fast as naval ships, since they couldn't use the jump channels, but they were built to be fast. A twenty-four-hour delay could easily mean the difference between the success or failure of the mission.

"Wilkes," she said, turning to the navigator. "Please chart us a course." She tapped the screen. "Well jump to just the outside of the hazard zone for the solar flare. We'll take the ship down to cruising speed through the flair path."

The woman turned to stare at her.

"You can't do that." Emmett's voice was blank with shock. "Do you know what will happen to the ship if we take it at cruising speed through an active flare?"

She spun on him. "Yes, I do. The power cells in the running engines will be hit by the electromagnetic particles. As the ship has been built to the correct naval specs, this energy will not destroy the cells outright, but they will increase the heat to the system by a factor of ten. You will instruct the ship's engineer to monitor the cells closely. As soon as they begin to heat up, we will increase the power to the engines."

He frowned, and opened his mouth to comment. She didn't give him the chance.

"We will then pull all power forward, so we're running at our top cruising speed." She gestured to the screen in front of her. "When we pull all the power forward, it will channel the additional power to the FTL jump engines, correct?"

The navigator nodded, but her face was pale. "Yes, Captain. But the power—"

"Will be defused if we jump immediately after the power transfer."

The woman looked at her for a moment. "I ... Captain, that's technically possible, but it will require exact measurements. If we don't do the jump correctly, it will risk a full meltdown of our FTL drive. We'll be stranded until another ship can pick us up."

"Then we'd best be sure we do the jump correctly," Hollis said, her tone sharp. "I'll remain on the bridge. You'll jump on my mark."

"Captain! You can't …"

"Mate Greene." Her voice was icy. "I am the captain of this ship, am I not?"

There was a long moment's pause, and she could see the battle on his face. "Yes, Captain," he said at last, resentment in his tone.

"Give the order, Mate Greene," she snapped.

Her palms were sweating, but she didn't dare wipe them dry on her trouser leg.

She wasn't concerned about her calculations. They were correct. She knew the specs of this class of ship inside and out, knew exactly the predicted effects of the energy burst of a solar flare.

But if her crew hesitated, for even a moment, to obey her orders, there was a very good chance they would be stranded. And if that happened, she knew well enough that she'd have lost more than the *Agate*.

She'd lose her command. The Admiral herself wouldn't be able to get her back on a ship, even if the woman was inclined to try.

"Yes, Captain." Emmett turned away.

"Mate Price, please assist Mate Greene," she snapped.

"Aye, Captain." Foster's voice was as neutral as always, but there was something comforting in the familiar acknowledgement that calmed Hollis's nerves, just a little.

She could only hope she was right to trust them.

The navigator was setting the coordinates into the system, glancing over her shoulder at Hollis.

Hollis watched, face impassive.

Her heart was pounding.

"Jumping to the onscreen coordinates. Prepare for jump." Wilkes's voice rang out over the noise of the bridge. "On my count. Two. One. Jumping."

There was the familiar sensation, not an acceleration as much as a pull, the feeling of your insides suddenly, momentarily, becoming your outsides, weightless and scrambled.

She kept her gaze fixed on the screen in front of her.

"Coming out of jump, on my count. Three. Two. One. Coming out."

Again, that odd, scrambled feeling.

The navigator looked at Hollis, and Hollis nodded brusquely.

The woman swallowed hard. "Setting cruising speed."

Now there was a sense of acceleration. Hollis gritted her teeth, her feet apart for balance. But she'd had years of experience keeping her balance on a shifting ship's deck.

"Captain." It was Foster's voice through her earpiece. "Cells are heating up."

She tapped her communicator. "Thank you. Advise when the cells are at ninety percent heat capacity."

There was another moment of silence.

Outside the wide plex windows of the bridge, the stars glittered bright and cold, and she could see the hot energy of the solar particles, burning as they hit the ship's shielding and turning it momentarily visible in their brilliant pin-prick glow.

"Eighty-five percent, Captain," came Foster's voice.

"Acknowledged."

"Eighty-seven percent."

"Acknowledged." She turned to the navigator. "Be ready to pull all power forward, Wilkes."

"Aye, Captain."

"Eighty-nine percent."

"On my mark," Hollis said, holding up a hand.

"Prepare for jump," called Wilkes over the bridge comm.

"Captain. Ninety percent."

"Now!" Hollis dropped her hand in the signal, and the navigator shoved the controls forward. There was the increasing hum of the jump engines powering up, shunting all the excess power from the solar flare through the ship.

"Jumping," Wilkes snapped.

Hollis held her breath.

For a brief, disconnected moment, it felt like the entire ship was holding its breath.

And then there was the tugging sensation of an FTL jump, and she had to hold herself back from putting out a hand to support herself on the control table and sagging in relief.

Instead, she straightened, and glanced over at the navigator. "Well done, Wilkes," she said.

The woman's face was pale, and she was making no effort whatsoever to hide her relief. "It worked, Captain!" Her mouth was turning up into what could only be called a grin.

"Yes." Hollis was trying, very hard, to keep her own voice steady. "It did. Thank you."

The air on the bridge was almost celebratory, the navigators and pilots grinning and exchanging excited whispers.

Even when they cast glances in her direction, the air of celebration didn't noticeably diminish.

Hollis closed her eyes for a moment, drawing in a long, steadying breath.

They still had a chance to make the *Agate*. She still had a chance to bring this mission in successfully.

"Captain."

She opened her eyes to the voice at her elbow.

Foster stood there, face and voice as respectful as ever.

Hollis cleared her throat. "Thank you, Mate Price. You did well."

Foster hesitated a moment. "That was … well done, Captain. I wouldn't have thought of it."

For the briefest moment, Hollis stared at her first mate, not entirely sure how to respond.

"Thank you," she said at last, gruffly. She glanced around the deck. "Sailors. If you have this under control, I shall be in my cabin charting out our next jump path."

There was a quiet murmur of, "Yes, Captain," and "Aye, Captain,"s, and Hollis turned back towards her cabin. But for the first time since she'd come on board, Hollis heard a hint of actual respect under the words.

13

Silas had sharpened his cutlass and checked his pistols and sparker at least a dozen times in the last twelve hours since their jump from the solar flare. He'd been in the navy for long enough that he was used to swallowing down his restless need to move, the way his muscles ached to be doing something, anything, other than sitting still, but something about the easy informality of the pirate crew had worn the edges off his stoicism.

And the fact that no one on the crew seemed to mind made it worse.

The tension in the *Sweet Jenny* was palpable, and it was almost a relief when Gracie called them up to the main deck.

"We'll be coming out of FTL in just over twelve hours," she said, once they'd gathered. She, at least, seemed just as calm as usual. "I want you ready for anything. If we had our heavy weapons, I wouldn't worry about whatever the navy wanted to throw at us— you're a good crew, and the *Sweet Jenny's* guns'll take down most navy shielding. But we don't have our heavies, and our light weapons aren't enough. With luck, we get in before the naval ship, but best be ready for trouble at any rate. *Agate's* a fifty-crew vessel under normal circumstances, but the Naval High Command don't take chances. They've got a good fifty extra navy sailors on board to protect the cargo, from what we've been able to intercept. Won't be an easy cargo to take, and you'd best bet you'll see ghosts. Don't want to lose any of my crew, so you'll damn well be ready for a fight." She gave a small smile. "And remember. We'll be coming in close to a black hole. We've got our stabilizers, so we should be alright, long as we run in slow and keep an eye on the engine strain. But running in close to a black hole ain't a place you can afford to lose focus."

"You ever run in close to a black hole, lad?" Temple asked, when he and Silas were on watch.

Silas shook his head.

Temple laughed grimly. "I have. When you're that close to one of 'em, things don't work the way you expect them to. Time slows down, yeah, especially if you get too close. But it ain't just that. Messes with your communications, messes with your weapons aim. The *Agate* is damn lucky they could get a communication out at all. They'll have been using the quantum comms as they use on the Level, figure those ain't affected as bad by the grav field. Only way they'd have got word back in time. But I've been right close to a black hole before, and I'll tell you—" He shuddered. "Not just weapons and communicators. Messes with your head, it does—you sitting in so close to something that'll turn you into streaks of matter, pull your atoms apart and crush your cells, and you can feel it, tugging at you. You can feel it, every moment you're near it, and it gets in your head. Scared the living hell out of me, I'll tell you that."

He shook his head. "You're working with Freddie most times, lad, and you may not think it's that important, work you do. But I'll tell you, you'll be glad of it when we get in close to the *Agate*. Because when you're that close to a black hole, your life and the life of every sailor on board comes down to your stabilizers. Those're the only things that are keeping you alive, and you'd damn better be sure they're running well. Because I seen a ship lose her stabilizers near a black hole once, one of our merchant convoy back when I was sailing for them. Stabilizers went, and she got pulled right in, us hearing her crew screaming through the comms, the sound all warped and strange from the grav field, until the comms went. Then we just watched them go, and nothing a damn one of us could do about it."

A week ago, Silas might have thought the man was pulling his leg. But he'd been on the crew long enough to recognize the very real fear in Temple's face.

He'd sailed in the navy since he was twelve years old. He'd never been near a black hole, for better or worse, but the old sailors told stories about them, and he'd heard his share.

He fought back a shiver of his own, and nodded, checking over the starboard sensors one more time.

They weren't close enough to the hole yet to feel the pull of it, but the unease of the crew was contagious.

Freddie felt it too—when he was off watch, she had him shoulder-deep in the stabilizers, greasing and polishing and checking and re-checking every component.

"Much as all our lives are worth, to make a mistake on the stabilizers when we're coming in on a black hole," she muttered, when he cast an irritated glance at her over his shoulder. She'd asked him to check the alignment for the third time in an hour, and sweat was dripping down his face and plastering his hair to his forehead. "You'll thank me when we get the *Sweet Jenny* close enough to the

Agate to get her cargo off her, and you feel the grav field for the first time."

The loss of the heavy weapons had done nothing to improve her mood, and by the time he was finished the tasks she'd set him, he thought he might simply drop from weariness and fall asleep on the engine room floor.

Even after he dragged himself to mess and ate the cold supper Vee had prepared, the crew quarters were uncharacteristically silent. No one seemed in the mood for dice, and for the first time since he'd signed on to the crew, the others who weren't on duty were at their hammocks, or else sitting quietly sharpening cutlasses or cleaning and reassembling pistols.

Silas fell into his hammock, but he couldn't sleep.

It wasn't just the loss of the heavy weapons, or the threat of the black hole, that kept him staring up at the ceiling long past the time when the cramped quarters had gone silent.

It was the realization that, after everything, the moment he set foot on the *Agate*, he'd have done something irreversible.

It was one thing to talk about the injustices perpetrated by the Level and the Admiral.

It was another to step onto a dying naval ship, not to assist, but to loot her cargo for a pirate crew.

With the navy scout ship, he'd had no idea what was happening until after it happened. But this time—well, this time he knew exactly what he was doing, and who Gracie and the others were. They'd made no pretence of it. As much as he hated to admit it, even to himself, he knew that in that, at least, Gracie was right—no matter how just his cause, once he'd done that, the navy would never take him back, even if they forgave him the crime.

He almost laughed at himself.

From the moment he'd taken the documents and fled the Academy, he'd known, intellectually, that he could never go back. But it wasn't until now, staring up at the ceiling of a pirate ship on its way to the edges of a black hole, that he realized it in his bones.

And he wasn't sure what his life would look like, without the one constant thing that had shaped him from his earliest memories.

At long last, he sat up with a sigh, swinging his legs over the edge of his hammock. He glanced around quickly—the others, at least, seemed to have been able to fall asleep—and picked up his weapons, walking as silently as he could to avoid waking anyone.

It wouldn't hurt to disassemble and clean out his energy pistol thoroughly before they came out of jump, and if anyone on this damn crew could sleep, he wasn't cruel enough to risk waking them.

He stepped out onto the main deck, the weariness of the day dragging at his limbs and seeping through his brain, making his thoughts thick and sluggish. It wasn't until he was half-way across the deck that he realized he wasn't alone.

"Can't sleep, lad?"

He recognized the voice instantly. "Captain?" he asked, turning.

She was sitting at the edge of the deck, leaned up against the rail, and it was only the faint glow of the charts hovering over her wrist comm that let him see her at all.

She chuckled, the sound soft and amused in the darkness. "Aye, lad, it's me." She gave him a one-shouldered shrug. "With what we're going into, I'd rather not leave anything to chance more'n I can help."

He nodded, and after a moment, sat down on the deck a little way away and, in the light of his wrist comm, began his methodical disassembly of his pistol, cleaning and wiping each part as he put it aside.

He found he was watching the captain from the corner of his eye as he worked. Trying to read the woman who'd risked her own life to save his with as little hesitation as she'd killed the captain of the scout ship.

He wasn't certain he'd ever be able to, truth be told.

At last, Gracie said, "A week on a pirate ship, and I still see the navy in you." The words weren't accusatory, just faintly amused.

"I've been in the navy since I was twelve," he said shortly. "I hardly think a few days on the *Sweet Jenny* is enough to counteract that."

She chuckled again, and for a while, neither of them spoke

"I know you hate the Level, Captain," he said at last, in a low voice. "I know you hate the navy and the Admiral. What would it take for you to come with me, take the documents I stole and use them to take the Admiral down, and those on the Naval High Command who were complicit? You killing captains on naval scout ships won't do that. You know that." He shifted, so he was leaning forward a bit. "I know you don't want to risk what you already have. But you built yourself up from nothing after you turned pirate. How would this be any different?"

She was quiet for a bit. At last she shook her head, and even in the dark he could see her small, amused smile. "I'm a hell of a lot older now than I was when I turned pirate," she said at last. "Maybe I'm just too tired for revenge."

"I don't believe it." He shook his head. "I've seen how much you hate them. Why not take it out on the people who deserve it? The sailors before the mast don't. Navy or not, most of them are just trying to survive, like everyone on the *Sweet Jenny*."

When she spoke, her voice was low, but sharp as a cutlass-edge. "Because, lad, one thing you learn when you live like we live, out on

Blackrock—there are no heroes. And there are no innocents. There's you, and there's your crew, and there's them as want you dead. And you'd best learn that before we reach the *Agate,* because you forget it, and you die." She paused. "When you were in the navy, lad, and you went after a pirate ship, you ever stop to think about the ones you were killing? You ever stop to think that maybe the people you cut open with that cutlass of yours had stories like Temple's, or Toothpick's, or Ari's? Or is it only the naval soldiers as deserve that consideration?"

He closed his eyes for a moment, gritting his teeth. "We're protecting ourselves," he said at last.

"Ourselves? The ones as would have hung you for treason if you'd taken this to them?"

He blew out a long breath.

He could feel Gracie's eyes on him. At last, though, she turned back to her charts, and he turned back to the half-disassembled pistol in front of him.

"I heard you were just as much a navy sailor as I was," he said into the silence.

She didn't answer.

He hesitated a moment. But perhaps it was the cool anonymity of the dark, or perhaps it was his residual irritation that made him say it. "I heard how the *Sweet Jenny* got her name, too. Maybe you were more a navy sailor than I was."

Gracie went still. It wasn't that she'd been restless before—she'd been bent over her charts, studying—but there was something about the sudden absence of all movement that made Silas stop dead, an instinctual reaction from the depths of his animal brain.

When at last Gracie spoke, her voice was deceptively mild. "Tell me what you heard, then, lad."

He closed his eyes a moment, his heart pounding quick and hard in his chest.

He'd heard Gracie speak to the captain of the scouting ship in that same tone, right before she'd pulled out a pistol and shot him through the head.

"I heard you had a lover, back in the Academy," he said. "Jenny. And that losing her was the one thing you'd never forgive the Level for."

She was still motionless, with the stillness of a mountain cat before it kills.

"Aye, Sil. You heard right," she said finally. "But then, that's the sort of history as gets people killed when they dig it up." She smiled a little in the darkness, the faint glow of the ship's emergency lighting glinting off the tips of her teeth. "Don't particularly like discussing my Jenny with people as never knew her. And I figure you have enough things trying to kill you at the moment. I'd go back to working on my weapons, if I were you."

He held her gaze for just a moment, and in that moment, he realized exactly what the scout ship's captain had seen the instant before he died.

And then he turned away, and Gracie leaned back against the rail, and the release of tension in the air was almost tangible.

He finished the pistol, then reassembled it, checking it to be sure he'd put everything back in the correct order. Gracie glanced up as he stood. "Sleep well, lad," she said. "We'll all have plenty to keep us occupied tomorrow, I have a feeling."

He nodded, and headed back to his hammock. But he doubted he'd be getting much sleep.

14

Gracie

Gracie frowned, blinking her eyes hard against the exhaustion.

Despite the damage from the solar flare, they were making good time. Whoever the Admiral had sent out after them was probably still sitting out the flare, if she recalled proper naval protocol.

She sighed, and pushed the heels of her hands into her eyes.

Damn that boy for bringing up Jenny. Damn him, and damn her that even after all this time, she couldn't simply let it go.

So much had happened, back then. So much hurt, and so much betrayal, watching the institution she'd given her life to turn on her. So many years after where she'd lived on the bloody edges of survival, where she'd finally drop from sheer exhaustion at night not knowing if she'd live to wake up.

And she'd managed to put all that behind her, somehow. She'd learned to live with those memories, like she lived with the scar on her forearm—something that would never heal, really, but that she could put out of her mind. She could make her decisions logically and rationally, put the well-being of herself and her crew over her own aching, desperate need for revenge.

But losing Jenny? She'd never managed to put that behind her. The best she could do was shove it out of her mind, make it clear to whoever tried to bring it back that that was one subject she'd not brook opening, not from anyone.

And then Silas had come, with his documents and his questions and his talk of revenge, and the cold fire of hatred, at the navy and at Admiral Usher herself, that she'd thought she'd long since banked, was flaring back to life.

She shook her head.

She was tired. The whole crew was tired. She'd only given them three days shore leave, and it had hardly been a leave—every moment filled with resupplying the ship and repairing the damage from their last voyage.

They'd need a long leave when she brought the *Sweet Jenny* in this time. And they'd have earned it.

Even Silas.

She allowed herself a small, reluctant smile.

Despite everything, the boy had done better as pirate crew than she'd expected. She knew he'd know how to sail a ship. He'd never have been recommended to the Academy if he hadn't. But the fact that he took the crew's hazing with as good grace as he had, without either complaining about the bum jobs that she knew would have left him exhausted and sore at the end of every day, or doing a poor enough job of them that they'd have to be redone, spoke to his self-control.

She'd seen his hot temper, back on Blackrock. The fact that he could control it was admirable. She'd known far too many otherwise promising sailors who couldn't.

It was possible she'd make a pirate out of him, sooner or later.

She shook her head wryly.

Assuming they all survived the next couple of days, of course.

There was a tap on the door—Ari, she recognized the woman's footsteps.

"Come in," she called.

Ari ducked through the door and stopped in front of Gracie's desk, legs apart and hands clasped respectfully behind her back. Gracie bit back a grin.

For all Ari's protests, there was still a bit of the Level left in the woman.

"Ari. What's the report?"

Ari shook her head and pulled back a chair, dropping into it. "It's not looking good, Captain. Freddie'n Sil and the rest of us been going over the guns since we made the last jump. Like Freddie guessed, not going to be able to get the heavy guns online in a fight, if it comes to it."

Gracie nodded. "Let's hope it doesn't come to it, then. What about the rest of the systems?"

"Freddie got Sil working with her on the thruster engines. We should be able to run fair enough when we come out of the jump, and the FTL drive is holding up fine. We'll want to look it over when we get back to a dry-dock, but Freddie says it'll wait until we get back. Stabilizers are good, at least, that's the most important thing."

Gracie nodded again. "Good. How's the crew? I want everyone ready for action. We're going to come out of FTL in—" she glanced down at her timepiece. "About three and a half hours, if my calculations are correct."

Ari grinned. "Never known you to have them wrong, Captain. I'll have the crew get ready." She paused. "What's the plan when we reach the ship?"

Gracie sighed and leaned back in her chair. "We'll be coming out of FTL a few hours' run from her. I don't want to come in too close and risk the *Sweet Jenny*. A naval ship could come out of jump closer —they'll have some shielding protection against the pull from the black hole, and they've got more stabilizer engines to kick in and keep her steady. But then, the *Sweet Jenny's* got a hell of a lot less mass than a ship of the line, so as long as we're careful, we can run in closer'n they'll be able to outside of FTL. Message we intercepted on the *Agate* says weapons are still functional, so we may have a firefight on our hands, but the event horizon will wreak havoc on any of their precision weapons." She glanced at Ari. "What about our light weapons? Are those functional?"

Ari frowned. "We still have the light weapons online. Freddie's checking them once she's done a once-over on the flight systems, but at a first look-through, she said they seem functional."

Gracie nodded. "We'll use those, then—we're not trying to shoot the ship down, we just want to disable it enough to let us get in close. Once we're close enough for boarding, I doubt we'll have anything to worry about, but it may come down to a bit of hand-to-hand fighting." She paused. "Do you think the lad Silas has it in him?"

Ari hesitated a moment. "I'm not sure," she said at last. "Do I think he can fight? Told you, I saw him take that ghost in an alley back on Blackrock, before I brought him to you. Anyone who can use a sparker like that'll be able to use a cutlass, if it comes to it, and he's naval through and through. They don't let people get near the Academy if they don't know how to use weapons from what I hear, not 'less they have an important last name. Sil may be Level, but he's not one as would get into the Academy without a service record."

Gracie nodded, still watching the woman. "Not what I asked, though, Ari."

Ari sighed and leaned back. "That's the part I can't answer, Captain." She shook her head. "Lad's the type to do as he sees fit. So I guess it depends on whether he sees fit that the crew of the *Agate* gets their heads lopped off at the shoulder."

Gracie nodded again, slowly, and tried to keep the amusement from her face at hearing Ari call the man "lad." He wasn't a year younger than Ari was, if Gracie was any judge. "That's the read I got on him as well," she said. "Any man who'll take documents from the Academy and come looking for Captain Mad Dog to lead an uprising against the Level is one who'll do as he sees fit." She paused. "Get the rest of the crew ready for boarding. I've about got our coordinates calculated, and I'll come out onto the main deck after that. I'll talk to Sil, take his temperature. Worst case, I'll get him standing guard on the *Sweet Jenny* while the boarding crew goes on."

Ari nodded.

"And Ari?" she asked. "What's your read on him otherwise?"

Ari paused. "To be honest, Captain, I don't know. He seems a good sailor, respectful enough. He didn't panic when he was caught out in the solar flare, which is better'n most sailors would do. But he's Level-born, and naval trained, and I don't know if that'll serve him on the *Sweet Jenny*." She looked up at Gracie. "You mean to keep him on, don't you?"

"If he'll work with the crew, I'm thinking of it," said Gracie, keeping her tone neutral.

"Well," said Ari at last, "not sure I'd argue with you there. Not sure the rest of the crew would either, but it'll depend on how he handles himself in a fight."

"That it will." This time, Gracie did let the smile reach her lips. "Go on now, get the crew ready. I want weapons checked and ready, and every sailor with a couple spares in case of an accident. I'm not willing to take chances on this."

Ari nodded and stood. "Aye, Captain," she said, turning out the door.

Gracie watched her go.

Ari may be young, but she trusted the woman's judgement. There was a reason Gracie'd put her over the crew, and it was because she was a damn good judge of character.

She sighed and pushed herself to her feet, glancing over at the charts pulled up on her desk.

Best to get her own weapons ready. If she couldn't trust Sil to come along on the boarding party, they'd be short-handed. There'd be at least fifty navy-trained sailors on the injured ship to keep the cargo safe, unless she missed her guess, in addition to the crew. She planned to send the skiff in under cover of heavy fire, and lock down the *Agate's* cargo hatch as soon as they got on, but even then there'd be a few sailors posted in the cargo hold. It'd be a bloody fight, and there was a good chance that at least a few would turn ghost when they died.

If any one of her crew were lost, they'd turn for certain. But she had no intention that any of her crew should be lost.

She checked the pistols in her belt, energy weapons that wouldn't puncture a ship's hull in a fight, and belted on the cutlass from where she'd hung it beside her desk.

She had a sparker in her belt, and a spare in her jacket pocket, and every damn sailor on the ship had better have at least two as well. Thing about ghosts was, they were just as likely to turn on their own former crewmates as on their attackers, so if you could keep your head around them, they could sometimes turn the tide in a fight.

She finished strapping on the cutlass, and stepped out the door.

Her crew was well-trained. By the time she reached the main deck, Ari had them assembled, all but Temple, who was in the cockpit.

Gracie glanced them over quickly. Their weapons seemed in good order, even the Level boy's.

"We're coming out of FTL in just over three hours," she said. "From there, we'll be just over a three-hour run from the ship. The ship'll be hot when we come in, unless I miss my guess, and we'll have to come in fast. The moment we're out of FTL, I want every one of you other than Temple on the light guns. We don't have heavies, but that shouldn't be a problem against a ship the size of the *Agate*. I want every one of you dead centre on a target before you get off the weapons, and if you can't get to dead centre after three attempts, you're off your grog rations for a week. I don't want slackers on this ship, and I don't want people who don't know what they're doing. You can't hit a target, you can go look for other work when we get back planet-side." She waited a moment for the good-natured grumbling to die down. "There'll likely be hand-to-hand fighting when we board, before we can block off the cargo hold. There'll be blood, and lots of it, and if there's not ghosts, I'll stop my own grog rations. Be ready for it."

She watched Sil out of the corner of her eye as she spoke. The speech was mostly for him, truth be told—her crew knew well enough how to skirmish.

His face was set, and his expression told her nothing, but there was a tension in his posture that indicated he knew exactly what she was saying.

Vee snorted. "I'll stop your sugar rations for your tea, is what'll happen, Captain," she called out.

Gracie grinned at her. "We don't have to deal with ghosts, I'll skip sugar in my tea for a week and be glad of it." She sobered. "I want everything on board this ship tight and running hot. I want the cargo deck open and ready for the weapons crates, and I want every last damn thing you can do to make our job easier done before we drop out of FTL. We won't have time to wish we'd done something when the time comes. Understood?"

There was a murmured chorus of "Aye"s.

She glanced over her crew one last time.

Good sailors, every one of them. Most of them she'd shipped with for years now. They'd die for her, every one of them, because they knew damn well she'd die for them if it came to it.

And every last one of them would kill naval sailors just for the pleasure of it, if she gave them the chance.

"Go on, then, you heard the captain," Ari snapped, and the crew turned back to their tasks.

Gracie watched them for a few minutes, then started back to her cabin.

They were as prepared as they could be.

Now, there was nothing to do but wait, and pray to Our Lady of the Ghosts they'd made it in before the ship of the line.

She tapped her communicator. "Sil," she said. "Come back to my cabin, if you would, soon as Freddie's got you off-duty."

"Aye, Captain," he said a moment later. "Freddie says she's done with me at the moment. I'll come up right away."

When she reached her cabin, Sil was waiting outside the door. He stepped aside at her approach, and she slid the door back, gesturing him in.

He stood stiffly at attention in front of her desk, and she pulled back her chair, gesturing to the seat Ari had vacated earlier. "Told you, Lad, we don't stand on ceremony here," she said, not bothering to hide her amusement. "Go on, sit."

He hesitated, then did as he was told.

His foot bounced restlessly against the leg of the chair as he sat, and she bit back a smile.

He hadn't done that when he'd first come on board.

She'd seen how the navy broke their young sailors, forced them into a mold. And for all Sil's protestations, the navy's mold was already crumbling around him.

For a few moments, neither of them spoke. Gracie studied him, letting the silence stretch, and he didn't seem inclined to break it.

Ari'd been right when she said the lad did as he'd see fit. She could see it in the set of his shoulders, the glint of determination under his grim expression.

"Well, Sil," she said at last, leaning back. "You've been on a pirate's ship for a solid twelve days now, haven't you? And what do you have to say about it?"

He shook his head. "I told you why I signed up, Captain. I haven't for a moment made a secret of my intentions."

She nodded. "You haven't. Justice from the navy is what you want, and me leading the holy charge." She paused. "You know the crew now, don't you? Know why Temple's here, why Ari's here. Vee and Freddie have similar stories—the resource planet you grew up on gets decommissioned, or there's not enough work to support the population, and where do you go from there? Merchant ships won't take you, not if you've got something in your past that'll wake you from nightmares." She shrugged.

"You live your life at the bottom of the heap for long enough, you end up with a story or three that'd turn someone's hair white. And once someone does for you like that, well, it's not them as'll suffer for it, is it? It's you as can't find work now, because it's you who'll turn ghost. And no one's going to take a chance with that." She gave a small, humourless smile. "Jumper and Toothpick—they're both from the Stacks. If you don't know why they signed on as pirates, you've been hiding yourself under a damn rock. So you see, lad, there's not a person on this ship don't hate the Level. Not a person on this ship don't want to see the Admiral hanged on Traitor's Gate with a tattoo on her arm to match mine."

He leaned forward, and now she could see the flash of temper in his eyes. "So why don't you do anything about it, then?" he said, his voice low and intense.

She shook her head. "Because the sailors on my crew trust me," she said. "They trust I won't throw their lives away over a grudge. I'm their captain. Thought you understood that, boy. I don't sacrifice my crew."

He was quiet a while, watching her. "Stories back on the Level say you're a monster," he said at last. "From the stories they told about you in the navy, I'd have thought you'd be happy to let a Level sailor die from radiation sickness, if he was stupid enough to get caught outside in a solar flare."

She smiled. "One of these days you'll learn that things aren't always the way they look from the deck of a naval ship." She shook her head. "We're going to board that ship, Sil. That was our bargain, and that's what I'll expect from you if you want me to hold to my side. You've been in pirate skirmishes before, I'm sure. This is the other side of it. We'll go in, and we'll take out the crew. Some of them'll be armed, some won't, and we won't have time to give them proper duelling warnings either. You fight from the bottom like we do, and there's nothing honourable about it—they die or we die, and I'm not letting my crew die if I can help it. But I need to know—are you willing to get your blade dirty? Or should I leave you to watch the ship, and I'll walk free of my bargain with you? Because I can tell you're a hand with a weapon, but one moment of hesitation could be the difference between life and death."

His jaw was clenched tightly, but at last he nodded. "I signed onto your crew, Captain. I accepted your terms. I'm not a man to break my word."

She watched him a moment longer. "Very well," she said at last. "You're my crew, and I'll keep you safe if I can. But know this—if for one moment you're putting the rest of my crew in danger, I'll slit your throat, and I won't think about it twice."

"I know," he said quietly.

Gracie was in the cockpit when they came out of FTL. Temple glanced up at her, and when she nodded, he hit the ship line. "Coming out of jump on my count," he said through it. "Three. Two. One. Coming out." Gently, he pulled back on the controls, and the *Sweet Jenny* lurched her way back into running speed.

Gracie glanced at the controls as they steadied, readjusting to the slower speed.

"Well done, Temple," she murmured.

He'd brought them in perfectly, on the hair's edge of the zone where the stabilizing thrusters would be able to push back against the inexorable pull of the black hole that loomed in the distance—a sucking, menacing thing that seemed to pull the gaze towards it in the same way it pulled at any ship unlucky enough to get trapped within its orbit.

She hadn't expected different. The merchant captain stupid enough to let a pilot like Temple go deserved their loss.

"How many hours' run are we?"

He glanced at the charts. "Three hours, seventeen minutes before we're in range of light weapons," he said. "We'll be in range of their heavy weapons in under an hour."

She nodded. "With luck, they've been in the grav field long enough that they won't pick us up on their sensors, but best not to trust to luck. I'll get Toothpick on the shields."

Temple nodded without looking up, bent over his charts in concentration.

And then Gracie frowned. "Temple," she said abruptly. "What's that?"

He glanced up at the screen. And then he turned to her, and she saw on his face that he'd seen the same thing she had.

The telltale shimmer of a massive ship of the line coming out of an FTL jump, a good hour's run closer in than the *Sweet Jenny* could have made it.

"How the hell'd they get there before us?" His voice was tight with shock.

"They must have run her through the flair field. Not protocol, but looks like this captain isn't hung up on protocol." Gracie's voice was grim. "Get Vee online, tell her to ID the ship, get me everything she can on the captain. Looks like we're going to have a fight on our hands after all."

15

Hollis

"Coming out of jump on my count. Three. Two. One. Coming out."

Hollis was on the bridge, one wrist clasped in the other hand behind her back, her face impassive. It was taking every bit of willpower to keep from pacing the deck, but she wouldn't show nervousness, not in front of her crew.

She'd instructed the navigator to bring them in as close to their target as possible—the least possible run-time would not only be the safest option, but the best way to avoid pirates.

When she glanced back up at the screen, she let out a quick breath of relief.

There, ahead of them, almost directly on the coordinates they'd predicted by calculating the *Agate's* last known position and the pull from the gravity field of the black hole, sat the ship.

They'd made it.

"Mate Price, prepare the tow-cables," she snapped. "I want to be ready to go in the moment we're close enough. Mate Greene, get the bay in the ship open. We're going to pull her onboard if she's in the shape to do so. If not, we'll send in skiffs to pick up the cargo and the crew, and we'll leave the ship."

The *Agate* was no ship of the line, just a merchant ship that had been converted into a short-term hauler for naval missions. Losing her would be unfortunate, but not a disaster. And depending how long the ship had been running within the black hole's orbit, she may not be salvageable anyways.

"Captain!"

She turned at the sudden panic in the navigator's voice.

Then she saw what the woman had seen, and her chest went cold.

A small ship, perhaps an hour's run-time distant, with a slim, sleek shape that she recognized instantly from years of whispered tales around dice games below decks, or in sailors' taverns in the poorer parts of the Level.

"Run the ship's codes," she said, although there was no need. Her voice sounded hollow in her ears.

Every person on the bridge knew to fear the shape of the small ship instinctively, like a child knows to be afraid of a hand reaching out from under their bed.

"It's the *Sweet Jenny*, Captain." The woman's voice was hushed, sick with fear.

Already, she could hear the murmurs on the bridge around her. And she'd shipped before the mast long enough to know—a few minutes at best, and rumours would be circulating through the crew, wilder and faster at each retelling.

She glanced back at the screen, eyes flicking through the ship specs.

The *Sweet Jenny* ran faster than any of the ships of the line, and she had weapons that could breach the shields on the *Verity* with relative ease.

"This is the *Sweet Jenny*, paging the *Verity*."

The words came through the ship's general channel, the pirate captain's laconic tones crisp and unmistakable.

The navigator glanced helplessly at Hollis.

Hollis drew in a quick breath and stepped forward.

Mad Dog was a legend. But Hollis was the first commissioned captain from the Stacks, and she'd be damned if she'd let the pirate frighten her.

"This is the captain of the *Verity*," she said, hitting the button to transmit. "You are in government space. Your ship reads as illegal. You may either surrender, or you may take yourself out of our space at once."

"That's a generous offer, Captain of the *Verity*." The woman's voice was dry and amused. "So I'll give you an offer of my own— I'm taking the *Agate*. If you stay back, I have no quarrel with you. But if you don't … best pray to Our Lady of the Ghosts that she lets you die before your crewmates turn ghost and rip you to shreds. Best pray to whatever you pray to for mercy. Because you'll get none from me." Her voice was still mild and a little amused, but there was a cold edge to it that told Hollis the woman was deadly serious. "I know what your navy does to pirates when you capture us. And I swear to you, Captain of the *Verity*—you'll be begging for a fate that easy."

Hollis tapped off the transmitter without bothering to respond. "Mate Price," she snapped through her comm. "Gather the crew, please."

"Aye, Captain." Foster's voice was still calm, but more strained than usual.

"And the rest of you." Hollis turned sharply on the gathered crew on the bridge. "Belay that talk at once, by God. What are you, sailors, or children?"

The frantic whispers stilled as the crew turned to look at her.

Her heart was beating a quick rhythm in her chest, like ship's drums beating to quarters.

She'd be damned to the blackest of hells before she let this pirate cost her her ship, her crew. Her command.

She smiled, a small, tight smile. "Sailors," she said, surveying the fearful group on the bridge. "I am going to speak with the crew, keep them from panicking. In the meantime, I expect each of you to carry out your duties. We are going on, and we are taking that weapons ship. And if that means we blow the *Sweet Jenny* out of the sky to do it, then that is exactly what we will do. Do you understand me?"

They were still frightened. Hell, she was frightened, the nervousness trembling under her skin. But this was a kind of fear she recognized, that she knew intimately from her lifetime in the Stacks, her lifetime being passed over, being underestimated, struggling to stay alive in a world that didn't want her there. It was the kind of fear you could take hold of in both hands, and squeeze into a cold core of ironclad determination—that you'd die before you'd let them win.

She clasped her hands behind her back and strode out to address the crew, the sharp sound of her boots clicking off the hard deck a comforting echo in her ears.

Foster had the crew assembled, and the sailors were waiting for her on the lower deck, watching her as she emerged from the bridge. She could see the terror in their faces.

They were on the edge of fleeing like frightened animals, and the only things holding them steady were their duty to the fleet, their fear of punishment, and their trust in their captain.

If one of those was lost, they'd break and run, and she'd be facing a mutiny. She knew it well enough.

"Crew of the *Verity*." Her voice rang out, sharp and clear over the restless murmurs, the rustle and movement of three hundred and fifty bodies packed onto one deck. "We've come to take back the *Agate* and rescue her crew. We are a ship of the line, and we are sailors in the navy. And I will be damned before we let a pirate ship best us."

"But Captain, it's the *Sweet Jenny*. Do you know how many ships of the line Captain Mad Dog's broken up? How many sailors she's left drifting in space?"

She couldn't tell who had spoken. But it hardly mattered. "It is. But Captain Mad Dog is no god. She's no Lady of the Ghosts. She's a sailor, like any of us. The *Sweet Jenny* would have had to come through the same solar flare we did, and without our shielding. She'll be limping, whether on weapons or running engines or both." She paused a moment. "Mate Greene. Prepare the ship for action. I intend that we will sail back to the Level with the *Agate* and the *Sweet Jenny* both in tow. And if not, I'll see to it that the *Sweet Jenny* is left nothing but a ghost ship that not even the salvagers will touch. Do you understand me?"

"Aye, Captain."

The chorus was weaker than she would have hoped.

But it would have to do.

She turned on her heel. "Mate Price. Follow me to the conference room, if you would, and instruct Wilkes and our weapons master to come as well. We have some pirates to deal with before we take the *Agate*, it appears."

16

Silas stared at the shape on the screen, his pulse pounding.

He recognized the ship by the telltale vis-tags—the *Verity*. A three-hundred-and-fifty-crewed ship of the line.

He swore quietly. He wasn't completely sure if the tightness in his stomach was for the crew of the tiny pirate vessel, gathered in the cockpit around him, or for the *Verity*.

Dammit, he'd been able to justify this, barely, when he thought they were going to use their guns on a hundred-crewed ship. But three hundred and fifty? He'd seen how ruthless Gracie was. And he'd heard rumours of what she'd done in the past. Crippling a ship like the *Verity* wasn't impossible.

Before this, he'd been able to tell himself that whatever Gracie did, whatever he helped her accomplish, it was for a greater cause. He was still doing his duty to the navy, to his family. What had happened twenty-five years ago, the disaster that had killed his parents and condemned Gracie, was a wrong that he had an obligation to right. But this? Taking on a three-hundred-and-fifty-crewed ship of the line?

He knew, had known since his earliest memories, that he didn't matter. His life didn't matter, in the grand scheme of things. When it was just his own life and reputation on the line, his duty had been to try to save the navy from its past sins, whatever the personal cost. But he couldn't argue, even to himself, that his duty to root out the corruption in the navy was worth the loss of the *Verity* and her captain and crew.

And the moment he refused to go along with this, he lost Gracie and his bargain both. Everything he'd risked, everything he'd sacrificed to get here, every chance to avenge his parents and clear his own name would be gone like smoke in the wind.

He gritted his teeth.

What he wanted didn't matter. But it wouldn't be a simple thing either way. Gracie had already made it clear she'd go ahead with or without his help.

"Temple. Chart us a direct course for the *Agate*." Gracie's voice was measured.

Temple didn't argue, just turned to the controls, but Silas could see the tension in him. It was Toothpick who spoke. "Captain," he said in a low voice. "A direct course will take us in range of the *Verity's* heavy weapons within thirty minutes. What are we doing?"

Gracie glanced over at him. "When we get to the other side of the *Verity*, the grav field from the black hole will throw off their aim. Once we have the black hole at our backs, we can turn and fight."

He nodded, but Silas could see on the man's face that he realized well enough what Gracie had left unsaid—that would leave them vulnerable for at least fifteen minutes, even at the fastest running speed. And a thirty-minute approach would give the *Verity* more than enough time to aim in.

"Jumper." Gracie tapped through to her com. "I want you to get the light weapons ready to fire. Set them for maximum range, even if we lose a little accuracy and power. We'll reset as we get closer, but I want to be able to fire on the *Verity* as soon as possible." She turned to the rest of the crew, gathered in the cabin. "Freddie, you get the shields up. I want max power on our port bow shields, that's where they'll hit us first."

"Aye, Captain." Freddie's voice was grim. "I'll take the Level boy with me."

"Do that. And you'd best dig for every scrap of power you can find, or we're not going to last long enough to fire back." Gracie paused a moment, calculating. "I want our waste gasses venting out the port side exhaust the moment we're in range of their guns. It'll do something to confuse their sensors, at least, and it may keep their precision weapons from locking on."

Freddie nodded and turned her hover-chair, jerking her chin at Silas. "Come, boy, we have work to do."

He hesitated, every muscle in his body tight. But at last, reluctantly, he turned to follow her.

There was nothing he could do right now. And this would at least give him time to consider his options.

Ari appeared at Gracie's elbow. "Captain. I have the information you asked for on the *Verity's* captain."

Silas paused despite himself, tension aching through him.

There was a cowardly part of him that wanted to simply step through the door after Freddie, not know the name of the captain Gracie was, in all likelihood, planning to take down.

But he couldn't do it. The navy might already consider him a traitor, but at least he was sailor enough not to hide from the damn fact.

Gracie glanced over at him, but didn't comment.

"Hollis Ives," Ari continued. "This is her first command, fresh from the Academy."

Silas sucked in a quick breath.

Damn it. Damn it to hell, of course it had to be Ives. The captain from the Stacks.

She'd been a year ahead of him in the Academy. He hadn't known her personally, but he'd heard of her. When she'd been given a captain's posting, the news had been all over the Academy, people talking in hushed voices, spreading rumours that were foul enough to make his blood boil.

"What's her history?" Gracie's voice was still mild, but it carried in the small space, and he caught himself wondering if she'd meant for him to overhear.

It would be like her—gauge his reaction, decide if he'd make trouble.

He closed his eyes.

Damn this all to hell.

"Shipped on with a merchant ship at fourteen, joined the navy at sixteen," Ari was saying. "Recommended to the Academy by the Admiral herself."

Gracie raised her eyebrows. "Her family was important, then?"

"No, Captain, it wasn't." Silas had crossed the small cockpit to Gracie before he had time to think through his words. "Hollis Ives was a year ahead of me in the Academy. She was a damn good student, too, from what I heard, and she's never backed down from a fight once in her life. But that's not the important thing about her."

"Then what is, lad?" There was a hint of steel under Gracie's mild tone. "What do you know about Captain Ives?"

"She's the first commissioned captain from the Stacks." His voice was low. "The Admiral put her in as a test case. You know what that means, Captain."

Dammit, this was Mad Dog Gracie Madox. She wouldn't care about something like that. But he did. He couldn't bloody help himself.

Because that could have been him. In a year, if he'd stayed on, that could have been him on his first mission, his first command. But at least he'd have been able to take the respect of his crew for granted. He'd been in the navy long enough to know that Hollis would have had to fight for every scrap of respect she received.

Ari gave a low whistle. "She'll have something to prove."

Gracie nodded thoughtfully. "Means the Admiral needs this captain. She'll have to have put her reputation on the line to get a Stacks woman a position. Won't look good for her if Ives loses her life and her ship on her first command, will it?"

Silas sucked in a breath. "Captain—"

Gracie turned to study him. "Careful, lad," she said. Her voice was still mild, but he'd shipped with her long enough to hear the danger in it. "You signed on to my crew. You struck a bargain with me. You willing to let that go now?"

He gritted his teeth. "This is her first command. She fought like hell to get here."

"Take that up with the Admiral, Sil." Gracie bit off her words. "She'll have known damn well there were pirates after those weapons, and she sent your Captain Ives in after them anyway. You have your orders. Get after Freddie, and don't let me see you back here until she tells you you're done." She paused. "That, or you tell me our bargain's off, and you'll go in the brig until I have time to deal with you. Won't matter either way, you know that, lad. Me'n the crew will do what needs to be done. Hardly matters whether we shoot her down or not—Ives loses the *Agate*, she's lost her command. The Admiral's already doomed her."

He held her gaze for just a moment.

He knew what he should say.

But saying it would lose him everything, and win him nothing but a place in the damn brig.

Gracie was right. There was nothing he could do about this, not right now.

And underneath the thought, there was the stirring of guilt. Because he wasn't nearly certain enough, if there had been something he could have done, that he'd have done it.

"Aye, Captain," he muttered through clenched teeth.

Gracie turned back to Ari. "Best get the crew prepared. If it'd been a seasoned captain, chances are they'd let us take the weapons ship, make an official report that the *Agate* had already been sucked into the black hole by the time they got here. But someone with everything to prove and nothing to lose? There's no chance she'll take the intelligent route. There'll be a fight, and it'll be bloody."

Silas turned away to follow Freddie from the cockpit, cursing under his breath.

Damn everything.

He knew exactly where his duty lay. No matter what he wanted, he couldn't argue that his own mission out-weighed saving a ship of the line, rescuing the life and reputation of a captain the navy desperately needed.

But he couldn't help the nagging coldness in his gut at Gracie's reminder—it had been the Admiral who'd sent Hollis out here to face pirates, on her first command. He couldn't help the memory of Ari's words, playing over and over in his mind: *You don't like the Captain's morals, maybe, but hell, she's not going to see her crew in trouble and cut their line.*

And he couldn't help the sickness in his stomach at the memory of Gracie on the outside of the ship, her hand wrapped around his anchor line to hold it steady as the solar storm blasted closer, and the knowledge that, if he'd been on a ship of the line, he'd have died out there in the black.

17

Hollis

The bridge was silent, every set of eyes glued to the screen.

Hollis stood where she was, clenching her jaw so tightly that her teeth ached.

The pirate's ship was running fast, faster than she'd seen a ship run.

Not faster than what she'd have expected from the *Sweet Jenny*, though. She'd heard the stories of Mad Dog as much as any of her crew had.

"Shields are up, Captain." The voice came through her ear comm, and she barely managed a distracted acknowledgement.

Mad Dog should have fired on them by now. If she had, Hollis knew well enough that the ship's weapons would cut through their shields after only a few hits.

She could adjust the power, of course, adjust the shield's positioning, but that would only delay the inevitable. And as much as she trusted her navy-trained gunners to be competent with their aim on the heavy weapons, she knew well enough that the pirates would be better.

Their lives depended on it, in a way that was much more immediate and intimate than gunners on a ship of the line.

But the pirate ship couldn't have made it through the centre of a solar flare without damage, and if they'd made the time they had to get here, they'd have passed within a few light-minutes of the event. The *Sweet Jenny* was running injured, she had to be. And the most likely system to be affected were either her running engines, or her heavy weapons, depending on how the ship was set up. The speed she was running meant her running engines were in strong shape, so her guns had to have been compromised.

They had to have been.

She closed her eyes for a moment, praying to Our Lady of the Ghosts that she'd guessed right. Because if she was wrong, if she'd misjudged …

"Captain. The approaching ship is five minutes from firing range, if she continues on her current course."

"Prepare the heavy weapons," Hollis snapped. "Have the gunners sight in. Instruct them to fire the moment they can lock onto target."

"Aye, Captain."

The bridge was tight with a restless energy, and Hollis could feel it crawling up her spine, injecting itself under her skin.

The *Sweet Jenny's* heavy weapons would be able to lock before the *Verity's* could, if they were still functional. She'd know in a matter of seconds whether she'd been right, or whether she'd just doomed her ship and her entire crew.

"Two minutes, Captain."

"Lock in the aim." She tried to keep her voice steady.

The silence around her was broken only by breathing, by the muttered prayers of someone behind her.

She didn't take the time to guess whether they were praying to God, or to Our Lady of the Ghosts. She'd served in the navy long enough to know that no matter how pious an officer might appear back on the Level, how often they sat down in the pews of a church, out here, on the edges of the known universe, the prayers people offered up were offered to Our Lady—the patron of those who were no longer trying to avoid death, but only to make sure their deaths were avenged.

"In range!" The sharp voice rang through her comm, jolting her out of her thoughts.

"Fire!" She snapped out the command, and a second later, the sharp bolts of energy that were the long-range weapons shot out from the side of the *Verity*.

There was no answering shot.

Hollis closed her eyes, sagging with relief.

She'd been right. The *Sweet Jenny* must have lost her heavy weapons. That meant at least fifteen minutes of unimpeded firing on her.

She felt shaky, almost lightheaded with relief. Around her, she could hear the collective release of breath from the others on the bridge as they realized the same thing Hollis had.

The gunners were getting into their rhythm now, the shots streaking out from the *Verity* in a steady pattern of death that was stark in its cold beauty.

The first of the shots had struck the pirate ship, although now that Hollis was watching, it appeared they were venting something from the ship that was affecting the aim.

Still, it looked like the ship wasn't trying to fight, simply trying to avoid the gauntlet of shots, running with her engines wide open.

"Captain! We have them running." Emmett came up beside her,

his voice triumphant. "I've never seen Mad Dog run from a fight."

Hollis was still staring at the screen.

And suddenly, ice formed in her stomach.

"Dammit," she hissed, turning on her heel. "She's not running, she's gunning for better ground. Price! Where are you, damn your eyes?"

"Here, Captain." Foster materialized at her elbow a moment later, their usually calm face tight with strain.

"Organize a boarding crew, immediately," Hollis snapped. Her pulse was pounding in her ears. "She's coming around behind us. She can run in closer to the event horizon than we can, and the grav field will affect our aim. She'll tear us to pieces. We're sending out a crew to board her."

Foster was staring at her, shocked out of their diplomacy for the first time since Hollis had met them. "We can't send a crew to board the *Sweet Jenny*! They'll be slaughtered."

"Look at this," Hollis hissed, keeping her voice low enough that the rest of the bridge wouldn't overhear. She jerked her head at the screen above them. "Once Mad Dog gets around us, she'll take our shields apart at her leisure, even without her heavy weapons. You don't want every damn sailor on this ship killed? Then find me a crew who can handle themselves in hand-to-hand combat and get them on a skiff."

Foster looked to where Hollis had gestured, then back at Hollis. Their expression was more grim than Hollis had ever seen it. "We'll need a crew of at least twenty if we want any of them to come back."

"Then damn well get me a crew of twenty, Price," she snapped. "And I'll have a word with them before they leave."

18

Silas

Silas glanced grimly around at the others.

They were crouched at their places, weapons at the ready, watching the airlock hatch.

He closed his eyes and tightened his grip on his cutlass.

He'd been in plenty of skirmishes before. But this was the first time he'd be fighting on the side of the pirates.

But this wasn't taking down the *Verity*. This was the simple, brutal fact of skirmishes—you killed the people who were trying to kill you, or you died. And he'd be no use to Hollis, or to the navy, dead.

Or, a voice in the back of his mind nagged, to Ari, or Freddie, or Jumper, or Gracie, or the rest of the crew who'd befriended him when they'd had no reason to.

"Four minutes out." Freddie's soft whisper cut through the silence. "Least the ship won't be firing on us while they're sending their own out to slit our throats."

There had been complete shock on the faces of every one of the crew when they first caught sight of the skiff. Hollis had been smart, hiding it behind a barrage of shots, so that they didn't see it coming until it was in close.

But after the first jolt of surprise, Silas hadn't been nearly as shocked as the others.

Of course Hollis Ives, of all people, would have sent out a boarding party. He'd never met her in the Academy, but he'd known her by reputation. He hadn't considered it, because the idea of sending out a boarding crew to the *Sweet Jenny* was so starkly insane that it hadn't occurred to him. But there was a reason Hollis had gotten to where she was, and it wasn't because she did the expected.

"Two minutes out." Freddie's voice was still soft. "Jumper, you on the guns?"

Three clicks through the general line, which Silas had taken to understand meant "Yes."

The skiff Hollis had sent was a small thing, and it was in close enough by now that the *Sweet Jenny's* light weapons wouldn't do much good.

"Fire." Gracie's voice was somehow still measured, and a moment later the ship shuddered at the weapons fire of at least a dozen light weapons. "Again," she said, and again, the ship shook.

Silas could picture the scene on the skiff—they'd be shielded, but no shield would save them from something like that.

"Again."

"Jumper says they're in too close, Captain. Can't fire without risking the ship." Vee's voice was tight with strain.

"Stand down, then, and prepare to repel boarders." Gracie's voice was still calm.

"Aye, Captain."

After a few more long, agonizing minutes, the *Sweet Jenny* shook again, and Silas could hear the tortured scrape of metal on metal as the skiff locked itself on.

"Everyone tied in?" snapped Ari through the general line.

A chorus of "Aye"s answered her.

Silas double-checked his own tie-in.

He'd been on his share of boarding parties. It was as much a battle of wits as it was a battle of weapons—when to cut the gravity, when to open the airlock, whether to engage on the inside or the outside of the ship.

He tightened his grip on his energy pistol as the seal-lock cutters worked on the outside airlock door.

"Open the airlock." Gracie's voice was curt.

It was a good call—they'd not hold out for long enough for it to be worth the damage of the lock-cutter.

There was the unmistakable hiss of the outer airlock door opening, then the confused sound of mag boots, people scrambling inside.

Gracie was watching over a screen Silas couldn't see.

"Now!" she snapped.

The outer door hissed shut, cutting off the remainder of the boarding party, and a moment later the inner door hissed open. Silas dove through after Ari and Jumper and Temple and Gracie, firing his energy pistol as fast as his fingers could move on the trigger.

He had just a moment to catch a confusing glance of naval sailors, most of them panicked, cut off from the rest of the boarding party by the outer door, the sound of the seal-lock hammering at the airlock, and then he was in the middle of it.

An impact from an energy pistol knocked him backward, but the shielding on his suit was enough to protect him from the worst of it. He caught himself against the wall and yanked out his cutlass. The tiny airlock room was too close quarters for an energy pistol to be effective—he was just as likely to hit one of his companions as he was one of the boarding party.

He swung his short sword, felt it cut into someone's space suit, and he twisted the blade and drove it in with all his strength. There was a scream of pain, muffled by the helmet, and he yanked his sword back out of the body, just in time to bring it up to deflect a blow from someone to his right, a hard arc that would have taken off one of his limbs if it had landed. He turned it aside, barely, and then jumped back, dodging another strike.

From the corner of his mind, he noticed the reinforced walls of the airlock—the *Sweet Jenny* may not be a ship of the line, but she was built for a fight like this.

From outside, there was still the sound of the lock-cutter hammering at the airlock seal.

"They'll be through in a minute." Ari's voice through the general line was sharp and crisp. "Make sure your suits are sealed, we're going to lose pressure."

Silas lunged forward, knocking his attacker's arm aside, and shoved his cutlass through their stomach. They grunted in pain, falling back as their suit sealed itself around the wound, but he pulled the blade up as he pulled it out, ripping the suit as far up as he could.

And then the seal broke, and he could see through the open airlock door and out into the boarding skiff as more sailors piled through the opening, trying to find their footing on a deck already slippery with blood.

Temple was waiting at the entrance, and he threw a percussive explosive into the centre of the boarders. The sharp blast of it knocked them staggering, and then the pirate was in the middle of them, a cutlass in one hand, his shiv in the other, cutting anchor-lines and puncturing oxygen tanks as the sailors staggered to their feet. Silas pushed himself up and leapt in after Temple, swinging his bloody cutlass. From the corner of his eye he saw Temple go down, and a sailor brought up their cutlass for a killing stroke, but before it could fall, Vee was there. She shoved her knife upwards in a vicious motion, opening the sailor up so a wet pile of intestines spilled out onto the floor. Temple finished the injured soldier off with a slice through the throat.

And then Silas heard Ari shout, "He's turning, get back!"

A blue shock of energy pulsed through the small space, and as it dissipated, the ghostly image of the dead man formed above the bloody body. Its features were human enough, except for the eyes—black pits of burning darkness that shot a jolt of animal terror through Silas, even though he'd seen ghosts more than enough times to be used to the sight—and the mouth, stretched impossibly wide, its teeth jags of darkness sharp enough to cut like knives and burn like fire.

The sailors around the dead man stumbled back in horror, fumbling for their sparkers. When a ghost turned, it didn't retain loyalties or friendships or memories or anything except the brutal, furious echo of the trauma that had created it, and it turned on anything it could find—friends, family, crewmates, anyone close enough for it to kill.

It sprang at the nearest naval sailor, its distended jaw opening impossibly wide, its ghostly fingers lengthening into claws. Its teeth tore through skin and flesh as its victim screamed, its claws ripping through the space suit and into muscle and viscera like it was wet paper. The sailor screamed again, a hoarse, horrible sound, and for a moment everyone, sailor or pirate, turned instinctually towards the noise.

The ghost's victim fell to the deck, suit and flesh shredded and hanging in bloody fragments from the visible white of her bones, and the soft implosion of blue light over the body told Silas she was turning as well.

"Get back!" he shouted, grabbing Toothpick by the arm and hauling him away.

By now, everyone had scrambled far enough away from their dead companions that a space had opened up around the two ghosts, and for a moment, all motion in the cramped airlock ceased. Ghosts would attack anything, but they were attracted to sound and movement, and no one wanted to be the one the ghosts would come for first.

And then Vee staggered, foot slipping on the wet blood, and both ghosts sprang for her at once. Ari, beside her, shoved the woman backwards and yanked out her sparker, the tiny, glowing blue tip the only thing standing between her and certain, horrible death.

Silas was shoving his way towards her before he had time to think, pulling his own sparker out of his belt.

The ghosts hung back warily, their burning black eyes fixed on Ari's sparker, but they'd spring in a moment. Even the best-trained sailor could miss their mark as a ghost sprang—the point where a sparker's burst of energy would break the ghosts apart was a tiny thing, difficult to find even if the ghost wasn't trying to tear your throat out at the same time. Against two, there wasn't a chance.

The ghosts lunged forward, and Ari shoved her sparker up, her hand shockingly steady, and then Silas was beside her. The ghost Ari struck dissolved, and at the same time Silas shoved his sparker into the side of the second ghost as it grabbed for Ari's arm. He yanked it free and tried again, and this time the thing dissolved as well.

Ari shot him a grateful glance, and then the sailors from the boarding party were on them, and they were separated in the shoving mass of bodies.

A sailor managed to get a stroke past Silas's guard, her cutlass slicing through the shoulder of his suit. He cursed as the shock of it turned from ice to pain, his suit trying to seal the wound to staunch the flow of blood. He stumbled backwards as she swung again, and tripped over the body of a fallen sailor, landing on his back on the slippery deck.

"Gravity going off," a voice snapped through his earpiece, and from the corner of his eye he could see his crewmates anchoring in to the walls, but all his attention was focused on the blade coming for his head. He rolled out of the way, and the edge of the cutlass hit the floor with a resounding clang, and at the same time there was an odd, disorienting feeling of weightlessness, and the sailor was drifting backwards, shoved up and away by the energy of the strike as the gravity cut.

He grabbed her arm and yanked her back towards him. She pulled her cutlass up, but not quickly enough—in one quick motion, he'd sliced her throat, his cutlass slipping between the helmet and the edge of her suit. Blood sprayed out, the spray turning into a shimmer of red globules floating in the air between them, and he shoved the body away.

The sailors seemed to have mostly readjusted to the change in gravity—they were moving more carefully now, keeping their lines hooked to the walls, but they'd been trained well. Despite the fact that he was fighting on the other side, Silas couldn't help a small glow of pride at the sight of them.

The guilt of it would hit him at some point, he knew it, and he wasn't sure how he'd live through it, but that was something to worry about after this was over.

"Gravity on." Freddie's voice through the general line was brusque, and Silas just had time to shove himself towards the ground when the gravity flickered on again, sending the sailors stumbling.

He looked around quickly as he dove for them—some of them had kept their footing, but others were staggering, trying to regain their balance, and Gracie went through them like an avenging angel, her short cutlass dealing death to everyone within range.

"Three of them slipped past me!" Ari shouted, her voice tight with strain. "Freddie, watch your back, you have incoming!"

Silas whirled, just in time to catch a glimpse of the boot of one of the sailors as they ducked under the cut seal of the airlock and into the main cabin.

"Toothpick! Get in there and help her. Freddie, be ready with the seal in case the outer seal breaks." Gracie's tone was short, but still calm, oddly incongruent in the chaos surrounding them.

"Aye." Toothpick turned, disappearing after the fleeing sailors.

The hiss of an energy pistol made Silas's head jerked up, and he dived out of the way, staggering as the shot impacted off his suit. And then he was too busy fighting to pay attention to anything else.

The muscles of his arms swung the cutlass almost without input from his conscious mind, the years of training taking over. He could feel his brain going into that quiet, calm place it always did in the middle of a battle, where everything was sharp, and alive, and the world slowed down so that there was time between each stroke and parry, a millennium where he could study the opponent's move, calculate a counter move, let his arm slide up smooth and automatic to parry the blow. The pain when one of the sailor's weapons slipped past his guard, slicing across his arm, was something odd and distant. He'd have to reckon with it the moment the fight was over, but it wasn't yet, and his mind could still focus on nothing but the battle.

And then he lifted his arm to parry another stroke, and realized it wasn't coming—the sailors had turned, and were running back for the ship.

"Go after them, kill as many of them as you can." Gracie's voice was clipped and hard, and again Silas heard the voice of Mad Dog, the pirate captain feared by every sailor in the navy for the last twenty years—cold, merciless, and completely unyielding.

Ari lunged after the retreating soldiers, her cutlass slicing through the back of one as he screamed and collapsed, and Temple was in front of the door, and he jabbed his shiv up through the chest of one of the sailors, yanked it free, and then drove it through the back of another, shoving the injured sailors after their companions so that if they turned ghost, they'd turn on the skiff.

And then it was over, and the skiff's hatch slid closed, and Gracie shouted, "Anchor in!"

The ship pulled away, the icy vacuum of space sucking the air from the airlock. Jumper was running across the floor to the opening, and he grabbed Temple by the back of his jacket and yanked him inside with one hand as the fingers of his other hand danced across the controls.

A moment later, an emergency airlock door slammed shut, leaving the six of them gasping and panting in the small space, the floor slippery with blood.

19

As the lights flickered on, Silas glanced around, his body still buzzing with adrenalin.

If any of the bodies lying on the floor were only injured, there was a chance they'd turn as they died, and the crew would be facing another ghost.

Sure enough, he could see a haze of blue forming around one of the dying sailors. But before it had time to coalesce, Gracie was there, the point of her sparker dissipating the ghost as it formed.

"Are we sealed?" asked Freddie through the general line. "If we are, I'll cycle the air back in."

"Toothpick?" Gracie asked, not lifting her head as the pressure in the small airlock compartment returned. "Did we get the three off?"

"Depends on what you mean by off," came Toothpick's laconic voice. "One of them turned when she died, took a bite out of Freddie. But there's not a living one left among them, not anymore."

"What were they after?" There was a grim note to Gracie's voice. "They must have known they'd never make it off the ship."

Vee had already crossed to the airlock door. "Captain, I'll get the med bay set up. Guess I have plenty to do." Her voice, too, was grim.

"I'll see to Freddie the minute she's finished checking out the damage."

Gracie glanced around the small airlock. "Thank you, Vee. And all the rest of you, get in there and get bandaged up enough that you won't be passing out on me. We're not finished here yet."

At her words, Silas glanced down, and had to shove back a quick wave of lightheadedness.

Blood soaked the front of his suit from a cutlass wound, and his shoulder, where he could vaguely remember being cut earlier, throbbed and ached.

When he glanced around, none of the others looked any better.

Gracie turned back to them. "Come on, get in to see Vee before anything else. We may be facing more boarders, I don't want anyone who can't hold a weapon."

Silas glanced around, his body still in shock from the pain, and then started after the others for the airlock.

He'd hardly stepped through when he heard Freddie's vicious swearing through the comm.

"Freddie? What is it?" Gracie's voice was sharp.

"Not good news," said Freddie grimly. "They were after the stabilizers."

There was a moment of silence. And then Gracie cursed, her voice hard with anger.

"How many of them did they take out?" she snapped, stepping through the airlock and striding over to where Freddie sat. Even from here, Silas could see the blood dripping from Freddie's injuries and soaking her suit, but the mechanic hardly seemed to notice it.

"They got all of them. Someone must have got past me and Toothpick while we were fighting the others, that must have been why they sent the boarding party in the first place. Without stabilizers, we can't run in much closer'n we are right now, and we'll be sitting dead in range of the *Verity's* guns."

Dread sat like a stone in Silas's stomach.

Gracie tipped her head back, and he could see the weary exhaustion in her posture. When she spoke, though, her voice was as calm as ever. "Very well. They've damaged our stabilizers, and at this point, we'll have to assume they're not repairable."

Ari cursed. "No chance we get in close enough to take the *Agate* without the stabilizers, is there?"

"No chance." Freddie's voice was just as grim as Ari's. "I've taken risks in my time, but that ain't a risk. That's a certainty, this close to the hole. Even now we're too close for my comfort."

"We've the black hole to our back now, at least—Temple and Freddie kept us moving while we were fighting off the boarders." Toothpick had come up behind them. There was blood streaming down the man's arm, and he was limping heavily. "Means we're too close in for them to use their heavy weapons anymore, and the grav field should throw off their aim on the light weapons—good. That's what we were going for. But if we try to get out the way we've come, they'll be ready for us. We don't have a way back, and without the stabilizers …" he paused. "Well, don't see as we have a way through, either."

There was a long silence, as the crew took in his words.

He turned to Gracie, with a forced smile. "Sorry, Captain. Don't see a way we live through this."

Again, there was a moment of silence.

At last Ari shook her head, determination on her face. "No, Toothpick. I don't believe that. This ain't the end, not yet. Captain got through onto their skiff." She turned to Gracie. "Didn't you, Captain? And you planted something, I saw you. You plant a percussive? We can set it off the moment they get back to the ship. Blow one of the airlock doors, that should keep them busy enough that they won't have the time to come for us."

Silas glanced at Gracie, his body gone suddenly cold with horror.

If Gracie had set an explosive on the skiff, held off until they opened the door to bring back the injured before she set it off—she could very well damage the *Verity* so badly that it wouldn't be able to hold itself back from the black hole itself.

"Move like that wouldn't work on an experienced captain, but then, that's not what we're dealing with, is it?" Ari gave Toothpick a sharp smile. "Any new captain crazy enough to send a boarding party onto the *Sweet Jenny* isn't one who takes too many precautions. We might die, but we'll damn well take her down with us."

Silas swallowed back bile.

It was exactly what he should have expected from Captain Mad Dog. It was the reason, after all, that he'd come to her, hoping that she would agree to take her revenge—because Captain Mad Dog was the only one he knew of vicious and ruthless enough to do what would need to be done.

Taking out a ship of the line was three hundred and fifty souls aboard would be nothing to her.

The others had turned to look at Gracie, and reluctantly, not wanting to do it, Silas followed their gaze.

She watched them all for a moment. Then she turned, deliberately catching his eye. "No, Ari."

She was addressing the girl, but her eyes never left Silas's.

"I didn't send back a percussive. Just a mag-lock."

There was a long moment of utter silence.

A mag-lock.

It would do ... something, at least. If they couldn't get the stabilizers back online, it could possibly hold them tight enough onto the naval ship that they'd avoid being sucked into the black hole, as long as they weren't already caught in its gravity—if they could find a way to escape the *Verity's* guns, that was.

But they'd lost the *Agate*, and they'd lost the weapons.

Silas closed his eyes and let out a long breath. The fact that the ship of the line wasn't about to be ripped to shreds was an almost shaky relief.

Maybe Gracie had actually, against all odds, listened to him—taken pity on a young captain on her first command, saved the three hundred and fifty souls on board the *Verity*.

Or maybe this was just another trap. He had no damn idea at this point.

Either way, it didn't matter—as Temple said, unless they came up with something to deal with the *Verity's* guns damn quick, everyone on the *Sweet Jenny* was dead.

And the tradeoff—a ship of the line and her shiny new captain, against the lives of Ari, Freddie, Jumper and Toothpick and Vee, against every chance he'd ever have of finding justice for his parents —left a taste in Silas's mouth that was more bitter than he'd expected.

"Well," said Toothpick at last, shaking his head. "I guess we'd best get to work on the stabilizers, see what can be done." His voice was short, his words clipped, and Silas looked around at the others, frowning.

They didn't seem particularly surprised at Gracie's revelation. Only Ari looked vaguely disappointed.

"Captain!" Temple shouted from the cockpit. "We're in range of their light guns, and they'll be firing on us in a minute. Need someone on the guns for covering fire if we don't want to be turned into damn space dust."

"Jumper, get on the guns." Gracie turned to the boy, her words tense, but still measured.

Jumper jerked to attention, his fingers flying quickly enough that Silas couldn't begin to make out what he was saying.

Gracie gave a short nod and turned to the others. "Vee, when you're finished bandaging up Freddie, get in the medic room. We may need you soon." She turned to Silas. "Sil, you're with Freddie. Temple, evasive manoeuvres, if you please. I'm not quite ready to give up just yet. Let's take care of the light guns before we worry about the rest."

"Aye, Captain," Temple murmured, turning back to the controls.

"There," Vee said, sealing a bandage over the bleeding wound on Freddie's arm. "I'll have a look at it when we're done, but this'll keep you from bleeding out in the meantime."

Freddie nodded impatiently and pushed her chair forward. Silas started after her, then had to pause a moment, swaying on his feet.

Gracie glanced at him and cursed. "Vee, best bandage up the boy, too." Her voice was grimly amused. "Won't do Freddie any good if he's passed out."

"I'm not about to pass out," Silas mumbled, but he had to blink against the wooziness when he tried to straighten.

Vee chuckled grimly. "Boy, there's being heroic, and there's being stupid. Right now, you're being the latter. Don't know what they teach you in the navy, but we uncivilized pirates know that if you lose enough blood, no amount of stubbornness will keep you on your feet." She crossed over to him, slicing through the sleeve of his suit expertly with a medical knife. A moment later, she had a compression bandage sealed over the two shallow cutlass wounds, and a quick tape seal over the slit in the suit. "Should hold you until we have time to look at it," said Vee. "Now go!"

Silas nodded and took off after Freddie.

He'd barely slid into the engine room when the ship shook from the impact of the first of the *Verity's* light weapons.

"We've got more incoming." Temple's voice over the line was grim. "I'm doing evasive manoeuvres, but they've locked onto us too tightly."

"Jumper." Gracie snapped out.

A moment later, Silas felt the familiar shudder of a ship loosing its own light-range weapons.

"Don't have time to get distracted, boy," Freddie muttered, shoving a wrench into his hands. "We get this ship running, or we die for it."

He nodded, and set to work on the damaged stabilizers.

The ship jerked again as more weapons fire hit, and he could hear Ari cursing steadily through the general comm line.

Ten minutes in, he knew it was hopeless. He turned to Freddie, shaking his head. "The stabilizers aren't coming back online, not unless you've got a hell of a lot more extra parts than it looks like you do."

She nodded grimly, but didn't speak.

"Captain! We're close enough in that we can start returning fire!" Ari's voice over the comm was tense.

"Get firing, and keep firing while we lock in. If we can damage their shields, we may get them to back off a moment."

Silas glanced up at Freddie.

She was clearly thinking the same thing he was—mag-lock or no, if they didn't take care of the Verity's light weapons, they'd be space dust long before they had time to worry about being sucked into the black hole.

Silas yanked on the wrench, pulling a bolt tight. "There, Freddie," he said through clenched teeth. "It's as good as it's going to get."

She glanced at his work, then nodded. "We've done everything I can use you for. Get up to the gun room, help Ari. She and Jumper'll need an extra set of hands."

Silas nodded, thrusting the wrench back into Freddie's hands and taking the ladder up to the main deck two rungs at a time. He got out on the main deck, glanced around, and then swarmed up the ratlines, hardly paying attention to where he was putting his hands and feet. He could do this in his sleep—he had been doing it since he was twelve. At the moment, the only important thing was to get up to the gunner's tower as quickly as possible.

Freddie must have called ahead, because when he reached it, Ari was waiting for him. She gestured him over impatiently, pointing at the gunner's seat next to her. "You're on the top two radial guns," she snapped out. "Hope you're a good shot."

He grinned at her as he slid into place. His heart was pounding, but it was more from excitement than he'd ever want to confess. "Best in the Academy, two years in a row."

This was what he damn well lived for—things moving too fast to let him sit and think about where his damn duty lay, or what his family would expect of him. Action, and reaction, nothing else, clean and clear and simple,

Ari scoffed. "Fastest horse in the glue factory," she muttered, and he laughed despite himself.

"Ari." It was Gracie.

Ari's head came up. "Captain?"

"I've got Temple bringing us around and in close. I need you to take out as many of her upper shields as you can."

"On it." Ari's voice was as strained as the captain's, and she glanced at Silas to make sure he'd heard. He gave her a quick nod and turned to the weapons.

They weren't exactly the same as on a ship of the line, but Jumper had shown him around earlier, and everything he didn't know, he could figure out.

"My guns are the heavy power," said Ari through her teeth as she lined up. "Yours are precision weapons. I'm going to make sure they won't be able to disable us, on account of their target-locks won't work, on account of I'll be bombarding them with enough damn heat that they'll wonder if they took a wrong turn and ended up in hell. While I'm doing that, you need to take out the shield generators. I'll send you over the pattern."

Silas nodded again, bending quickly over his weapons.

This would be sharpshooting. But he hadn't been lying to Ari—he had a reputation in the Academy, and before that on the ships he'd flown with.

Now, he supposed, it was time to put it into practice.

At least now he didn't have to think about the morality of the thing—they were shooting out the shields, yes. But without stabilizers, there'd be no chance they'd hold off long enough to damage the *Verity* herself.

"We're in range." Ari's voice was still strained, and faintly annoyed. "You don't watch Jumper, you're damn well going to get us shot to space dust."

Silas jerked his head up. He'd momentarily forgotten Jumper's sign language.

The young man was on the overhead weapons. A good weapons master was worth half a dozen good gunners, Silas knew that well enough—make sure each gun had the correct amount of power for the shots to hit true, judge the enemy's shields and figure out where additional power was needed, adjust their own shields to the enemy's shots.

Jumper signed a string of rapid signals that took Silas a split second too long to decode.

"Fire, damn you!" hissed Ari through her teeth, and then she was shooting, and Silas turned back to his controls, keeping an eye out for Jumper's signals from the corner of his eye.

He lined up his first shot, zooming in on the target. Carefully, he squeezed the trigger, and two short bursts of energy shot out from the ship's nose. Ari's cover fire was blistering and unrelenting, and Jumper's fingers played over the controls, dancing along the shield and the weapons powering. Silas turned back to his weapons, lining up another shot.

His first two shots had hit just wide of the target, and he adjusted his aim, firing again, then again, then again. At last, he could see in his controls the bright red of a hit target, and he gave a quick exclamation of satisfaction. Ari glanced over, scowling, but he could see from the dangerous gleam in her eyes that she was just as excited about this as he was.

"One down, seven to go, Level boy," she said with a grin, then turned back to her work.

Silas lined up his next shot. Now that he had the guns sighted in, it was easier—it took in less than a minute before his next target dissolved.

The Sweet Jenny shook as one of the *Verity's* weapons struck home, and Jumper hissed out a sound of unmistakable disapproval.

Silas gritted his teeth and turned back to his work. He'd have to re-line up his sights, but he'd got the hang of the guns now. It wouldn't take him long.

Ari had redoubled her efforts, but the gunners on the ship of the line had dialled their sights in as well, and another shot hit the Sweet Jenny, shaking her.

"Anytime you feel like it, Sil," Ari snapped. He gave a short nod, to focused to bother trying to answer.

It was only a few minutes before the next two targets were gone.

"Temple, I need to get a few degrees to port. Won't be able to hit them straight on at this angle," he snapped through the general line.

"Give me a minute." Temple's voice was terse. A moment later, the ship had adjusted course, and Silas had an open sightline.

He was grinning. He couldn't help himself. He took close aim, and this time his target exploded at the first rapid-fire burst. He turned to the next.

"Three more to go, Ari," he said over his shoulder. "How's that for sharpshooting?"

Ari snorted. "Took your damn time."

Another target exploded.

The *Verity* must have finally figured out what they were gunning for, although it wouldn't have been obvious—the shield pattern Ari had given him wouldn't take the shield out completely, just weaken them enough that it would pull too much power to keep the ship fully shielded and fire the guns at the same time.

It was a brilliant manoeuvre, honestly, and he didn't blame them for not seeing it at first. But now they had, and with only two shielding ports left to hit, their firing became increasingly frantic.

"They're moving," he hissed through the line to Temple.

"On it," came the man's laconic voice, and the *Sweet Jenny* moved with the ship of the line, keeping just out of range of her heavier weapons as Jumper and Ari kept up their blistering counter fire.

"Hurry up." Freddie's voice was worried. "We're taking damage."

Jumper tapped something in reply through his comm, and Silas made a mental note to damn well put in a few more hours of study in whatever the hell code Jumper was using.

Another of the shipping ports exploded, and before the *Verity* could respond, Silas sighted in on the last one.

"Watch and learn, Ari," he muttered, and caught her irritated glance from the corner of his eye before he turned, pulling back on both triggers and sending a long burst of shot towards the final gun port.

It exploded, and he whooped, throwing his hands up off the gunner's controls and shoving back his seat.

When Ari turned back to him, she was grinning. "Not bad work for an Academy boy," she conceded.

He laughed. "You're impressed. You may as well admit it."

She laughed as well. "I'm just surprised you managed to figure out which button you had to hit to shoot things."

Jumper was watching their banter, grinning, and he flicked his fingers in a rapid message, glanced at Silas, rolled his eyes, and tried again, more slowly. *"You only took about twice as long as you should have. Better than I expected. Congratulations."*

Silas raised an eyebrow at the boy, who smirked at him.

Ari laughed. "Don't let Jumper's mild manners fool you—he's got a wicked sense of humour."

Silas chuckled and shook his head. "Noted." He sighed, shoving himself to his feet. "I guess we best get back, see what Gracie wants with us."

Ari nodded. "Suppose we may as well, at that."

When they reached the cockpit, Gracie was waiting for them. Temple was next to her, his face grave, and it wasn't until then that Silas remembered—no matter how well they'd done shooting, unless they could figure a way out past the *Verity*, they were as good as dead.

20

Gracie

"Captain. We've stopped them shooting us out of the sky for now. But it won't last. What's the plan?" Temple's voice was grim, like he wasn't sure she'd want the others to hear the answer.

Gracie glanced around her at the rest of the crew. Ari and Silas had come in. Jumper was presumably still on the weapons, and Freddie would be working frantically to repair whatever damage they'd taken in the firefight.

Not a soul of them looked like they expected to come out of this alive.

And yet, here they were. Ready to take her orders, whatever those orders might be.

She gave a short sigh, a mix of affection and strain.

"I'm sure you've seen, Captain," Temple continued, his voice still low, "but they've had a chance to lock their weapons on. Be hard to get out past them now. Not sure we'll stand much of a chance, even with the shields taken out."

Gracie nodded. "We wouldn't. But we're not going out past the

Verity. Set us a course for the *Agate*, please."

Silas's dumbfounded expression might have been funny, in other circumstances.

"Captain," he said at last, and she heard the anger in his tone.

She turned to him, her expression still mild. "Sil. You've sailed under a captain before, I assume. Are you questioning my orders?" She made her voice soft, soft enough that he could pretend, if he wanted, that he was the only one who could hear her.

There was a moment of hesitation. Then, at last, he shook his head, teeth still clenched. "No, Captain," he said in a low voice.

"Good." She turned back to Temple. "Chart us a course, please."

Temple nodded, his expression tense. "Aye, Captain," he said softly. "Charting a course for the *Agate*."

For a few minutes, no one spoke.

"Captain." Freddie's words came in over the general line. "Stabilizers won't be coming back on, not until we get back somewhere we can do a full repair, and those last couple of hits got our engines pretty good. We won't have much in the way of running power, I'm afraid."

"Thank you," said Gracie. She'd learned well enough over the years that it was the captain's job to stay calm. Everyone else may be panicking, but the captain didn't have that option.

"I've charted the course." Temple's voice wasn't loud, but in the utter silence of the cockpit it was easily audible.

She turned to study the screen. "Very good, Temple. Please proceed at half speed."

Silas was still staring at her, his expression challenging, but she ignored him.

Either the boy would learn to listen, or he'd try to mutiny. And whatever else she knew about her crew, they were impossibly, absurdly loyal. He wouldn't have time to pull his cutlass before someone, probably Ari, would shoot him dead.

He didn't try, though—maybe he'd been thinking along the same lines. Instead, he stayed where he was, jaw clenched, watching her.

"Captain." Temple's voice was strained. "We're on course, but we're caught in the pull. I won't be able to keep us straight on for much longer. You want me to pull the power up to keep us on course?"

Gracie didn't take her eyes off the screen, watching the *Sweet Jenny* crawl towards her destination. "No," she said absently. "No need for an exact course, Temple. Adjust as necessary."

"Aye, Captain."

The line marking their course on the screen was being dragged inexorably towards the dark black of the hole.

The silence in the small cockpit was almost tangible.

"Captain." Freddie sounded just as tense as Temple. "Engines are working hard to keep us back. Won't take long before we don't have the power to hold."

"Acknowledged, Freddie," she said through the line.

Again, the cockpit was silent.

"We're about half an hour out," said Temple. "We could get there faster, but I'm holding us back to keep at a steady pace."

"Thank you, Temple," she murmured.

On the screen, she could see the *Agate* getting closer.

"Jumper," she said through the general comm line. "The *Agate* is preparing to fire on us. Stand by on the shields."

Jumper's quick staccato acquiescence tapped through the comm in return.

In the distance, she could see the quick stutter of weapons fire from the injured ship, aimed for the *Sweet Jenny*. It didn't get close—

the energy beams were sucked backwards the moment they were fired, pulled off course by the massive gravity of the hole that loomed behind them.

To one side, she heard Silas's sharp intake of breath at the sight.

"Steady on course," she murmured.

She could feel her own heart rate, quick and sharp in her chest.

It wasn't fear, though. It'd been a long, long time since Gracie had been afraid.

It was a sharp, bright adrenaline, the thrill of testing yourself against something that could crush you as easily as you might crush a fly.

"Engines are working at full power. I can't hold us back anymore," came Freddie's voice through the line.

"Acknowledged," said Gracie. "Temple, how far out?"

Temple's hands were strained on the controls, the tendons in his wrists and hands visible. "Twenty minutes out."

She nodded, and tapped the comm line. "Jumper. Check your aim to adjust for the gravity, but I want you to send two blunt impact missiles at the ship. Hook them up to a mag-lock, if you please. Can you do it at this range?"

There was a pause. Then Jumper tapped through her line the quick staccato taps of his code. *Aye, Captain. Can fire off blunt impacts from here and hit, even with the gravity field.*

"Good," she said. "Go ahead, please."

Again, there was a short, tense pause. And then she saw the two impact missiles, showing up on the screen as a bright flare, shoot out from the *Sweet Jenny's* guns.

Instantly, the gravity from the black hole sucked them in, but Jumper's aim was true—even with the additional pull, it was instantly clear the missiles would hit their target.

"Captain?" asked Temple. "We're approaching the point where I won't be able to hold us back at all."

"Acknowledged," she said. From the corner of her eye, she could see Silas, his entire body stiff with tension.

He was afraid. He had to be afraid. But he wasn't going to show it in front of the others.

Through the screen, there was the brief burst of an impact, and the *Agate* rocked, knocked backwards.

"Captain!" It was Freddie. "We're too close to hold! I'm running the engines on full, but they're burning up, and we're going to lose them in a minute if I don't cut them back."

"Acknowledged." Gracie could hear the tension in her own voice. "Cut them back, please, let the grav field pull us in, but give us enough power to stay on course for the *Agate*."

She waited, counting quietly in her head as the ship moved closer.

And then she turned to Ari. "Ari. Activate the mag beam from the skiff, please."

Ari stared at her a moment. Then the woman's face lit up in a huge grin. "Aye, Captain," she said, jumping to her station.

Silas was staring at both of them. "What the hell—" he began.

"Didn't put a bomb on the skiff, remember?" called Ari over her shoulder, still grinning. "She sent it back with a mag-lock. If we're going into that hole—the *Verity's* coming in right along with us."

21

Hollis

Hollis stood on the bridge, her posture tense.

She'd been there when her boarding party had returned She'd had to. Because she'd been the one who'd given the order. She'd been the one whose fault it was that the exhausted, horrified sailors who'd stepped back through their airlock had gone out in the first place. The very least she could do was be there when they came back.

There hadn't been nearly as many of them as she'd hoped. Foster had told her, but it was one thing to know abstractly. It was another to see the sailors staggering back, the horrified, haunted look in their eyes, the ghost injuries on some of them, the sword injuries on others. Every last one of those was her fault. It was her choices that had put them there, and despite that—despite the horror of it, despite the dead—she'd do it again. Every time, given the choice, she'd do it again. And she wasn't sure if that made her a monster or a hero, and in the end, she wasn't sure it mattered.

The important part was, they'd completed the mission she'd

assigned them. They'd taken out the *Sweet Jenny's* stabilizers. It had been a costly victory—more costly than she really wanted to think about. But without stabilizers Mad Dog would have no choice but to turn around. And when she turned, the *Verity* would shoot her out of the sky.

The others on the bridge looked as tense as she felt, their postures tight as they stared at the screens, waiting.

"What the hell are they doing?"

Hollis's head whipped around to find the speaker. It was the navigator. She was watching a blip on the screen that showed the *Sweet Jenny*, her face tight with horror.

Hollis followed her gaze.

Then she swore under her breath, trying to keep her own horror in check.

The *Sweet Jenny* hadn't turned around. She was still heading straight for the *Agate*.

"What the hell is Mad Dog doing?" It was Emmett this time, but Hollis could tell he was voicing the thoughts of every person on the bridge. "Did she not realize she's hit? Maybe they didn't realize we'd taken out their stabilizers."

For half a second, Hollis dared hope it was true. Maybe the pirates hadn't noticed their stabilizers were gone. Maybe that meant they'd get caught in the black hole's gravity before they realized they were unable to pull out.

But even as she thought it, she knew it wasn't true. Another pirate captain, maybe. But not Mad Dog. If the woman was that easy to fool, she'd have been dead a long time ago.

"Stay on the weapons," she snapped. "If they try to make a break for it, I want you to show them how we handle pirates."

"Aye, Captain," her gunner said, their voice quiet.

Hollis found she was holding her breath.

What the hell was the pirate up to? Did she really believe she could somehow pull out of a black hole without stabilizers?

No one spoke—every eye was glued to the screen.

The *Sweet Jenny* would turn around at any moment. She had to.

And then there were two bright flashes on the screen from the *Sweet Jenny*, and Hollis opened her mouth instinctively to call for her gunner—and then she realized. The shots weren't aimed at the *Verity*. The *Sweet Jenny* was firing on the *Agate*.

She thought, for a moment, that the black hole's gravity would pull the shots off course, but whoever was on the *Sweet Jenny's* guns had taken that into account. On the screen, the *Agate* rocked as the missiles impacted.

"Bloody pirates," the navigator grumbled. Her voice was still tight with strain, but now it carried a hint of disgust as well. "Want to kill as many good sailors as they can on the way down."

Maybe that was all this was. After all, they all knew about Mad Dog Gracie Madox—deadly, erratic, completely ruthless. It made sense that, if she was facing death, she'd take as many people down with her as she could.

But there was a cold unease in Hollis's chest.

She'd underestimated Gracie once. She wasn't sure if any of them would survive her doing it again.

And then came the frantic shout through the communicators. "Captain?" The sailor's voice had taken on a tinge of utter panic. "Captain! We just had an alarm on the sensors—there's a mag-lock activated."

For a moment, Hollis stared in disbelief, trying to make the man's words make sense.

A mag-lock. That would be deadly, if it were true—but you had to get practically onto a ship in order to set a mag-lock, and despite all the damage she'd done, the *Sweet Jenny* had never got close enough …

She cursed viciously.

The boarding party. She should have guessed. The pirates had let the ship come back. They could have wiped out her whole boarding party, easily, and they hadn't, and she'd been so sickeningly grateful that she hadn't paid attention as to why they might have left the sailors alive to bring the skiff back.

She was already striding off the bridge and back towards the airlock controllers before she had time to finish the thought. "Where is it hooked on?" she snapped into her comm.

"Down here, Captain, hooked onto our airlock."

"Can we get it off?" she reached the Captain's Deck and slid down the rat lines, not bothering with the ladder.

"Sorry, Captain. The way this one's locked on, it'll take us hours to disentangle it."

She swore again.

Not unexpected—if the pirate had gone to the bother of sending back a mag-lock, it wouldn't be an easy one to undo.

"Do you know what the mag-lock is hooked onto on their side?" she snapped.

"No, Captain." The man's voice was tinged with worry. "I don't. But—but it's pulling, a hell of a lot stronger than a ship the size of the *Sweet Jenny* should pull."

There was a moment, just one moment, where Hollis almost stopped walking, the dread cutting so deep that she couldn't force her legs to keep moving.

"Captain?" Foster was at her elbow still, a perfect first mate, their bearing still absurdly calm.

"Mate Price," she said. Her voice was distant, odd—as if, somehow, the part of her that reacted had been shut off, and the only thing left was the cold, clinical part of her. "Please go check the trajectory of the *Sweet Jenny*. I need to know how close she's getting to the hole, and when she'll get far enough in that her running engines won't hold her back. And I need to know how much additional pull that would put on the *Verity's* stabilizers."

Foster turned to her, and for a split second, Hollis could see the confusion on her first mate's face.

And then, abruptly, it was replaced with horror, and she knew that Foster had understood.

"Aye, Captain," they said quietly, and disappeared back towards the bridge.

Hollis stared after them for a moment, her mind still reeling. Then she forced herself forward, forced her pace back to its normal briskness.

Of course. For someone like Mad Dog Gracie Madox, pulling a broken-down weapons ship into a black hole wouldn't be enough. Hollis had had the audacity to challenge her, and as punishment, Mad Dog was going to take the *Verity* down with her, and every soul of the three hundred and fifty sailors on board.

She wanted to swear. She wanted to scream.

But she didn't do either of those things. She knew damn well it wouldn't change anything.

When she reached the deck where the mag-lock had been affixed, she looked it over clinically.

The man at the airlock hadn't figured out what was happening yet. She could tell, because despite his alarm, he seemed relatively calm. As if this was an inconvenience that could quickly be got rid of, instead of a death sentence.

She almost laughed. In other circumstances, it would have been—a minor inconvenience, nothing in particular to worry about.

"Get to work on it, sailor," she heard herself say, her voice calm and emotionless. "Get it off quick as you can."

He wouldn't live long enough to finish, but keeping her crew busy, keeping them from panicking at the end, was probably the last kindness she could give them.

"Captain." It was Foster's voice through her comm link, and she could tell, by the sound of it, what the news would be.

"Yes, Mate Price?" She wasn't sure how her voice was still calm. It shouldn't be.

"It's—not good news, I'm afraid, Captain." Foster's voice was measured, and somehow, that made Hollis even angrier than if her first mate had berated her for her decision to send the boarding party.

"Out with it, if you please," she snapped.

There was a moment of quiet, then Foster's voice again. "Their ship is already past where they'll be able to get out, with their stabilizers damaged."

Somehow, Foster was delivering the news as if it was an impersonal, impassive thing. As if they themselves weren't going to be killed by it.

"I'm on my way back to the bridge," Hollis said brusquely. "Have we done the calculations? Weight ratio?"

There was a pause. "If it was just the *Sweet Jenny*, we're still back far enough that we could pull out," said Foster slowly. "But—the *Sweet Jenny's* hooked onto the *Agate*. That was what they did with their impact missiles—shot out another mag beam."

This time, Hollis did curse, a long, blistering stream of invectives, every foul word she could remember.

Her heart was racing, nausea twisting in her stomach.

They'd lost the *Sweet Jenny*, they'd lost the *Agate*. She'd lost her command, and her crew. She should, she knew, be more concerned about her own life. She should be more concerned about the fact that she was going to be sucked into a black hole, along with every soul on the *Verity*.

But instead, all she could think of was the crew staring at her, half in admiration, half in horror, when she'd told them to go through the solar flare—and they'd done it anyway. The boarding party, staggering back to the ship, injured, faces haunted and horrified by what they'd seen and what they'd done. She'd sent them there. They'd gone, because she was their captain.

She'd done it, because she'd believed she'd be able to save them.

And she couldn't. Every person under her command was going to die.

When she reached the bridge, everyone turned to look at her.

It was only natural. She was the one that was supposed to find them a way out of this, after all, their captain from the Stacks.

She ignored their gazes, and turned to Foster. "Show me the calculations."

Wordlessly, Foster pulled up the screen, and Hollis glanced it over.

Again, she felt the quick, tight nausea gathering in her stomach.

Foster had been right—if it had only been the *Sweet Jenny*, the *Verity* had enough mass, and was far enough back, that they could pull both ships out.

But Mad Dog hadn't stopped there. Instead, she'd tied both their fates to a dying ship.

Hollis stared at the screen for a long time, trying not to see the eyes of the others watching her, trying not to see the painful hope in their expressions.

Anger was welling in her chest, bright and hot.

Mad Dog, the famous pirate captain, and she'd doomed her own crew, and Hollis's too, because Hollis had had the audacity to stand up to her. She knew damn well the pirate captain hadn't expected that she'd send her boarding party to take out the stabilizers, or she'd have stopped it somehow. She'd expected Hollis to do exactly what Foster had suggested, stand back, let her help herself to the *Agate*, and send a hundred good sailors to their death. And just like every person Hollis had challenged in her lifetime, every person she'd stood up to, when they'd expected her to back down—when she'd refused, Mad Dog had decided to teach her a lesson, show her her place.

"I will be damned before I let that pirate take down the *Verity*." She didn't realize she'd spoken out loud until she saw Foster look over at her in surprise.

She raised her chin, and spoke louder, loud enough that the entire bridge could hear. "I will be damned before that pirate takes my ship and my crew into a black hole."

The others were looking at her now, their expressions a blend of terror, and desperate hope.

"I am the captain of the *Verity*, and by God, I will see Mad Dog in hell before I let her win this."

They were staring at her as if she were mad. "Captain?" said Foster carefully, as though wondering if the strain had sent Hollis entirely off her head. "What—"

Hollis shook her head sharply. "Prepare a skiff please, Mate Greene. We're going in, and we're taking those sailors off the *Agate*, Mad Dog be damned."

"Captain—" Emmett sounded stunned.

She turned on him impatiently. "A skiff, man! We may have lost the weapons, but we're not losing the crew. We're going in, and we're going to pull off the sailors. And then we're going to blow the *Agate* into space dust. I expect that that should break the mag-lock, am I correct?"

There was a moment of stunned silence, and then, on the faces around her, the looks of people who'd been given a second chance at life.

"Well?" she snapped. "Don't just stand there! I told you to get a skiff."

"Aye, Captain," said Emmett, and she heard the respect in his tone. "Right away, Captain."

22

Silas

"Captain!" There was a repressed excitement in Freddie's voice. "Captain, the *Sweet Jenny's* holding!"

"Very good. Keep the engines running and pull us back a bit, but don't put too much strain on them."

Silas glanced around at the cockpit. The others seem perfectly content to trust Gracie's judgement.

"Captain?" he hissed, crossing over to her and keeping his voice low. "You expect the *Verity* to pull us out of this once we're this far in?"

Gracie glanced up at him, her expression mild. "Of course not. Don't think they could if they wanted—Jumper's mag-locked us onto the *Agate*. The combined mass'll be too much for the *Verity*."

He stared at her, then turned and stared around the crew. No one else seemed even mildly taken aback by their captain's suicidal pronouncement.

She chuckled. "Come, lad, I've seen you face death before."

He shook his head and cursed violently. "You knew we weren't going to make it out, so you decided to kill them along with us? Is this who you're going to take your revenge on, Hollis Ives and her crew?"

He felt sick to his stomach.

This wasn't even a battle. This was vengeance, pure and simple.

Exactly the sort of thing, he realized, that he'd come to Blackrock to ask her for.

But not like this. Not against a crew of three hundred and fifty souls whose only crime had been to sign onto one of the few jobs that would accept people from the Stacks, or people down on their luck and with trauma in their pasts.

Again, Gracie shot him a small smile. "I have no intention of sacrificing the *Sweet Jenny*, and I told you how difficult it is to replace crew." She paused, glancing at the screen. "If your Captain Ives plans to save her crew, she'll work out a way to cut the *Verity* free. And while she's busy with that—" She shrugged, and turned to her first mate. "Toothpick, prepare a skiff, if you please."

"Aye, Captain," said Toothpick, straightening, and he limped towards the exit.

Gracie raised her eyebrows at the expression on Silas's face. "We came all this way, lad. You don't think I'm leaving without my weapons, do you?"

He stared at her, speechless, as she turned away, calling out her orders as she strode towards the airlock.

After a moment, Silas strode after her. "Captain?"

Gracie turned to him. Her expression was still mild, but there was something in her face that told him that he had just about run through his quota of patience from her. "Listen, lad. The *Verity* is holding the *Agate* steady for the moment. That won't last forever— either Ives will realize she's got to blow the *Agate* to get the *Verity* out, or she won't. She doesn't, we'll use the *Verity's* mass to leapfrog out as the *Verity's* getting sucked in. She blows the *Agate*, she'll be able to pull the *Verity* free, and she'll pull us out with her. The *Verity'll* be using all her engine strength to do it, so if we're fast on our feet, they won't have time to shoot us down before we leave. But either way, that's going to happen sooner rather than later, and I want my weapons before we go. Now, you can either keep to your bargain and help out, or I can ask Ari to throw you in the brig until it's sorted. But either way, I've got too many things to do to babysit you."

She turned and continued towards a skiff.

Silas narrowed his eyes at her retreating back, his breath coming sharp and short.

She was right. She was exactly bloody right—if Hollis was smart, she'd figure out how to save the *Verity*. And if she was stupid—well, if a ship the size of the *Verity* was being pulled in, the *Sweet Jenny* should be able to get close enough to use her thrusters, push off the *Verity* and get away themselves.

It was brilliant, really.

And he wished, desperately, that he didn't understand how brilliant it was, or what this might mean for the crew of the *Verity*, if Hollis was even a fraction less quick on her feet than she might be.

When he caught up with Gracie, she was already standing in front of the skiff. She still wore that mild expression he'd grown accustomed to, but now he could see the quiet ruthlessness of the woman.

"I'll take two with me on the skiff," she was saying.

Silas followed her gaze.

It wouldn't be an easy choice—Freddie would be needed on the engines, and Gracie wouldn't want to take Jumper off the guns, not with how close they were to the *Verity*. Temple was a navigator, she likely wouldn't want to risk him, and Toothpick, although he was doing his best to hide it, was clearly injured badly enough that he'd be next to useless.

"Ari," said Gracie. "You're with me."

"Aye, Captain." Ari stepped forward smartly. Silas wasn't sure if she was afraid or excited, and in Ari's case, he wasn't sure it would make any difference, or if there even was a difference.

Gracie paused, glancing at Silas. "You're my best choice for a second, Sil. But I've told you before—I won't sacrifice my crew. So what'll it be? Do you have the stomach for this?"

He hesitated.

He knew his duty. He'd known his duty since the *Verity* came out of jump ahead of them. He had a duty to sacrifice everything he so desperately wanted—his naval career, the mission he'd been willing to give up everything for, his own damn life—to save it. And even if he couldn't save the *Verity*—and he was intelligent enough to realize he couldn't—he had a duty to, at the very least, refuse to go along with this.

He could picture Hollis, the crew of the *Verity*, their utter, abject terror, the naval ship of the line, necessary and needed and vastly expensive.

But that was already done, and nothing could change it. Either Hollis figured out a solution, or the *Verity* and all three hundred and fifty souls on board died. And in the meantime—

Jumper's small smile when Silas had first made a clumsy attempt at signing, the way Freddie had taken him under her wing. Ari's irreverent grin and sharp tongue.

He closed his eyes a moment.

Damn it to hell.

You don't like the Captain's morals, maybe, but hell, she's not going to see her crew in trouble and cut their line.

He blew out a breath and straightened. "Aye, Captain," he said, trying not to think too hard of the implication of his words. "I believe I do."

She watched him for a moment, calculatingly. At last, she nodded. "Good lad." She turned to the rest of the assembled crew. "Toothpick, ship's yours until I get back. Hold her steady, don't let the *Verity* get a jump on you. Be ready on the guns, and be ready to haul us back in if need be. I've set a mag-lock on the skiff, figure we'll need it on the way back."

"Aye, Captain." Toothpick's voice was grim. "Good luck."

The skiff was small and cramped, barely big enough to fit the three of them.

"I'm on the guns," Ari snapped, sliding into place.

"I'll chart us a course, if you think you can steer us in, Sil," said Gracie.

Silas gave a short nod, not bothering to answer aloud.

It wouldn't be easy, not on a skiff like this, not when he could already feel through the controls the way the skiff was jumping, pulling towards the gravity of the black hole.

"Good." There was a tension under Gracie's mild tone. "Start us off then, lad."

A starchart popped up on Silas's screen, the course marked in a red line. He glanced over it quickly, then pushed the throttle gently forward, his palm resting lightly on the controls.

The skiff responded instantly, and he raised his eyebrows in approval—he'd expected the battered craft to respond sluggishly. But then, if Gracie was willing to trust her crew's life and her own to it, it would have to be more than it looked.

The controls were tugging against his hand, the ship pulling into the draw of gravity.

"Alright Sil, point us in the right direction. The course I charted takes the grav pull into account, so it'll bring us in around sideways. That should keep us off the *Verity's* sensors."

He nodded, not taking his eyes off the controls.

He hadn't realized until they were out here how close they were to the hole, how strong the gravity would catch and pull at them. He'd heard about black holes, been briefed on them plenty of times, even gone through simulations in the Academy, where they talked about what to do if you got too close, and the calculations you needed to run to see how far to stay back. He knew, logically exactly how this all worked.

But they'd never told him about the raw, cold terror that rose in your chest at the sucking, inexorable power of the thing. It was one thing to read about sailing near a black hole. It was another altogether to be in the middle of it, trying to push a tiny craft, barely big enough to fit you and two others in the cockpit, through a force that could crush you like fine porcelain.

He pointed her nose towards the coordinates Gracie had set out, calculated the angle, and hit the thrusters on full to keep them in the right direction.

Behind him, the *Sweet Jenny* was receding into the distance, a pinprick dot against the limitless swirl of stars and nebula around them.

The ship jerked under his hands, and he turned back to the controls.

Then he swore.

The controls were going haywire, the readings jumping and lurching, pulling the skiff off and then back onto its set course like a frightened horse.

"Lad?" Gracie's voice was sharp.

"The grav field's messing with the controls," he said through his teeth. He paused. "I'm putting her on manual. That's the only way we'll get through this."

"Aye, lad," said Gracie, but he could hear the strain in her voice. "You do that. But best be sure you have a solid grip. This skiff needs a steady hand to keep her pointed in the right direction."

"Noted," he said. He tightened his hands on the manual controls and drew in a deep breath. Then he nudged the bar that would switch them to manuals.

He knew the moment the ship switched over. It balked and jerked, almost yanking the stick out of his hands.

"You alright there, lad?" There was still a hint of humour in Gracie's voice, and he wasn't sure how—surely even she was frightened of dying. Surely even she could feel the merciless strength of the grav field.

"I've got it, Captain," he said, still speaking through his teeth.

"We're coming out of the *Sweet Jenny's* grav control field," Ari snapped. "It's going to get worse before it gets better. I'll try to keep us off the *Verity's* sensors in the meantime. I'll count you down."

Again, Silas gave a quick nod.

"Eight. Seven. Six. Five." He could hear the strain in Ari's voice.

He glared down at the screens. The *Agate* was straight on. If he could hold their course, the skiff would run right into the back of her.

"Four. Three. Two. One."

It felt like the whole world was holding its breath.

And then the skiff shook itself like a wet dog, and Silas fought to keep it under control.

"Steady as she goes," Gracie murmured. Her eyes were still fixed on the course she was charting. "Steady as she goes, lad. We're almost there."

Silas was swearing under his breath, his hands on the control stick tight enough that his knuckles were white.

The skiff balked again, and he wrestled it back on course.

"Have they caught us on their sensors, Ari?"

How the hell was Gracie so calm? How the hell was she not just as panicked as the rest of them?

"Not yet, Captain." He could hear in Ari's voice the same hint of fear that he felt, the exhilaration mixed with terror.

The skiff was almost pulling itself out of his hands.

The force was too strong. There was no way he'd get her back, not like this. He needed more power to be able to pull them back on course.

"Ari." He was speaking through his teeth. "I need you to fire off all weapons, straight to starboard. On my count."

Ari glanced at Gracie. The captain nodded. "Do as he says, Ari." She glanced at Silas. "I'll re-chart the course."

He nodded, not bothering to answer. He wasn't sure he could have had he wanted to—every bit of his concentration was focused on keeping them from slipping off-side any further.

"Three," he said, tightening his fingers in the controls.

"Two." He closed his other hand around the stick. He'd get one chance at this. One chance, or they'd all die.

"One. Now!"

With one hand he yanked all the power forward to the support engines, and with his other, he jerked back on the steering column, wrestling it with every bit of strength in his body.

The skiff jumped as the weapons fired, and the stick fought to escape his grasp. And then, at last, it settled back on course.

He sighed, almost boneless with relief, but he couldn't afford to let up. In the background, he could hear Ari's whoop of triumph, hear the soft release of breath from the captain.

"Not bad," she said, but there was relief in her tone. "Straighten her out and bring us in."

He glanced up at the screen, and realized they were close enough that Ari could start the boarding procedures.

"Cargo hatch is to starboard," Gracie said, and he glanced down at his controls again.

It only took them a moment to line up, now that gravity was pulling them the way they wanted to go. Really, at this point the most difficult thing was holding the skiff back while he lined up.

"Alright," he said at last. "I'm locked in. Are we ready?"

Gracie glanced at Ari, who gave a quick nod.

She turned back to him with a small smile. "Bring us in, lad."

23

Hollis

"Captain."

She glanced up to see Emmett standing in front of her.

"They're preparing the skiff. I've asked the sailors to assemble, so we can choose a boarding crew."

She caught the hint of hesitation in Emmett's tone, and found herself glancing, without really thinking about it, towards Foster. "Mate Price, if you would?"

Foster gave a brief nod. "Of course, Captain." Their voice was smooth.

Hollis sighed, biting back her irritation. It wasn't Foster's fault they were so bloody unflappable.

"What is it, Mate Price?" she snapped, as soon as they were out of earshot.

Foster sighed a little, and shook their head. "Captain." There was something in their voice that, on anyone else, she would have called wryness. "You're asking the sailors to go into an injured ship currently in the process of being sucked into a black hole. To do so, they'll have to get past Mad Dog Gracie Madox and the *Sweet Jenny*. A boarding party just came back, half of them killed, the other half injured, and we're currently on a collision course with that black hole ourselves."

Hollis narrowed her eyes. "If my crew are too much of cowards to —"

Foster held up a hand. "Please, Captain," they said in a low voice. "I know you've fought for everything you have. I've heard the stories about you as well as anyone else, and whether you'll believe me or no, they're not all bad. There are more than a few sailors on board who were bragging about serving under Hollis Ives when news came. But you have to understand—not everyone is used to what you're used to. Not everyone is used to having to fight for their lives. I know these sailors. They aren't ones to disobey orders, not usually, but they're frightened."

Hollis's heart was pounding, her pulse beating in her ears.

She had never, not once since the time she'd signed on to the merchant ship when she was fourteen, been able to say "no" to an order. It didn't matter how unreasonable, it didn't matter how dangerous, she'd never been able to afford to be afraid. Even if she was. Even if she was bloody terrified, she'd never had that luxury.

"Captain." Foster's voice was still quiet, but cut with something that could have been sympathy, or could have been admiration, or could have been something else entirely. "All of us here have seen what you can do. We've all seen that you're fearless, and smart, and a damn good captain, if I may say so. But—" they broke off, shaking their head. "I can't tell you what to do, Captain. But your sailors are terrified."

Hollis closed her eyes a moment.

As much as she hated it—Foster was right.

Back at the Academy, they would have called what she was about to do irresponsible. They would have said she had a duty to stay with the ship, come what may.

But she was facing a possible mutiny, and a ship being dragged to its destruction, and she didn't, at this moment, give a damn about what they'd say at the Academy.

This was her best option. Perhaps her only option.

At last, she turned. "Mate Price," she said, her voice brisk and businesslike. "Your ship."

Foster stared at her. "I—" they began.

Hollis glowered at them. "Your ship, Mate Price. I will be going with the boarding party."

Foster stared at her for a moment before they regained their equilibrium. "Captain," they began.

"Mate Price." She kept her tone cold, so Foster wouldn't hear her voice shaking. Knowing Foster, they'd probably guessed anyway. "I have every confidence in your ability to captain the ship in my absence. And I have given you a direct order."

For a long, long moment, Foster stared at her, as if they were trying to read something in her she couldn't see. At last, though, they nodded, their expression going neutral once more. "Aye, Captain," they murmured.

"In the meantime, please come with me to help pick out my boarding crew. I believe some of the sailors have sailed under you longer than they have under me."

"Aye, Captain," said Foster, as if the familiarity of the snapped orders had done something to bring them back to themselves. They paused. "Captain—" they began.

She turned, face cold. "Yes?"

They cleared their throat. "Nothing, Captain. I'm sorry." They stood brusquely to attention. "Ready to inspect the crew, Captain."

Hollis nodded—she couldn't quite trust herself to speak—and the two of them started for the ship, where Emmett had gathered the crew.

When they reached it, Hollis could tell at a glance that Foster had been telling the truth. The faces of the sailors showed a blank fear she would have recognized even without Foster's assistance. Although, some part of her whispered, without Foster's assistance, she wasn't sure she'd have had the time to think over her reaction. And the fact was—Foster was right. She was asking the sailors to go out on a mission that could very well mean their death.

She was looking into the face of a mutiny—not because they hated her, not because they mistrusted her, but because they were terrified.

And she was their captain. This was her responsibility.

She cleared her throat and stepped forward. "Sailors." Her voice wasn't loud, but it carried in the utter silence. "I'm certain Mate Greene has explained the situation to you. We disabled the *Sweet Jenny*, but it appears Gracie Madox intends to take the *Verity* and the *Agate* down with her." She paused a moment, long enough to let the murmuring subside. "Sailors," she said. "I do not intend that she succeed. We are neither children nor cowards. And we will not go peacefully to our deaths, nor abandon the crew of the *Agate* to theirs. I'm prepared to lose the *Agate* and its cargo, but we're going to bring that crew back, and we're going to save the *Verity*." She glanced around. "I will not ask my crew to take a risk I am not willing to take myself. Therefore, I will lead the rescue party. Mate Price will captain the ship while I'm gone. If we succeed—if we reach the *Agate*, evacuate the crew, and blow the ship, we'll give the *Verity* a chance to survive. I know this is dangerous. I'll need every hand fully committed. So I won't assign you. But anyone who is willing, I ask that you volunteer."

There were a few moments of silence. Then Blakely, the man she'd punished on her first day on board, stepped forward. "Captain," he said, his voice quiet. "I know I haven't—" he paused. "But I'm in, Captain, if you'll have me."

She looked at him a moment, trying to keep the astonishment from her face. Then, at last, she nodded brusquely. "Thank you, Midship Officer Blakely."

"I'll come as well, Captain." Another sailor stepped forward.

Another stepped forward after that, then another, then another, until there were a dozen sailors standing in front of her.

"And you'd best take me as well, wouldn't hurt to have another officer on board if things go badly," said Emmett, stepping forward as well.

She glanced over the sailors assembled on the deck. "Thank you," she said. She had to clear her throat. "You'll need your weapons. I don't know what we'll be facing when we get there. Get ready, get on board the skiff. We'll be pushing off in five minutes' time."

There was a chorus of, "Aye, Captain," and then the sailors left. Their faces were grim, their voices muted, but they moved with purpose.

Hollis turned back to Foster. "Mate Price," she said quietly. "As you know, the plan is that we go in, take off the crew, and blow the ship."

"Yes, Captain," said Foster. Hollis glanced around and lowered her voice further. "If it becomes apparent that our skiff will not make it back in time, and the *Verity* is in danger—your standing order is to leave without us. You will take full command of the *Verity* on my orders, and chart a course back to the Level. You will not put the lives of this crew at risk for a chance of saving mine."

Price was watching her, their face creased in a frown.

"Do you understand me, Mate Price?" she snapped.

Foster closed their eyes. For a moment, Hollis saw the weariness there, the exhaustion, the strain of the past few days. But all they said was, "Aye, Captain."

"Thank you." Hollis paused, then glanced up, clearing her throat. "And—Mate Price, should the situation not arise again for me to say this—it's been an honour to serve with you."

Foster nodded. "And with you, Captain," they said quietly.

Hollis turned away, closing her eyes a moment.

She should, she knew, be terrified. If she let herself think about it for long enough, she would be—she was heading out on a mission that was almost guaranteed to end in her death, trying to save her crew and the crew of the *Agate* from a bloodthirsty pirate and a black hole. She should be terrified, shaking.

But there was a tight grin spreading over her face that she couldn't quite help.

There was a reason she'd been sent to the Academy. It was because the Admiral had seen something in her, something she thought she could use. And it had been far, far too long since Hollis had done something like this.

She lifted her head, checked her weapons, and strode briskly towards where the skiff was being prepared. "Those sailors on the skiff, to me," she called out over the comm line. "The skiff is pushing off in one minute."

24

Silas

The echo of the seal-lock breaker was loud in the utter silence of the skiff.

At last the seal on the *Agate's* airlock popped, and the door swung free.

Silas tightened his hand on his cutlass. Ari, beside him, was holding an energy pistol, and Gracie had a cutlass as well.

"Best get moving. We don't have much time." Gracie's quiet voice was almost enough to make him jump.

He stepped through the opening, and into the cargo hold of the *Agate*.

The inside of the ship was as silent as the skiff had been, the cargo hold completely deserted.

Silas couldn't blame the crew—if his ship was in the process of being sucked into a black hole, he wasn't sure he'd have the attention to spare for his cargo either, no matter how valuable.

"Clear," Ari whispered. She'd stepped past him, making a quick circuit of the deck and clipping a lock seal onto the doors.

"Good. Then let's get this cargo loaded." Gracie's voice was matter-of-fact, but he could hear the strain under it.

He and Ari bent wordlessly to their tasks, lifting the heavy cases together and heaving them onto one of the small lift-boards Gracie dropped beside them.

Ari pushed their first load back towards the skiff as Silas turned to load another board.

He tried to shove aside the eeriness of the scene, the odd, uncomfortable quiet of the ship as they worked. From the other side of the cargo-hold doors, he could hear, muffled, the voices of the *Agate's* crew—shouts, raised voices, running footsteps. The hallmarks of panic.

He tried to ignore it.

Those sailors were going to die. They were going to die, and he knew it, and he wasn't doing anything about it, and he wasn't sure if he could live with himself after that fact. But the skiff they'd brought was far too small to take the sailors and the weapons both, and the *Sweet Jenny* was too small to hold the sailors even if they could bring them back.

He swore under his breath, and kept working.

He had finally managed to get himself into a rhythm when Gracie's voice pulled him from his reverie.

"How close are we?" The captain's voice was tense, and when he paused for a moment, Silas could understand why—the *Agate*, which had been holding itself steady, barely, was shuddering now, shaking under the strain of the gravity, held back only by the pull of the *Verity's* stabilizers.

"About halfway there, I think." Ari's words were clipped.

Gracie nodded and turned to Silas. "And how are you doing, boy?" Her voice was soft, but there was a sharpness in her gaze that told him he'd been more transparent in his thoughts than he'd meant.

He'd promised. He told her he could handle himself, even here.

But perhaps it was the remembered terror of just a few minutes ago, the inexorable drag of gravity on the skiff, the terror of not knowing if they'd survive, or be pulled in and crushed.

"Captain," he said at last, in a low voice. "We can't just leave them."

Even as he said it, he knew how ridiculous it would sound to the pirate.

Hell, it sounded ridiculous to him.

Gracie smiled a little, giving him time, maybe, for his own words to sink in. "I didn't start this war, lad," she said quietly at last. "Those that did knew damn well what they were getting into."

He cursed through his teeth. Gracie raised an eyebrow. "You'll not put the injustice of the Level on me, lad. You'll not ask me to pay the price for their inhumane policies. That's one thing I won't take on my name. The Level wants war with us? It can have it. And I'll not let the fact that they throw their dross out as cannon fodder keep me from taking my due." She paused, dropping her burden on the board, and Silas followed suit, striding after her as she brought her load into the skiff's hold.

"You feel sorry for the sailors on the ship," she said over her shoulder. "But do you think any one of them felt sorry when they signed up to fire on sailors like Jumper and Temple and Freddie?" She shook her head, and there was steel in her tone. "No, lad. They knew damn well what they were signing up for. Don't you dare ask me to sacrifice my crew to show them mercy." She grabbed another stack of boxes as he finished unloading the board, and shot him a sardonic grin. "Besides—you asked me not to shoot down your friend the captain. I didn't. If she finds a way to save the *Verity*, more power to her. But in the meantime—" Gracie shrugged. "Her ship's holding us in place while we grab our cargo. I don't suppose I could ask her for any more." She turned back to her work.

Silas closed his eyes.

Either Hollis would blow the *Agate* and save the *Verity*, or she wouldn't. Either way, the crew of the *Agate* was dead. And if Hollis wanted to blow it, with how close it was to the black hole—she wouldn't be able to simply shoot it out of the sky. She'd have to send a crew in close to set the explosives. She'd have to do it, knowing exactly what death she was dooming the sailors on board to.

He cursed again and turned back to his work, grabbing the crates with a little more violence than necessary.

The ship shuddered, and Ari glanced up. "Captain," she said. "We've got another skiff landed."

Gracie nodded. "You know what to do, lass." She turned to Silas. "Best hurry up. I'm not worried they'll blow it before their skiff gets clear, but we want to be clear before they are."

Ari shoved the last of the boxes she was loading onto the small lift-board, and shoved it towards Silas. "Sil, get those loaded," she snapped, and he grabbed the lift-board and pushed it towards the skiff. He was sweating at the exertion by now, even through the temp-regulated suit, but he couldn't slow down—they didn't have time to slow down. If they were to get the weapons loaded and the skiff off before the *Agate* went down, they'd be cutting it close already.

By the time he'd unloaded the boxes into the skiff's cargo hold and turned to bring the lift-board back, Ari was crouched at the door that led to the main body of the ship, tucking something carefully around the corners. She straightened and stepped back, her energy pistol ready in her hand.

He could hear a commotion from the other side of the door, the shouts of the sailors. There were footsteps coming down the hall. Gracie glanced up. "Ari, no one comes through that door and lives."

"Aye, Captain," said Ari, her voice tight.

"Sil, get moving unless you want to take a nice tour of the inside of a damn black hole!"

"Aye, Captain," he said, jerking his attention back to his work.

He glanced around quickly as he loaded cartons of weapons and weapon parts, calculating.

They had maybe ten solid minutes of work left—a little longer, if Ari was needed to guard the door. And from the way the ship was shaking, they'd have barely that before the *Verity* would be unable to hold any longer.

His heart was pounding, and sweat made his palms slick and slippery inside his gloves.

From the corner of his mind, he heard the boots coming to a halt, a sound at the door. The sound of someone's hands on the control.

He straightened, his hand finding his pistol, his eyes already going to the closest place to take shelter and set up a good counter fire. Ari was standing against the wall, pistol in hand, and there was a look on her face that told him she'd have no qualms whatsoever about killing whoever stepped through that door—terrified sailor, or Captain Hollis Ives herself.

And then from outside, a voice shouted, "Leave it! We don't have time for the cargo!"

There was a moment's pause. And then the footsteps receded down the passageway, and Silas felt himself droop in almost lightheaded relief.

Hollis had sent a skiff after all. And she hadn't abandoned the sailors. From the sounds of it, she'd take as many off on the skiff as she could.

The thought sent another twinge of guilt through him that he pushed back ruthlessly.

He was here because the navy would have hanged him for treason for demanding justice. And he'd still been treated better than Hollis Ives had been—he knew that well enough.

She'd chosen to stay on despite that. And the moment he'd agreed to get on the skiff with Gracie and Ari, he'd chosen his loyalties. They'd both chosen their paths, and it was far too late for second thoughts.

He pushed his cargo towards the skiff, unloading it quickly. But he found, in the back of his mind, he was reciting a sailor's prayer for Hollis.

Our Lady of Mercy, let her get the sailors off the dying ship.

Let her save them.

Let them get back to the Verity.

It felt like simultaneously hours, and mere seconds, before they'd finished loading the skiff. Ari was still in position by the door, pistol at the ready.

"Ari, we're done here," said Gracie at last, looking around.

Silas followed her gaze.

The *Agate's* cargo hold wasn't emptied, but they'd taken most of the weapons crates, at least.

The ship was shaking harder now, its engines trembling as they fought against gravity. It wouldn't last forever, and he knew it damn well.

"Aye, Captain," said Ari, holstering her pistol. She checked the locks and bent down to check the edges of the doors.

Then Gracie cursed. Silas followed her gaze, but she was sprinting forward before his brain could make sense of what she'd seen.

And then he saw it—a door on the far end of the cargo hold, pushed slightly open. And through the gap—

He swore as well, starting after her, but he was far too late. The ghost had already materialized through the opening. The dark pits of its eyes were glowing black, its mouth stretched wide, fingers elongated to claws, and there was another behind it. They were going to spring, he could see it; Ari was just straightening, she wouldn't have time to grab for her sparker …

And then Gracie was there, her shout drawing the ghosts' attention.

They turned on her as one, streaming around her as she backed into a corner between the stacks of boxes. Her sparker was in her hand and ignited, the blue tip glowing, but even Gracie couldn't take two ghosts at once.

Ari was on her feet with a wordless cry, but Gracie gestured brusquely. "Ari, belay that," she snapped, her voice harder than Silas had ever heard it. "Ain't going to reach me before the ghosts do, so get the hell back on the skiff. No point in wasting the weapons." Her eye caught Silas's for just a moment as she turned away, and the corner of her mouth quirked, just a touch.

"Captain—" Ari's voice was choked. But Gracie was right—there was no way Ari would get to her in time.

But he could. He knew it, and Gracie knew it too, he'd seen it in her expression. He could get to her before the ghosts did, even though it might mean dying for it.

His eye snagged on something in her hand, something small and black.

A controller.

Abruptly, he knew what Ari had been doing, crouched by the

door.

She'd been planting explosives, to send the Agate and every soul on board to their deaths.

His stomach twisted with dread.

If Gracie died, the controller would die with her—the controller that would mean the deaths of all the sailors on the *Agate* and whoever Hollis had sent to evacuate them. Hollis would be able to do whatever she needed to to save the *Verity*.

It was his duty. It was everything that had been drilled into him since he was too young to remember. All he had to do was leave.

But he was running even before he had time to finish the thought, grabbing Gracie by the arm and hauling her out of the way as the ghosts sprang. Ghostly claws ripped through the shoulder of his suit, burning ice-cold and hot at once, but he managed to keep his feet, yanking out his sparker with his good arm and spinning to face them. His teeth were barred in a grin, his whole body light with adrenalin, and he could barely feel the hot blood streaming from his injury.

And then Gracie was beside him, her own sparker ignited, and Ari had made it to the door the ghosts had come through. Gracie stepped forward with her sparker, and as the ghosts backed up cautiously, Ari yanked the door open, the eddy of air pulling them momentarily back into the empty space.

Ari slammed the door shut behind them, and for a moment, the three of them stood there, gasping for breath.

"Must have been the supplies entrance from the med bay," said Gracie, shaking her head. "Don't figure there's anyone alive in there, at any rate, not with two turned ghosts like that."

The ship shuddered, and her expression went grim. "You think you can still pilot us, lad?"

He nodded, and the three of them sprinted for the skiff. Silas slid into the pilot's seat and grabbed for the controls as the hatch slammed shut behind Ari, and Gracie hit the lever to un-seal them from the airlock.

He shoved forward on the thrusters, and the skiff shot away.

The drag of the grav field hit them like a physical blow the moment they were away from the *Agate,* and he wrestled with the steering column for a moment while Ari activated the mag-lock they'd set to the *Sweet Jenny.* Then the skiff steadied on its course, managed on the other side by Temple and Freddie.

Silas let out a breath of relief and glanced down at the screen.

The skiff from the *Verity* was still clinging to the side of the *Agate.*

And he knew, well enough, that the controller for the explosives Ari had planted sat in Gracie's hands.

Guilt sat in his stomach like a stone.

He'd saved Gracie. He'd saved her, knowing exactly what the result would be.

The *Verity* would be able to pull herself free once the *Agate* blew, and she'd pull the *Sweet Jenny* out with her. But the moment Gracie hit the controller, the *Agate's* crew, and the crew of the skiff that had risked their own lives to save them, would be hurled into the crushing heart of the black hole.

He closed his eyes for just a moment, bracing himself for the click of the controller. Bracing himself to look back down at the screen and see nothing but debris.

But no sound came.

"Were you planning on flying us in blind, lad?" Gracie's voice was faintly amused, and he glanced over at her in shock.

She'd placed the controller down beside her, and was watching him, eyebrows quirked.

He cursed under his breath, glancing back down to make sure the skiff was still running on course. It was.

And behind it, the *Agate* still teetered on the edge of destruction, still barely holding back from being pulled into the black hole—but there, still.

"Why?" he asked through his teeth, without looking at her.

She was still watching him. At last, she shrugged and turned back to the view screen. "Looks like your Captain Ives has things under control. If the ship starts to go and we can't use the *Verity* to jump ourselves out, I'll blow it. But in the meantime, I suppose we can afford to give them a fighting chance. Won't hurt us either way."

He turned to stare at her. "I thought you said this was a war," he said at last. "I thought you said those that signed up for it knew what they were getting into."

She chuckled softly. "Aye, lad, I did. And I believe it. But wasn't it you told me they might not have had any more choice than our crew?" She shook her head, still watching the screen. "The Level is a nasty place, lad, filled with wolves. You know that, you've seen it. Although maybe not as intimately as my crew's seen it. I don't hold any pity for those as started this war, and if it were the Admiral and her ilk on that ship, I'd blow it without a second thought. But she won't stop to mourn a few dozen sailors going to their deaths, and there are families back in the Stacks as might. No point in doing the Admiral's dirty work for her." She paused. "You're bound and determined to bring us in blind, aren't you, boy?"

He yanked his attention back to the screen, and made a quick correction to their course.

The mag beam was holding them steady, and the trip in was a thousand times easier than the trip out had been. Even if the *Verity's* skiff were to break loose now, they'd make it in well before she had time to disengage and start back for the ship.

But he couldn't help but watch Gracie from the corner of his eye as he flew.

And if she noticed, he could only tell by the hint of humour tugging at the corner of her mouth.

25

Hollis

At least, Hollis thought grimly, getting the skiff to the weapons ship had been easy enough. At the angle the *Verity* had been forced to take in its straining efforts to keep them all from being pulled into the black hole's gravity, all they'd had to do was detach from the ship and nudge the steering column once or twice. The force of the gravity field had pulled them directly into the *Agate's* starboard airlock, almost without input from the skiff's engines.

"Page the *Agate*," she snapped, as the ship loomed up in front of them. The gravity had scrambled communications out of the ship, but this close they should be able to make contact. "Let them know we're from the navy, and we intend to get the crew off."

"Done, Captain." The grim-faced young woman at the controls snapped.

"Good. Wait for their response. Edgeworth, you get us in front of the airlock. If we can't make contact before we reach the ship, we'll break the airlock seal."

And they'd hope like hell the sailors on board weren't waiting with pistols and cutlasses to cut down the rescuers they'd mistaken as attackers.

"Aye, Captain."

Hollis watched the control screen, her hands clasped behind her back, and prayed her crew couldn't see the whiteness of her knuckles.

The skiff's comm crackled. "This is the *Agate*, paging the skiff. Message acknowledged. Report to the airlock, we'll have it open for you."

Hollis let out her breath in a quiet sigh of relief. At least they wouldn't be fighting the people they'd come to save, battling ghosts as they tried to evacuate the dying ship.

There was enough chance of them all dying before the end of this already, without any further complications.

She turned to her small crew. "We're here to rescue the crew," she said, her voice low. "Do not go after the weapons, do not go after the supplies, and any sailor who insists on going back to grab something, shoot them. We don't have time for anything but getting this crew off, and damn little time we'll have to do that. I'm not risking the *Verity* for someone's belongings." She turned to the two technicians. "You're to plant the explosive charge. With the grav field distorting everything we throw this direction, I don't want to count on the *Verity's* guns to take down this ship once we're off it. Place the explosives, then get back to the skiff. If things go badly, I will expect you to set them off, regardless of who is still onboard the *Agate*. The *Verity* is our top priority at the moment, and if she's pulled in, every soul on this ship and skiff will be pulled in after her. Do you understand me?"

"Aye, Captain." The technician's naturally pale skin had gone a shade paler, but he nodded.

"Very good."

The skiff shuddered as it hooked on to the outer airlock door.

"Be prepared to move, the moment that door is open," Hollis snapped.

There was a scattered murmuring of "Aye, Captain,"s.

And then there was a hiss as the airlock door cracked open and slid wide, and the skiff sealed on.

"Go!" she called, and all but sprinted off the skiff and into the dying ship, her small group of sailors at her heels.

The technicians split off—they'd clearly already discussed where they'd set the charges, as they didn't even stop to consult—and Hollis stepped off into the centre of the terrified sailors.

"Where's your captain?" she asked, her voice brusque.

"Here." A man who appeared to be in his late forties stepped forward. His face was weary and lined with strain, and he looked like he hadn't slept in days.

"I'm Captain Hollis Ives, of the *Verity*," said Hollis, stepping forward. "Captain Brown, please instruct your crew to get the hell onto that skiff."

The man's face relaxed into an expression of such exhausted relief that it was almost painful to see. "Aye, Captain Ives. Thank you." He turned and began barking orders to his crew.

"With your permission, Captain, I'll send my crew to help round up stragglers," she said.

"Permission granted, of course," the man said, turning back to her. "Thank God you've come. After that damn pirate ship hit us with the missiles, I thought we were done for."

"Oh, she did more than hit you with her missiles," said Hollis grimly. "She tied you to the *Verity* with a mag-lock. I believe she was hoping we'd be forced to shoot you down or go into the black hole with you. We may yet, but I wasn't going to leave without saving those I could." She glanced over her shoulders. "*Verity's* crew, to me. Spread out, get everyone onto the skiff. It's going to be a tight fit, and we won't have time to count heads, so when I give the final call, you'd damn better finish up with whatever you're doing and get yourselves back here."

Her crew were already herding the terrified sailors from the *Agate* into the skiff, and the captain was holding order, barely.

"The skiff doesn't leave until I give the order," she snapped over her shoulder. "Mate Greene, you have my permission to shoot down anyone who tries to take her off early."

"Aye, Captain," he said, saluting, and she strode out into the depths of the dying ship.

Even if she hadn't known how close they were to destruction, it would have been an eerie scene—the electric lights had dimmed as the ship's power was sucked out, and now they flickered and buzzed in a way that reminded her more of the Stacks than a naval ship of the line. The ship itself shuddered, creaking and groaning ominously as it fought against the deadly pull of gravity, and her boots rang off the hard surface of the corridors.

Most of the sailors, it seemed, had seen the chance for salvation and run for the front of the ship, but she found the ship's mechanic, along with two or three of her helpers, in the engine room, the noise of it loud enough that it was no wonder they hadn't heard the broadcast.

"Go on!" she shouted over the noise. "Get the hell out of here, now!"

The woman jumped to her feet, brown skin pale, and grabbed her two assistants by the shoulders, shoving them for the door.

"Is there anyone else down here?" Hollis shouted.

The woman glanced around quickly, then shook her head. "Not in the engine room, no. But check the med bay, there'll be people down there for sure."

Hollis nodded and turned. "Get your people onto the skiff," she called over her shoulder, and started for where the woman had indicated.

The noise of the engines' fight with gravity grew louder the deeper into the ship she went, and she could feel the strain of it through the soles of her boots, through the tremble in the walls when she put out a hand to steady herself around a corner.

They were almost out of time.

She reached the mess-hall, and started another terrified group of sailors for the airlock and salvation, then turned back to the med bay.

When she reached it, she paused at the door. "Hello?" she called. "We're here to get you off the ship. Is there anyone in there?"

There was no answer, but she caught a flicker of movement through the opaque plex glass.

The noise of the ship in its death throes was enough to make it almost impossible to hear at any rate.

She pushed the heavy door open, and cautiously stepped inside.

When the door closed behind her, the sudden absence of sound was almost shocking.

Even in a merchant ship, the med bay would be fully sealed off.

"Hello?" she called again, glancing quickly around.

This ship had been well fitted-out—there were half-a-dozen sickrooms off the main corridor, and she started down it, tapping at the doors as she passed them. "Hello? We won't be able to stay for much longer. If you're coming …"

She stopped abruptly, staring down at the sight in front of her.

A man with black hair and light skin lay face-down on the floor, his body contorted, blood oozing and pooling under his chest.

She stared for a moment.

Then she caught a flicker of movement on the edge of her vision, and she jerked her head up.

Her entire body went cold.

The ghostly, translucent shape of a young man watched her from the hallway ahead of her.

She was suddenly certain that if she turned the young man's body over, she'd see the same features, the same ragged clothing, as the ghostly figure.

And behind it …

She felt her stomach drop, felt the beginnings of a sick panic starting in her chest.

Behind the first ghost, two more.

She froze, not moving a muscle, as the ghosts watched her with their burning black pits of eyes.

A ghost would be attracted to movement. If she moved, they'd spring.

But staying still didn't mean they'd leave you. It just meant your death would take longer.

From the corners of her eyes, she caught the details she'd missed before, too caught up on finding any living sailors still in the med bay —the smears of blood on the walls, the crumpled body, fallen behind the operating table. The dark shape slumped against the inside of one of the sickrooms, the door just barely ajar.

She'd seen this type of scene play out before, more than once in her time in the navy.

There was a reason the med bays were so carefully sealed. And usually the medics were careful, but no matter how careful you were, you couldn't always prevent something like this.

One of the patients had turned, and now everyone in the sickroom was dead. And at least three of them had turned ghost as they died.

The ghosts were drifting towards her now.

If she didn't know, if she hadn't had the experience with ghosts that she had, she might have thought the expressions on their faces were wistful, sorrowful. But she'd seen how quickly those expressions turned to rage and hate, the moment they were close enough to their quarry.

Slowly, the movement so minuscule that it hopefully wouldn't attract attention, she closed the fingers of her hand around her sparker.

A sparker wouldn't give her a chance, not against three ghosts like this. Probably not even against one—you had to have perfect aim or incredible luck to kill a fully-turned ghost with a sparker quick enough to keep it from killing you. And even one of the absurdly expensive plasma guns the peacekeepers on the Level used wouldn't have been enough to save her from three ghosts at once.

With her free hand, she tapped her wrist comm against her hip. "Greene," she said quietly. "I'm in the med bay. They were wiped out by ghosts. I may not make it back. If I'm not back in five minutes, leave without me. Do you understand?"

There was a moment's hesitation.

"Aye, Captain," Emmett said at last, his voice thick with dread.

"Get everyone onto the skiff in the meantime. If I make it back, we won't have long."

"Aye, Captain."

She turned her attention back to the ghosts ahead of her.

Even as quietly as she'd been whispering, the sound had drawn their attention. They were drifting towards her more quickly now, the expressions on their ghostly faces sharp with a dangerous interest.

She tightened her fist around her sparker, whispering a silent prayer to Our Lady of the Ghosts.

And then they sprang, and she yanked the sparker free, igniting it, and shoved it into the chest of the first ghost.

The sparker passed through it harmlessly, and then the ghost had her by the arm of her suit, the material shredding like paper under the ice cold of its grasp.

She gasped out a curse and stumbled backwards as the second ghost sprang at her, its fingers raking along her cheek, burning and deathly cold at once. Her legs hit the edge of a low medic table, and she fell backwards, her arm jerking from the ghost's grasp.

For one heart-stopping moment she was falling, and then she hit the ground hard and rolled under the table, scrambled to her feet as the ghosts slipped under after her, and ran for the door.

Blood was dripping down her face, and her arm burned where the ghost's fingers had grazed it, but the door was in front of her.

She risked a quick glance over her shoulder, and her heart almost stopped in terror. The ghosts were streaming after her, their jaws stretched wide, teeth shards of blackness in the pits of their mouths, eyes glowing dark with hunger and rage.

And then she was at the door, and her hands fumbled for the key-lock. She heard the click, at the same time as she felt icy fingers grasp the back of her coat, wind around her shoulder, and then she'd shoved the door open, slipped through, and slammed it behind her, locking it with shaking hands. She paused a moment, leaning against the wall, gasping for breath, then glanced around quickly to be sure she hadn't let any of the ghosts loose.

There were none—if there had been, she'd be dead already. They wouldn't leave fresh prey, already injured and bleeding as she was.

Under her feet she could feel the ship shaking, breaking itself to pieces, and now that she was outside the sealed-in med bay, the grinding and clanking of the engines, the scream of the dying ship beneath her, was almost deafening.

She steadied herself on her feet and sprinted back towards the airlock.

When she reached it, it was still a tangled, twisted mass of bodies, all trying to shove themselves onto the skiff at once, pushing and trampling each other in their panic. She could see over the heads of the crowd Emmett and the captain of the *Agate* standing at the door to the skiff, trying to keep order, but there were too many people and too much raw fear for them to hold long.

"Enough!" she shouted over the noise.

No one paid her any attention.

She yanked out her energy pistol and fired into the ceiling, the blinding, shocking brilliance of it like a flash of lightning in the small space.

For a moment, there was utter stillness.

"Listen to me," she shouted. "There's room on the skiff for all of you, but by God, the next person I see try to push their way past someone else I will shoot dead. Do you understand me?"

There was another moment of silence.

Then someone called out, "Captain, it's not the room we're worried about, the seal is breaking!"

She swore under her breath, turning to find the speaker.

The noise and clamour began to rise again, and she shouted, "Quiet, all of you! Mate Greene and your captain will get you on board the skiff, follow their damn orders! I'll deal with any other problems."

Her head was starting to spin, the terror and the pain of the ghostly attack of minutes earlier finally sinking through her consciousness, and she had to shove it back, brushing her arm across her face to wipe away the blood that dripped down across her suit and spattered off the floor in a red trail behind her.

She saw the problem a moment later—one of the clamps had come loose, knocked aside in the frantic scramble for the entrance to the skiff, the end of it bent so it wouldn't seal.

She crossed to it quickly and shoved it closed, and the worrying sucking sound of dropping pressure ceased. "I'll hold it down, get on board the skiff, nice and orderly," she snapped at the sailors behind her.

She leaned her weight against it, holding it shut by main force. She could feel through her fingers the shuddering of the ship, the way it fought and bucked against the pull of the black hole's gravity, trying to knock the skiff off like a horse shaking off a fly.

"Edgeworth," she said through her comm, keeping her voice low. "Are you and Wilson on the skiff? Ready to hit the explosives if need be?"

"Aye, Captain," came the voice through her earpiece. "I've set it so that if we lose pressure, the explosives will go. That way, if we don't get off and something should happen ..." He didn't finish the sentence.

"Good man," she said grimly.

He was one she'd want to keep an eye on for promotion, if they all lived through this.

The press in the airlock was slowly subsiding as the captain and Emmett finally imposed order on the struggling crowd, and the sailors were trailing in quickly and quietly, finding their places and moving aside to let others in.

Her arms were shaking, and she shifted, letting her shoulder press up against the seal lock.

It wasn't just her shoulder—her whole body was shaking, and she wasn't entirely sure why. She'd been hurt worse than a scratch across her face before, had faced ghosts on more than one occasion, and it would usually take something much more serious to leave her weakened like this.

She glanced down.

It took her a moment to understand what she was seeing.

And then she swore, closing her eyes to keep from passing out.

It hadn't been just the cut on her face that had been leaking blood, leaving the bloody trail behind her. She'd have guessed that, if she'd had the time to pay attention. It was far too much blood for a simple scratch like that.

It must have happened when she'd gone over backwards, the force of the impact of her fall enough to distract her from the pain, or as she was stepping out the door, ducking out from the grabbing fingers of the ghosts.

There was a long slash across the front of her suit, from the edge of her ribcage down to her hip. The suit was doing its best to seal, but she could see, through the translucent material, the shiny purple-grey of intestines, of things that you shouldn't be able to see on a living person.

She kept her eyes closed, swearing quietly under her breath.

If she'd been on the *Verity*, she could have survived this. If she'd had access to a medic, and to the medical tech carried by a ship of the line, maybe. She'd seen people hurt worse pull through.

But she wasn't.

Now that she'd seen the wound, her body had taken that as permission to feel it as well. The icy-hot ache of it curdled in her stomach, crept through her limbs, making her shaking worse.

She shifted position again, bracing herself against the seal.

"Captain! Captain, come on, we're loaded. We've got to ..." Emmett's voice from behind her trailed off.

She opened her eyes and managed a small smile. "Mate Greene. I think I'd best stay here and hold the seal, no?"

For a moment, he was silent. Then his face took on a look of determination. "Come on. I'll carry you if I have to. We'll have a few seconds once you let go of the seal, and I can get you there quick enough."

"And if I turn ghost?" her voice was barely a whisper.

He gave her a grim smile. "That'll motivate the others to move quickly, I guess." He paused. "I have my sparker, Captain. I'll be watching. I'll take out your ghost while it's forming, I swear it."

Her head was spinning now, and she could feel her muscles loosening off the seal.

"Very well, Mate Greene," she murmured. "I don't suppose we have time to argue about it."

"That we don't." His voice was sharp with strain, but she was having a hard time making out his face. "Ready?"

She nodded, and then she felt herself being lifted. Emmett staggered under her weight for a moment, and then he was sprinting for the skiff, and behind her she could hear the hiss of a cracked seal growing louder.

"Get the door shut, quick-time," she heard him shout, and his boots were clattering up the gangplank, and then it clicked shut behind them, and she sagged against the wall of the small cabin as he set her on her feet.

She could sense, dimly, eyes on her, hear whispers, but she ignored them, closing her eyes, forcing her brain back into coherence.

She straightened with an effort. "Mate Greene, to me, please," she said, her words coming out barely audible.

"Aye, Captain," he said, but she could hear the worry in his tone.

She clenched her jaw tightly enough that her teeth ached, and made her careful way past the mass of sailors and into the tiny cockpit of the skiff.

Emmett would take her out before she had time to fully turn, if she were to die. She had to trust that he'd do that. And right now, the most important thing was making sure the *Verity* survived.

"Sailors," she snapped.

The others glanced up, then snapped to attention.

"What's our status?" she asked.

They were all staring at her. Finally, Edgeworth said, "We're away. I want to give us a minute to get out of the way before I hit the explosives—don't want to suck us in with the explosion."

She glanced at the screen, chewing on the inside of her cheek.

He was right—the skiff was close enough to the *Agate* that the shock of the explosion would shove them off course, possibly knock out their steering.

But even from here, she could see the *Verity* was in a bad way, fighting to stay back from the hole, and the skiff would be battling gravity on the way back. Even with the engines straining, at the rate they were moving, by the time they got clear, it may be too late for the *Verity*.

"I think," she said quietly, "that we'll have to set it off regardless."

There was a moment where they all looked at her, then stared at the screen, as if trying to make the calculations come out differently than they had.

"Captain," said Edgeworth at last. "I think we can safely hold out for another two minutes."

She closed her eyes, then nodded brusquely. "Very well, sailor. Carry on," she said. "Set the explosives to go off in one hundred and twenty seconds. I shall inform the *Verity*."

"Aye, Captain," he said, his tone muted.

She allowed herself a small smile.

Pity, really, that they weren't going to make it back. He would have made a fine petty officer, given the opportunity.

"This is Captain Hollis, paging Mate Price," she mumbled into the comm. She was leaning up against the wall, the waves of dizziness that were washing over her now enough that she was unsure she'd keep her feet otherwise.

"Captain!" Foster's voice through her earpiece was sharp with worry. "Thank God you're alive. I'm holding the ship for you."

"Mate Price." She forced her voice steady, forced herself not to look out on the crammed hull of sailors she was condemning to death. "We have the sailors off, but my calculations say that if the *Agate* isn't gone in the next two minutes, the *Verity* will be in too far to pull out."

There was a moment of silence. "Captain?" Foster began.

"I have instructed the technicians to blow the ship. It will happen in—" she checked her timepiece. "In seventy seconds from now. I presume that at that time, our skiff will be knocked off-course by the explosion, and our steering will be knocked out." She paused. "You are to take the *Verity* off the moment you see the explosion. Do you understand me? You are to take command of the *Verity*, and you are to head back to the Level to report back to the Naval High Command. You are to lay the blame for the failure squarely on me, as that is where it belongs. But regardless, you are not to wait when you see the explosion."

There was a moment's pause. "I'm sorry, Captain." Foster's voice was undergirt with iron. "I didn't quite catch that. I will proceed to send out a mag-lock to bring the skiff in."

She stared at her comm blankly for a moment. "Mate Price!" she snapped. "You will obey orders, or I will have you court-martialed for insubordination. I order you to leave the skiff and bring the *Verity* in safe."

"Captain. I believe the grav field is interfering with the comm signals." Foster's voice had reverted to its usual bland politeness. "If you can hear me, prepare for the incoming mag-lock."

"Price, damn your eyes …" she began.

"Good luck, Captain, if you can hear me." The line went dead, and Hollis was left cursing, leaning up against the wall, her body shaking.

The pain had turned from a dull ache to boiling lava in her gut, and she could feel herself going into shock, her mind slipping on the edges of consciousness. She squeezed her eyes closed and bit down on the inside of her cheek, the sharp bloom of pain and iron blood on her tongue enough to bring her mind back to the present, just for a moment. "Mate Greene," she mumbled.

"Here, Captain," he answered instantly, and she almost smiled.

Of course. He was right next to her, waiting for her to die so he could keep her ghost from slaughtering the crew.

"That damnable idiot Price is sending out a mag-lock." She had to concentrate to form her tongue around the words. "Have the crew prepare for incoming. You stay with me."

She didn't have to explain why.

"Aye, Captain," he said, but his words were strangely distorted, like radio-waves with a weak signal.

"Captain, the explosives will go off in fifteen seconds."

She managed some response.

"Ten seconds."

Her head was spinning, and she thought she might faint, or she might vomit, and everything around her felt odd and distant and not quite real.

"Five seconds."

"Prepare the crew for the impact," she mumbled.

Blackness encroached on the edges of her vision, but she couldn't. She couldn't lose consciousness, because her crew still might need her, and she couldn't die, because they couldn't afford a ghost, not right now. Emmett needed his wits about him.

"Two. One."

There was a flash of light on the screen, like a miniature star going supernova, and then the light was swallowed up, crushed into the black of the black hole. The skiff shook, and she almost lost her footing, clutching onto the corner of the wall with fingers white with strain.

"We've lost steering." The voice was panicked. "Captain, we've lost steering, we're being pulled in …"

"Prepare for incoming!" Emmett's voice was sharp, cutting through the fog in her head for just a moment. "Mag-lock incoming."

The skiff shuddered again.

"They missed us, we're going to die, we're going to die …"

Hollis couldn't tell who was shrieking, but it didn't matter. They were going to die, and for a moment the thought was almost peaceful.

"They're trying again." Emmett's voice was so tight with strain she almost didn't recognize it. "Stand by."

Again, the skiff shuddered.

And then there was a whoop of triumph, and the entire cockpit was screaming and shouting, and blackness danced in front of her vision.

"Captain! Captain, can you hear me?"

She forced her eyes open.

Emmett's face was in front of her, wavering and unsteady, like something seen through running water.

"Captain, they've managed to fix a mag-lock. They're pulling us in. Captain?"

She couldn't force her tongue to form an answer.

She could feel, faintly, arms catching her as she collapsed, propping her up against the wall. "Captain, hold on." Emmett's voice was faint and distant. "We're almost there, it'll only take them a minute to pull us in. Just hold on, we'll have you in the med bay."

Time passed. She didn't know how much, and she didn't know what was happening around her. She was conscious, she knew she was because it hurt far, far too much for this to be a dream, but the world around her was tinged red and the pain shot through her like fire, the noises and sounds distant and far-off.

The skiff shuddered under her, and it took her a moment to realize that it was the impact of them docking, and then Emmett had leapt to his feet and was striding out of the skiff, shouting, and people had surrounded her and were lifting her, and she didn't have the strength to protest, or to help them.

She caught brief, disconnected glimpses of her surroundings—the ship corridors, the main deck, the hallway that led down to the med bay. And then she was laying down, blessedly still, with no one grabbing at her and no hands hauling her anywhere, and she almost sobbed in relief, despite the pain screaming through her body.

"Captain?"

She blinked her eyes open.

A face she recognized, vaguely, as one of the ship's medics hovered over her, and beside it, another familiar face—paler than usual, but still holding its usual bland politeness. "Captain. The *Verity* is on her way back, and as per your orders I am acting as captain in your absence."

"Damn you, Price," she muttered. "I ought to have you court-martialled."

Foster smiled, and for just a moment she caught the hint of genuine affection in their face. "Aye, Captain, you do that," they said. "But you can't court-martial me unless you're alive, so focus on staying that way. In the meantime, Mate Greene and I are getting the remainder of the rescued sailors to their bunks. I thought you'd like to know."

For a moment, she just blinked up at them, trying to focus on the words through the hot blur of pain.

Then, at last, she managed a small smile. "Thank you, Mate Price," she whispered.

And then, at last, she felt her eyes falling closed, and the only thing on the other side was blessed unconsciousness.

26

"Temple. Are you ready?" Gracie's voice was sharp. "The moment the *Verity* pulls out, we'll want to get ourselves away."

"Aye, Captain." Temple sounded far too composed about this whole thing, in Silas's opinion.

Still, there was something about the calm in Gracie's manner that was infectious.

He stared at the screen, watching the *Verity's* tiny skiff as it broke away from the *Agate*, and then, a couple of minutes later, the explosion.

Despite everything, he could feel an odd sinking in his chest.

The skiff had been much too close. There was no way something as small as that could escape the grav field, not after the explosion would have knocked out the controls.

But a moment later, he saw the tiny marker on the screen that marked the skiff reappear on the screen, moving rapidly towards the *Verity*.

He let out a quick breath of relief, and glanced over to see Gracie

248

watching him, amusement on her face. "I'll say one thing for your Captain Ives," she said. "She has nerves of steel. Not everyone would have sent a skiff out in the first place, and certainly not everyone would have managed to pull the thing back." She glanced over at Temple. "Temple?"

"Ready on, Captain," he said, his gaze still focused on the controls. "I'm guessing we'll be pulling out in sixty seconds or less."

"Better be—the engines don't like this," came Freddie's voice through the general line.

"And … there she goes," said Temple quietly, his fingers dancing over the *Sweet Jenny's* controls.

There was the quick rush of acceleration, and Silas almost staggered backward at the jolt of speed.

"Unhooking the mag-lock," said Freddie. "Stand by …"

"Ready when you are," Temple replied. "I've set jump coordinates into the system, just give the word."

"Mag-lock releasing," said Freddie, and the ship shuddered.

"Temple, if you would?" said Gracie.

There was the quick, strange disorientation of an FTL jump, and the vis-screens fuzzed out. The last thing Silas saw through them was the *Verity*, bringing her nose around towards the jump-tunnel that would lead back to the Level.

He let out a long breath of relief, sagging against the wall for just a moment. Then he pushed himself upright. "Captain. I'm going to head down to the engine room. I'm guessing Freddie'll need a hand, after all that."

Gracie glanced over. "Best go talk to Vee first, get yourself patched up." She paused, watching him for a moment. "Thank you, lad," she said at last, quietly. "Wasn't sure what you'd do back there."

He smiled reluctantly. "We're crew, Captain. You'd have done the same for me."

She studied him a moment longer. Then she gave him a quick smile in return. "Good lad," she said turning back to her work.

He almost bumped into Ari as he stepped out of the cockpit. She'd stayed back to secure the skiff, and he hadn't seen her since they'd come back on board.

"Sorry," she said, stepping out of his way.

He paused, and she turned to look at him.

He managed a small grin.

The adrenalin from their close call was still humming through his body, and he could feel the way it jittered through his muscles, making his hands shake just a little and his stomach tighten. "We made it," he said. "I honestly wasn't sure we would."

She cocked her head at him, then grinned back. "Told you, Level boy. You're shipping with Captain Mad Dog."

He chuckled. "You have to admit, she's not exactly what I was led to expect."

Ari rolled her eyes. "You've got to stop basing your life off what the idiots on the Level tell you. Far as what they'd say, we're all a bunch of hopeless reprobates or bloodthirsty ghosts, who can't feel the warmth of human kindness."

She was standing very close to him, and grinning up at him, and for a moment, the adrenalin buzzing through his body turned warm and liquid, pooling in the pit of his stomach.

Ari winked and stepped past him into the cockpit, and he realized he'd been standing there, staring at her like an idiot.

He sighed and ran a hand through his hair, suddenly more shaky than he'd been a moment ago.

Shaking his head at himself, he turned and started for the med bay.

Best get himself patched up and back to work. Freddie almost certainly had something for him to do, and if he didn't get down there quick-time, she'd probably think of something even more difficult than what she already had planned.

Hollis

By the time the *Verity* was within hailing distance of the Level, Hollis could stand and walk, albeit haltingly.

She'd had a long time, laying in her med-bay bunk and trying to fight off the night-terrors brought on by pain and stress, to consider how she'd handle her first mate.

In the end, though—well, in the end, Foster had saved her life, and the lives of almost a hundred sailors from the *Agate.*

And at last, she'd decided she'd simply ignore it. Foster had given her, after all, the perfect excuse—grav fields like those around a black hole were notorious for interfering with communications. It was plausible that her orders had not, in fact, made it through the line. It was plausible that, with the stronger signals coming out of the *Verity*, Foster had been able to communicate with the skiff, but that Hollis's attempts to relay orders in return had been fatally affected. She'd been only half-conscious at the time at any rate, and delirium and pain were a potent mix. It was entirely plausible that Foster had done their best to anticipate her orders, and behaved accordingly.

And the fact that she knew it wasn't true didn't have to come into consideration.

Foster had come to visit her several times in the sick bay. They had been nothing but polite and deferential, just like always. And if there was a tension in their posture as they watched her, it was disguised enough that she likely wouldn't have noticed it if she didn't know them as well as she did.

Now she made her careful way up the lift, made for sailors who were injured or unable to use legs or arms. Without the *Verity's* advanced medical tech, she wouldn't have stood a chance of even being on her feet so soon, she knew it well enough. No matter how much she wished to, she'd not be using the ratlines any time in the near future, and would likely be confined to the captain's deck.

If, something in the back of her mind whispered, she'd retain her command at all.

She'd done the best she could have, under the circumstances, and she knew it. But she knew well enough that her best may not be enough. She'd been sent to bring in the *Agate* if she could, or the weapons and the crew if she couldn't, and she'd completed half the task, if that. The least important part of it, if the Naval High Command had their say. And on top of that, she'd been in firing range of the *Sweet Jenny* and hadn't taken her down.

She could argue that she'd kept the pirate from taking the *Agate*, that she'd gotten the crew off and blown the ship to prevent it. But that would hardly make a difference if they wanted to prosecute her.

When she reached the bridge, Foster was waiting for her, polite as ever. "Captain," they said, turning at her entrance. "I'm happy to see you up and about."

She managed a small smile at them. "I've received word that I'm to be called before the Admiral to explain myself the moment we dock. I very much doubt Admiral Usher will take the excuse of something as minor as having my stomach torn open as an excuse."

Foster flashed her a quick smile in return, but there was a small flicker of defiance in their expression that she hadn't expected. "You did everything that could have been asked of you, Captain. If they're asking for a witness, Mate Greene and I are more than willing to—"

Hollis held up a hand. "Thank you, Price. But that will not be necessary. I believe I am sailor enough to stand or fall on my own testimony."

She paused, then gestured with her head. "Walk with me a moment?"

"Aye, Captain." Foster's eyes flicked around the bridge quickly, ensuring everything would run smoothly in their absence, and for just a moment, Hollis felt a sudden swell of gratitude.

She'd thought, when she first set foot on this ship, that there was no one here she could trust.

It was an inexpressible relief to have been proved wrong.

"Mate Price," she said, once they were off the bridge and out of earshot. "I believe we need to speak about what transpired when I was on the skiff." Her language was stiff and halting, and she knew it, but she was taking refuge behind the formality of the words.

She could sense the sudden minute stiffening of Foster's shoulders, but their voice, when they spoke, was still bland and polite. "Yes, Captain?"

She cleared her throat. "I simply wished to say that … I am impressed with your actions, in consideration of the fact that the grav field interfered with the communication and you were unable to hear my orders. Your actions were not, perhaps, what I would have wished. Nonetheless, you carried out what was a difficult and dangerous maneuver in a situation where judgment on the correct course of action may have varied. And I must commend you for that."

There was a long moment of silence. She didn't look at her first mate, but she could feel their eyes on her. At last they said, their voice carefully neutral, "Thank you, Captain."

She let the silence stretch for a moment. At last, she turned to look at them, letting her expression go steely. "However, Mate Price, this will not happen again. Do you understand me? I expect that in the future, you will do whatever is necessary to ensure my orders are carried out."

Foster was still watching her. At last they dropped their gaze. "Yes, Captain," they said, tone once more polite. They paused and glanced up at her, and for just a moment, she could see something that looked like genuine gratitude in their expression. "Thank you, Captain."

She nodded briskly. "Of course. Now. Shall we head back to the bridge? I'd hate for the powers that be to see us make an untidy landing."

"Aye, Captain," said Foster, falling into step beside her, and matching their strides to her unsteady ones. "That would be a shame, after everything."

Docking a ship after a mission was always a chaotic affair—no matter how much order a captain managed to impose on their crew during docking procedures, the moment the gangplank was down and the sailors given leave to go, it was a mass of comings and goings, friends and family waiting at the dock, sailors bustled away to boarding houses on the port, where ghosts were more plentiful and landlords and tavern keepers more amenable to sailors with the potential to turn ghost than elsewhere in the Level. And added to that, there was the string of naval medics who'd been sent to inspect the injured from the *Agate*.

One of them made an attempt to inspect Hollis, and was turned away sharply. If she couldn't trust her own ship's medics to care for her, she'd be no captain at all.

Besides, the pit of dread in her stomach at her upcoming appointment with the Admiral was enough to send adrenalin through her body with enough potency that she could hardly feel her injuries.

And then, at last, the ship was empty enough that she no longer had any excuse to delay.

The petty officers had been released, and now it was only the few mechanics and maintenance techs who'd come onboard to inspect the ship, and herself and her two mates.

"Mate Price, Mate Greene, you are dismissed," she said, turning to them. "We're to report to the ship in a week's time, baring other orders."

"Captain," said Foster, their voice low. "Are you certain—"

She turned on them sharply. "Mate Price. Did I somehow indicate that my orders were open to discussion?"

Foster dropped their eyes. "No, Captain."

"Very well. You are dismissed." She paused a moment, closing her eyes. But it couldn't be helped, and she'd rather have spoken now than have neglected it, and never get the chance. "I ... think you both are aware that I have been called before the Admiral. It is entirely possible that I will not be returning to captain this ship. If that should be the case, I ... I want you to know that I consider it an honour to have served with you."

It wasn't enough. Words couldn't be enough for something like this—for the way Foster and Emmett had trusted her, worked with her. Saved her damn life.

But this was the navy, and that was the most she could say, really, even if she'd had the words for it.

"And with you, Captain," said Emmett quietly. Foster nodded.

Hollis cleared her throat and straightened, grimacing. "Well. Whatever's in store, it won't be made better by keeping the Admiral waiting."

She turned and made her careful way across the captain's deck and down the gangplank, resolutely avoiding looking over her shoulder.

She stopped by the officer's rooming house for long enough to straighten up as best she could, splash water on her face and make herself somewhat presentable. Her captain's uniform smelled far too much of a long voyage in deep space for her comfort, and her working clothes had been thoroughly ruined by blood—despite the grumbling of the ships' medics, she hadn't been able to bring herself to sit quietly and recover, a fact which, an exasperated Foster had pointed out more than once, had probably increased her total healing time significantly, as well as ruining most of her clothing.

All she had left was the dress uniform she'd used in the Academy. Not a stylish choice, but an acceptable one, at any rate.

She pulled her hair back into a neat ponytail, polished the last bit of scuff off her boots—they, at least, had survived the voyage unscathed—and straightened her jacket, checking herself carefully over in the mirror.

And then, with no other excuse for the delay, she straightened her shoulders and started off towards the Naval Headquarters.

It was a long walk, and she'd barely made it off the docks before she was forced to call for a transport—a public one, and crowded at that, but at least it let her sit, and not think too hard about the fact that she'd been slit wide open by a ghost only days before.

She was still desperately broke, at least until her pay chit came in. But she had a few meagre credit chits left, at least enough to get her to the Admiral's office. And if she had to walk home, so be it. She'd simply have to make sure she took her time about it.

The hall down to the Admiral's office, where she was directed by an irritated-looking naval man, was impossibly long. Her midsection was aching before she'd made it half-way across the floor, but she refused to limp, refused to let the pain show in her face.

When she reached the door, she hesitated only a fraction.

Then she reached up and rapped her knuckles on the smooth wood surface.

"Come in." The Admiral's voice was the same sharp brusqueness Hollis had grown used to when sailing under the woman's command.

She gritted her teeth, grimacing at her own hesitation, and shoved the door open, stepping inside.

Admiral Usher's office was spare—a worn bookcase, scattered with yellowing texts, an ancient desk that showed the wear of decades. The woman herself was seated in a bare wooden chair with carved armrests and a thin horsehair cushion, but no other concessions to either elegance or comfort. The wooden chairs facing the desk did not appear any more comfortable.

The Admiral looked up at her entrance, pushing aside the cluster of holonotes hovering over her desk. "Ah. Captain Ives. I'd heard your ship had docked. I was expecting you." She gestured to one of the chairs. "Sit down, woman. You look like you're going to pass out."

Hollis did as she was told, and tried to bite back both the grimace at the Admiral's words, and the sigh of relief as she finally sank into proffered seat.

Admiral Usher was watching her, her expression sharp and calculating.

Hollis held her head high and returned the Admiral's gaze.

Perhaps she'd lose her command. But she'd be damned if she'd let herself be cowed.

For a few endless moments, Admiral Usher simply watched her. At last she leaned back in her chair. "Captain Ives. I received your mission report. Perhaps you have something you'd like to add?"

Hollis drew in a deep breath. "No, Admiral. We went out to retrieve the *Agate*, and were met by the *Sweet Jenny*. We were able to disable the pirate ship's stabilizers, but she caught us with a mag-lock and knocked the *Agate* farther into the grav-field. We were able to rescue the sailors on board and get them back to the *Verity*, but we were forced to destroy the *Agate* and everything on her in order to save the *Verity*. And when we pulled the *Verity* free, the *Sweet Jenny* cut her mag-lock and performed an FTL jump before we were able to damage her further. I'm afraid we lost both the ship and the weapons, and we were unable to capture or destroy the pirates."

The narration of it felt so foreign, although it was factually true— so impossibly distant from the fevered panic of those few hours, wondering if she'd lose her ship and her crew together, wondering if her first command would turn into a death mission for her and everyone sailing under her.

The Admiral nodded without speaking, and for a few moments, the office was once again silent. At last, Admiral Usher pushed her chair back a little. "Ives. I don't think I need to tell you that there are those in the Admiralty slavering over the idea of relieving you of your command." She grimaced. "Your appointment was far from popular among a certain type of naval person. And much as I hate the politics of the whole thing, there are times I must bow to their whims."

Hollis could feel her stomach drop.

It was no more than she'd expected. But the ice-cold devastation of it still left her speechless.

One command. One mission, then—that would be her legacy.

And then what? Could she ship out again as a sailor? Would she even be advanced to petty officer? Or would she simply be let go from the navy, with her termination pay and a history that meant she'd never work on the Level again, never again sail out into deep space?

The Admiral leaned forward over her desk. "But by God, Ives, I wasn't about to let them win this one."

Hollis looked up, startled.

There was the faintest hint of humour in the Admiral's expression, like she knew exactly what was going through Hollis's mind. "I told them they could go hang."

Hollis just stared. "I lost the cargo and the ship both," she said at last.

Admiral Usher chuckled dryly. "You did that. But you saved the crew. That may not count for much to the High Command, but I served as a captain once myself, and a sailor before that. That was bravely done. And you were facing up against Captain Mad Dog, and you lived to tell about it. There's not many seasoned captains as can say the same."

Hollis was still staring.

The Admiral's expression turned serious, and she shook her head. "I can't protect you from everything, Ives, and nor would I if I could. If you can't handle a command, you deserve to lose it. But I've heard your report, and the reports of your first and second mate, and I'm willing to say that as far as I'm concerned, you did your best with the situation you were dealt." She paused a moment. "I'll expect you back on the *Verity* in a week's time to receive your mission orders.

You're dismissed."

It took Hollis a moment to recover her wits. When she did, she pushed herself to her feet. "Admiral—"

The Admiral had already pulled the holonotes back across her desk, and was studying them intently. She glanced up, a hint of annoyance in her voice. "You are dismissed, Captain Ives."

Hollis swallowed. "Aye, Admiral," she said at last. "Thank you, Admiral."

The Admiral looked up at her, and there was an expression on her face Hollis couldn't entirely read. "No need to thank me, Ives. Get along with you. If you want to be ready for action in a week, you'll need to rest up, from what I hear." She paused. "Officers rooming house will take you, they're obligated to, and since you're a captain, your credit will be good for meals and other necessities until your pay chit comes in. And in the meantime, you'll find a transport waiting downstairs. I need you on the *Verity* in a week's time, and that won't happen if you break that wound back open through your bloody stubborn pride. You'll take that transport, that is an order. Do you understand me?"

"Aye, Admiral," said Hollis. She felt stunned, as disoriented as she had when she'd learned the Admiral had recommended her for the Academy. "Thank you, Admiral."

Then she stepped out of the Admiral's office and made her way back to where the transport was waiting.

27

Silas

Silas leaned back against the Sweet Jenny's side on the half-open loading ramp, lifted high enough that it hung out over the docks like a balcony.

The place was exactly like he'd left it—a cauldron of unappetizing smells and a press of bodies shoving past each other, the noise and chaos of the drinking houses and whorehouses at the lanes at the end of the docks, all illuminated by flickering orange lamplight.

He sighed, shaking his head at himself.

He wasn't sure what he was feeling, exactly.

He'd given up everything he'd spent his life working for— honouring his parents' memories, making his family proud, doing his duty to them, to the navy, to the Level and the Admiralty. Not a one of them would be proud of what he'd done, he knew that damn well.

But … he touched his pocket, where the document chips still lay tucked away, waiting for him to hand them over to Gracie.

He couldn't have gone back to his old life even if he'd wanted to. Even if his choice hadn't been so utterly irrevocable, he couldn't have gone back and pretended that he didn't smell the rot underneath the glimmering high society, the legends of glory that went along with a captain's post in the navy. He'd made his decision back on the *Agate*. He'd consciously betrayed his duty, yes. But duty to something that had never been what he'd believed it to be.

He'd lost everything he'd believed, everything he'd been willing to give his life for. And he wasn't sure if it was his own fault or the navy's, and he wasn't sure it mattered. That moment he'd saved Gracie, and been ready to sacrifice the crew of the *Agate* to do it, he'd realized something he hadn't until that very moment.

Despite what he'd believed, despite what the navy had drilled into him his whole life, he wasn't willing to give up everything—he wasn't willing to give up the life of a captain who'd risked her life to save his —for his duty.

Maybe he'd never been.

His duty told him he should go back, give himself up to the navy, try to bring this through proper channels despite the near-certainty of failure, now that he knew what he knew about Mad Dog and her methods.

And he wouldn't.

He sighed and closed his eyes.

There was a noise from behind him, and when he looked up, Ari had come over. She shrugged out of her jacket, tossed it down on the dirty surface, and dropped down, laying back with her hands behind her head, staring up at the dark ceiling.

He smiled at her, and turned back to watching the dock.

"So, Level boy," she said at last. "What are you going to do next?"

He gave a humourless little laugh. "I've been wondering the same thing myself."

She rolled up on one elbow, watching him. "You could stay on, you know. Captain'd take you, I know she would. May not say much, but you've impressed her."

He raised his eyebrows. "You think I should turn pirate?"

She shrugged and lay back again. "I mean, you told me the Level is no better. At least here we look after our own."

They were quiet for a few minutes.

"The thing is, Ari," he said at last, testing the words in his mouth as he spoke them, "I always knew exactly where my life was going to go. Exactly what I had to do, exactly what the right thing was. I was going to sign on with a ship of the line as soon as I reached my twelfth birthday, I'd work my way up until I made petty officer, I'd catch the eye of a captain and get a recommendation for the Academy. And then I'd be given a captain's post, and I'd work my way up from there until I made Admiral, and joined the Naval High Command. I'd honour my parent's memory by doing what they never had a chance to. My aunt and uncle drilled it into me since I was a too young to understand what they were saying—my duty to them, to the Level. My responsibility to parents I never knew." He gave a small, bitter smile. "I still know what the right thing is. I know damn well what my life is worth. And … in the end, it didn't matter. I helped take down a naval scout ship, stole weapons meant for the navy, did nothing to prevent the *Agate* or the *Verity* and all souls on board from being pulled into a black hole—without Hollis, they'd have all been dead, and it'd have been on my hands." He snorted half-heartedly. "And for all my virtuous talk of doing it to root out the corruption in the navy, that was never what it was about, was it? Here I sit in Blackrock without anything to show for it."

She rolled up on one elbow again, studying him. "I mean, you have a cargo-hold full of illegal weapons to show for it. That'll take the wind out of a few sails back in the Naval High Command, I wager."

He grimaced. "That's the point! This wasn't supposed to be about just getting revenge. This was supposed to be about … about something bigger. More important. And it was all a lie, all of it." He shifted to face her, his expression going serious. "I'll take them down, Ari. Duty or not, I'll do it. I have to. I gave up my life for this, and I'm not going to let my duty to the navy or anything else stop me from seeing it through. But that's not Gracie's way, is it?"

Ari was still watching him. "Thing about the captain is, I don't think what you and she want is all that much different. Thing is, though, she's got other things to think about. Captain ain't going to ask her crew to sacrifice their lives for some ideal, like it sounds like you were planning on. Maybe that's what they expect from you in the navy, but this ain't the navy, and Gracie ain't the Admiral." She lay back again. "Here on the *Sweet Jenny*, you're a thorn in the navy's side, and … hell, at least it's a life, you know? Better than the charade you play up on the Level." She paused. "You ain't a bad sailor, Sil. Ain't a bad person, honestly. And the navy would've had you killed for trying to fix things, and you thought that was fair. Thought they still deserved your loyalty. Don't work like that around here. Don't need to be loyal to someone or something as is never going to be loyal to you back." She paused. "Not saying the captain won't help you, if you manage to persuade her. But whether she will or no—" She shrugged. "Figure you'll have a place on the *Sweet Jenny* if you want it. And figure we'll all be happy to have you."

They were quiet for a few minutes longer.

At last, Silas shook his head, shrugging out of his own jacket and laying it over his lap. "Here," he said. "Be a little softer than the deck, anyways."

She glanced up at him curiously, then scooted over, dropping her head down on his lap.

He watched her a moment, and found he was smiling.

She was pretty, yes, but it wasn't just that. There was something compelling about her, something that drew you in and held you. Something he was glad to have in a friend. Because for all she'd played him, more times than he could count, he'd never had to wonder if she'd have his back. He'd never had to check over his shoulder during a battle to see if she was still there. He'd never had to force himself to be something he wasn't around her.

And it hit him, suddenly, that perhaps the guilt that sat in his stomach like a stone over his choice back on the *Agate* was less about the choice itself than about the fact that he didn't actually regret it nearly as much as he should. He should regret choosing the people who'd, for the first time in his life, been loyal to him in return, over choosing his duty to the navy and everything that came with it—and he didn't.

And perhaps that was the worst part of it all.

"You know what you need?" she said after a few moments. "You need to get drunk and get laid. The world will look better after that." She shook her head and snorted. "I need to get drunk and get laid. Been a long damn time since we had shore leave."

Silas smiled. "You know, I have some rum down in my bunk. If you wanted."

She smiled back. "Nothing personal, Level boy, but I have a rule that goes, never screw a crewmate, on account of things might get messy and you'll still have to save their life afterwards if it comes to it. I need people I can hate if things go sideways. You know what I mean?"

He sighed, biting back the sharp jolt of disappointment—sharper than he'd expected—and nodded ruefully. "I can see the wisdom in that."

She peered up at him. "Don't mean to offend."

He smiled again, shoving back the regret. "No offence taken. A little disappointed, maybe, but nothing I can't live with."

They were quiet a little longer.

"Captain's already hard at work on her accounts, probably. Damn woman never rests." Ari laughed. "She needs to damn well get drunk and get laid." She rolled up to her feet and held out a hand. "Come on, best get off the ship before Mad Dog changes her mind and decides to haul us off somewhere without a moment of shore-leave." She watched him as he took the proffered hand and pulled himself up. "I'm guessing from your invite earlier that you're into women. Do you swing both ways?"

He nodded, and she frowned, glancing across the docks. "I know a very nice man who could show you a good time, but I don't see his ship." She shook her head briskly. "Never mind, I'll introduce you to a lady-friend of mine, she's a good girl, and she won't slit your throat and steal your purse while you sleep. And from the looks of it, her ship just docked as well, so she'll be looking for a lay as much as any of us."

She grinned and strode to the edge of the raised ramp, dropping lightly off it and onto the dock below, and he followed.

He'd have to face this soon enough. He'd have to face the irrevocable consequences of his decisions, face head-on what his newfound determination to take on the navy, without the benefit of his own self-righteous certainty, meant.

He'd have to face the fact that, after what he'd done, he'd lost every claim to any moral high ground he'd ever held.

But … hell. All that he could think about later.

He found he was smiling a little, despite everything, as he made his way off the docks after Ari.

Maybe this hadn't been where he'd thought his life would take him, back in the barracks. But he couldn't say, right at this moment, that given the opportunity, he'd change it.

Gracie

Gracie bent forward over the battered table in the small room over Abigail's tavern. The air was hazy with cigar smoke, curling and twisting in the candlelight like wisps of ghosts.

She never smoked on shipboard, but she made up for it on shore leave.

The haul had been a good one—they hadn't managed to take all the weapons, but they'd taken the most valuable of them, at least. It would turn a decent profit.

And more than that, it would give the *Sweet Jenny* and the other ships who bought from her something solid to use against the naval ships.

She was no romantic—there was nothing of the freedom-fighter in turning pirate. They were thieves and robbers and cutthroats, every one of them. But at least here, everyone knew it. And she'd met far too many desperate people on these docks. Who wouldn't turn to murder and thievery if they were driven to it? As far as she was concerned, the Level deserved no sympathy in dealing with a problem it had created for itself.

Behind her, she heard the sound she'd been half-expecting—the creak of the door opening, soft footsteps entering, the creak of the door again as it closed.

She didn't look up, just kept her eyes scanning through the

documents.

Her heart was beating a little faster than usual, and she wasn't entirely certain whether it was fear or anticipation.

Despite what the legends said, she wasn't impervious to fear.

There were a few moments of silence. And then a woman's voice said, "That's a nasty habit, Grace. I've told you, those cigars will kill you one day."

Gracie finished up the document she'd been skimming, then pushed it away and turned, leaning back in her chair. "Admiral," she said, smiling just a little. "And I've told you, always figured you'd kill me before I had to worry about it. Don't tell me you're doubting yourself now."

Admiral Judith Usher stepped out into the flickering candlelight.

She looked older than the last time Gracie had seen her, the lines of strain and worry cut more deeply into her face. She'd always been a powerful woman, but some of her muscle had started to go to fat, and the circles under her eyes were darker than Gracie remembered, the grey in her blonde hair more pronounced.

"I'd say it's good to see you, but we both know it'd be a lie." Gracie took a last pull on her cigar, and then snuffed it out on the small ashtray on the edge of her desk. "You didn't kill the guards Abigail posted, did you? Because if you did, I'll shoot you dead before I let you leave here."

Judith snorted. "I hope you know me better than that. They're sleeping peacefully, and they'll wake up with a dry mouth and a headache and the memory of sweet dreams to make up for it."

Gracie huffed a small laugh. "Always were that sort, weren't you?" She paused a moment. "So. To what do I owe the honour of this visit?"

Judith shook her head. "I know what you did, Gracie. The others in High Command don't, but I know you. You got away with the weapons, didn't you? There was no other reason Captain Ives and her ship came back home alive."

Gracie pushed her chair back and stood abruptly. "Meant to talk to you about that, actually." She kept her voice deceptively mild. "The hell were you thinking, sending in a brand new captain after me? You don't send a green pup after a fox. You were sending her to her death, and you knew it." She knew Judith would hear the cold anger under her tone. "I'd thought better of you."

Judith sighed, and for just a moment, Gracie could see the deep weariness in her expression. "I didn't know," she said quietly. "I didn't realize it was you that'd picked up the transmission, not until it was too late."

Gracie was still standing, one hand on the back of her chair. The feel of the rough wood grounded her, tamped down the white-hot fury that lit in her chest when she saw the Admiral. "You could have called her back."

Judith shook her head slowly. "She's from the Stacks, Gracie, first commissioned captain's candidate from the Stacks. If I'd called her back, I'd have been proving to Naval High Command that I didn't trust her. She'd never get a posting, not after that. She'd live her life out in shore-bound administrative tasks and routine near-space postings. I know Ives. She'd have preferred death."

Gracie took a step forward. "Be that as it may, she's alive because I left her alive."

"I know." Judith paused. "That's ... why I came. To thank you. And to give you something, in exchange." She hesitated. "We're sending out ships, in a week or so. Wasn't my decision, this came from the top, some politician who got tired of reading reports about merchant ships taken and naval ships shot down by pirates. One of the usual attacks on Blackrock, and they're sending the ships and the firepower to do damage this time. It's been in the works for some time, and I'm not telling you this because I think you can stop it. But you can warn the others here. They trust you. You can get them into the lower caves, keep a few more of them alive. I'm giving you that in exchange for the lives of Captain Ives and the crew of the *Verity*."

Gracie watched the woman.

She knew how to read people. She knew every one of Judith's tells, every small twitch or movement that no one else would have caught. Despite the sick wave of fury the sight of Judith Usher always called up, she knew damn well how to read the woman.

She was telling the truth, Gracie'd put her word on it.

"That's not all, though, is it?" Gracie asked, taking another step towards her. "That's not the only reason you came, is it, Admiral Usher?"

Judith had a pistol in her hand, pointed at Gracie's stomach. She'd always been quick, Judith had.

Gracie grinned, showing the tips of her teeth, and took another step.

Her heart was pounding faster than it should, but she hardly cared.

"Gracie, stay the hell back." Judith's voice was rough.

Gracie took another step, until the pistol was pressed into her stomach. She didn't glance down at it, just looked into Judith's face, still grinning dangerously. "That's not the only reason you came. Because you could have sent a message. You could have sent one of your loyal minions, couldn't you have? Would have been easier than finding some excuse to take a trip on your own, two day round-trip, isn't it, even with the shortcut and a fast ship? But you came yourself."

"Gracie, I'm warning you." Judith's voice was cold, but Gracie could feel the way the muzzle of the pistol trembled.

Gently, she pushed the pistol aside, lifting it from Judith's fingers and placing it on a chair beside her. She stepped in closer, still grinning, and lifted her hand. For just a moment, she hesitated. There was something hot and sharp in her chest, and she couldn't tell, exactly, if it was hate or anger or fear or longing, or some combination of all of them.

She'd never been able to tell, with Judith.

She wasn't sure it mattered, in the end.

"I've known you longer'n that, Jenny," she said, letting her hand slide down Judith's cheek, run along her jawline. "Don't bother lying to me."

Judith's eyes had closed, almost involuntarily, and she leaned into Gracie's touch. "Grace," she began, her voice quiet.

She was older. They were both older, but there was still that sense of aching familiarity in the feel of her skin against Gracie's hand, the warmth of her, the smell of her soap and her launderer's starch.

She let the backs of her fingers run down Judith's throat, pause for a moment at the jut of her collarbone.

"You could come back, Grace," Judith whispered. "There's a war coming, you know that as well as I do. We need you. I could work it out with High Command, I'm certain of it."

Gracie's hand stopped, her fingers flattening around the curve of Judith's throat. "I see. You'd keep me for as long as I entertained you, then sell me out. Just like you did back in the Academy."

Judith didn't drop her gaze. "I swear to you, I didn't know …"

Gracie snorted bitterly. "You didn't know I wasn't guilty? You didn't know you'd be condemning me to death?" She leaned forward, until her mouth was against Judith's ear. "I'd have lied for you, Jenny. I'd have let them drag me away in chains before I said a word against you, whether you were guilty or no, you know that. But you were always more loyal to the Level than you were to me."

Judith's pulse pounded hot and quick under Gracie's palm across her throat.

It would be a such a simple thing to tighten her hand, twist Judith around in one violent motion, choke the life from her. Leave her body limp on the floor.

God's eyes, she wanted to. She wanted to so badly it trembled through her muscles. She'd dreamed about it at nights—Jenny, Admiral Judith Usher now, her face tipped up, horror in her eyes as she choked and died.

"If I … if I could take it back, Grace—" Judith's voice was thick with emotion—regret, or longing, or fear, or all three.

Gracie closed her eyes and drew in a deep breath. "You can't take it back, though, can you? You can't undo the past. And I'll never forgive you for what you did, not as long as I live. One day, Jenny— one day I'll kill you for it. But first, I'll see you ruined. I'll see everything you care for and everything you fought for and everything you earned by betraying me crumble before your eyes. I'll take you down, Jenny, if I have to destroy the Level to do it." Her mouth was still close to Judith's ear, and she could smell the familiar smell of her —sweat and soap and something that was just Jenny.

"Grace." Judith's voice was a whisper. She leaned into Gracie, letting her head tip back. Making no effort to defend herself.

Gracie let her hand slide lower, cupping Judith's breast over her uniform. Judith shivered, and Gracie breathed in, letting her lips brush along the corner of Judith's jaw. "I've missed you, Jenny," she whispered. "God, I've missed you."

"Grace—" Judith's voice was choked, and her hands slid up

around Gracie's back, warm against the thin fabric of her shirt, fingers tightening as if she could somehow hold the two of them in that moment, never let them go. "Damn your eyes, Grace."

Gracie smiled a little, pulling her closer.

She'd have to deal with the information Jenny'd brought, sooner rather than later, figure out a way to use it. Figure out a way to save as many of this slovenly group of killers and thieves as she could, or better yet, use it to strike another blow at the Admiralty.

But not right now.

"I'll kill you one of these days," she murmured into Jenny's skin. "I'll kill you, or you'll kill me. Hardly matters, though, does it? That's why you came." She lifted her head, her mouth finding Judith's. The kiss was desperate, rough and sharp and bittersweet, and Gracie could feel herself melting into it, feel Jenny's body pressing against hers. And just for now, just for this moment, it was enough.

Thank you for reading!

I hope you enjoyed the book. Book two, Dead Reckoning, will be coming soon!

You might also enjoy the following, also by R.M. Olson:

The Ungovernable series:

Zero Day Threat
Jailbreak
Time Bomb
Insider Threat
Firewall
Trojan Horse
Security Incident
Threat Agent
Attack Path

A mouthy ex-smuggler pilot, a grumpy demolitions expert, a tech genius and a hacker. They're pulling a job on the most dangerous weapons dealer in the System. They're stealing tech that could change the course of history. And every one of them has something to hide.
What could possibly go wrong?
"Spectacular and thrilling! Olson's debut novel is filled with compelling characters and endless excitement." -SD Simper, author of the Fallen Gods series

The Singularity Series:

Redshift
The Observer Effect
Uncertainty Principle

R.M. OLSON

Quantum Entanglement
Event Horizon
Point Singularity

*A scientist searching for the cure to an uncurable disease, a canny elder
stateswoman in game of politics that could spell the beginning of a new era or an
end to humanity as we know it, and a cheerful assassin on the run.
A first contact with an unknown alien entity.
And a question: which of the three will be killed first?*

You can find the paperbacks on all major retailers.